JASON

BLUE HALO SERIES BOOK TWO

NYSSA KATHRYN

D1452897

An NW Partners Book
Cover by L.J. Anderson at Mayhem Cover Creations
Developmentally and Copy Edited by Kelli Collins
Line Edited by Jessica Snyder
Proofread by Marla Esposito and Jen Katemi

Danger throws them together. Attraction keeps them from parting.

Having lost her best friend, Courtney Davies lives every day like it's her last. Because if life has taught her anything, it's that some are cut far too short without warning. So when sexy former soldier Jason moves to Cradle Mountain, she shouldn't hesitate to express her immediate interest. Problem is, anytime she gets near the man, she inexplicably freezes, losing every coherent thought in her head.

Jason Porter has served his country, studied at one of the country's most prestigious schools, made groundbreaking strides in pharmaceutical science...but it was his time in captivity that changed him most. In irrevocable ways, both physically and mentally. Slowly, he's moving on, running Blue Halo Security with his team in Cradle Mountain, Idaho—where one of the best perks of the small town is coffee shop owner Courtney. She's friendly, spirited, vibrant... Everything he needs in his life. Too bad he seems to scare her senseless.

When Courtney wins an award, bringing with it media attention, she hopes it's the break her shop has been waiting for. Instead, strange things start happening. Unexpected things. Dangerous things. It's soon clear the award has put her in a spotlight for all the wrong reasons. And the one person she can trust? The very man who leaves her tongue, her body, and her heart tied in knots.

ACKNOWLEDGMENTS

Thank you to everyone who helped bring this book to life—Kelli, Marla and Jen, you guys are superstars. Thank you to my ARC team for reading this book before anyone else, giving me your honest and constructive feedback before taking the time leave a review. Thank you to my readers—you are amazing, and you are the reason the next book gets published. And lastly, thank you to my husband, you and Sophia are my world and none of this would be possible without your love and support.

CHAPTER 1

*C*ourtney's heels clicked in even beats against the polished concrete floors, the long hallway otherwise quiet. She couldn't repress a wide smile.

She'd just finished an interview with the Mountain Media Radio Station. Eep. She'd sat there and talked about her little coffee shop, The Grind, to hundreds of listeners for almost half an hour.

Someone needed to pinch her, because she had to be dreaming. The Grind was her baby, her seedling, grown from the ground up on nothing but sheer courage and hard work. Oh, and every last dollar she'd had. It could have sunk. It could have easily drained her savings. Killed her dream. It hadn't.

If possible, her smile widened.

Idaho's Most Unique Coffee Shop. Yep, that was the honor she'd won, awarded to her by *Living in Idaho Today Magazine...* and God, but it was everything. And it just went to show that hard work did pay off. Taking big, scary, I-might-lose-everything-but-I'm-doing-it-anyway chances could turn out great.

She turned a corner, smiling at a man who passed her.

Since the article had run, the shop had been beyond busy. It seemed like everyone in Idaho wanted to visit. Heck, everyone *everywhere.* The article being shared on most social media platforms hadn't hurt either.

Shaking her head, she turned the next corner. Her gaze zeroed in on the end of the hall—and her feet came to an abrupt halt.

No entry, maintenance in progress.

The sign sat in front of the staircase she'd used to reach the eighth floor.

What the heck? She'd just walked those stairs less than an hour ago.

Her steps slowed as she drew closer. She tried the knob. Locked.

Crap. Not good. Not for her, anyway.

Nibbling her bottom lip, she looked around. There was an elevator back the way she'd come. A small elevator that fit four, maybe five people, tops. She'd seen it on the way in, had almost stepped inside, but then her stomach had convulsed, sweat beading her brow.

Heck, she'd felt like she was on the verge of a mini panic attack.

Claustrophobia. It was new to her... and she had absolutely no idea how to handle it.

All because of what had happened to her less than a month ago.

She swallowed at the memory. She'd been locked in a walk-in freezer at The Grind, with a reporter's dead body beside her. Freezing. Unable to get out. The guy who had locked her in there had wanted her phone. He'd then proceeded to use that phone to hurt her friend Grace.

The man was now dead, but what he'd done to her was something she'd never forget.

She didn't want to get in the elevator. She didn't even want to *look* at the small space. But what choice did she have? She couldn't just camp out by the stairwell like a weirdo, waiting for whoever had locked the door to unlock it.

Could she?

No. Knowing her luck, one of the radio hosts would walk past and *boom*, her new phobia would be splashed all over the next talk segment.

Argh. Turning, she headed toward the elevator, every step feeling heavier than the last.

Come on, Courtney. Don't be dramatic.

It was an *elevator*, for Pete's sake. She'd traveled in the things her entire life. She should *not* be feeling like she was walking to her impending death.

When the elevator came into view, her breath actually halted in her throat. For a moment, she needed to work hard to get the air flowing again.

You've. Got. This.

Straightening her spine, she stopped at the doors, jabbing the button just a bit too aggressively. The doors slid open, and she tried to step in, but her feet wouldn't move. Hell, they might as well have been super-glued to the concrete floor.

Closing her eyes, she took a deep breath. When she opened them again, it was to see the doors closing.

Crap! Her arm shot out, stopping them in their tracks. Then, refusing to allow her ridiculous mind to prevent her from doing a completely normal, everyday task, she stepped inside and pressed the button for the first floor.

Good. This was good. Progress.

That thought lasted for about half a second. Then the door closed. Suddenly, her heart catapulted into her throat. Sweat beaded on her brow again, and for a second, she thought she might pass out right there and then.

Scrunching her eyes closed, she began to babble to herself.

"You're okay, Courtney. It's just an elevator. It's just eight floors. You're almost—"

The entire car jolted to a stop. Her bag slipped off her shoulder, and her ankles wobbled as the elevator shuddered. It wasn't a let's-pick-more-people-up stop, and it definitely wasn't a you've-reached-the-first-floor stop.

No. This was different. Wrong.

For a second, everything stilled. Her heart. Her breathing. Every thought in her head. Everything except her insides, which were twisting and turning. Then walls started to close in, the room shrinking before her eyes.

Oh, God. This wasn't good.

When she finally sucked in a breath, she could have sworn she smelled the same thing she had *that* day. The day when she'd been locked in the walk-in freezer...

The smell of Nicole's rotting body.

The reporter had been dead for days. And her body had lain right beside Courtney for over an hour... until the freezer had finally been opened.

Glancing up, she noticed she'd only just passed the sixth floor. Still so high...

She touched the blue gem hanging around her neck. A gem that had been passed down in her family for generations that she was rarely caught without. Usually, it calmed her. This time, it didn't.

She pressed against the wall and slid to the floor, then fumbled through her bag.

Phone. She needed her phone. Where the heck was it?

When her fingers slid over cold metal, she yanked it out, dialing the office where she'd just had her interview. The call immediately went to voicemail.

Oh, sweet Jesus. This could not be happening.

After leaving a quick message that she prayed was at least partially comprehensible, Courtney hung up. She sat there for a solid twenty seconds, trying not to pass out. Trying not to let the nausea that was stewing in her stomach crawl up her throat.

Grace. She needed Grace. Not only was the woman a good friend, she was also a therapist. If anyone could talk her down from near hysteria, it was her.

The phone rang three times before Grace picked up. "Courtney! How'd the interview go?"

"Grace. I need help." And maybe an oxygen tank. She sucked in a shuddering breath. "I'm trapped. I can barely breathe!"

Muffled male voices sounded in the background before Grace spoke again. "Where are you trapped and why can't you breathe, Courtney? Are you okay?"

Okay? Was a person okay when they felt like they were suffocating in a perfectly well-ventilated steel deathtrap box? Or were they just plain crazy?

She tried to steady her voice, but Lord, it was hard. "I just finished my interview and went to take the stairs, but they were locked or under maintenance or something stupid, so I had to take the elevator." Big breath in, big breath out. "I've been struggling with enclosed spaces since Kieran shut me in the freezer with... with Nicole's body."

Since he'd zip-tied the thing shut, plunging her into darkness. Freezing. Terrified. It had only been for an hour, but Heaven Almighty, it felt like a lifetime. The cold. The stench. And right now, her mind was trying to trick her into thinking she was living it all over again.

Courtney scrunched her eyes shut, trying to push the memory down.

More muffled male voices in the background. Logan, Grace's boyfriend, and someone else. His friend Blake, maybe?

"Courtney, Logan's calling Jason. He's right around the corner from the radio station and might be able to go to you."

Her eyes flew open. Jason? She couldn't let him see her like this!

The guy was one of eight former military men who owned and ran Blue Halo Security together. He was also ridiculously attractive. And sweet. And caused her to get tongue-tied and nervous every time she was near him.

But she couldn't give up help, either, not when she felt like she was seconds from suffering a heart attack.

"Courtney? Are you still with me?"

She opened her mouth to say yes, but nausea coiled in her belly, stealing her voice. Instead, Courtney nodded, knowing full well her friend couldn't see her. "Mm-hm."

"Logan's already on the phone with him. He won't be long. A couple minutes tops. Until he gets there, I want you to focus on your breathing, okay?"

Breathing. The one thing that should come so easily for her, but in this moment, she needed to relearn it. "Okay."

"I want you to take a deep breath in with me." She heard Grace suck in a large breath, and Courtney followed, filling her lungs. "Good. Hold the breath, two, three, four. Now breathe out, two, three, four."

Courtney listened to her friend's calming voice. It was the only thing keeping her stable at the moment. Each subsequent breath came easier. The anxiety was still there, trying to bubble to the surface, but Courtney used everything inside her to block it out.

They remained like that for long minutes, and Courtney was just about in a trance when she heard a thud on the roof of the elevator. Her gaze shot up and she was momentarily pulled out of her calm. Reminded that she was in a cube. Four walls boxing her in.

Her breaths shortened again just as a hatch in the roof of the elevator opened and Jason jumped inside.

Well, if she thought the space looked small before, that was nothing compared to now. It was absolutely tiny. Scratch her earlier thoughts of four or five people fitting in here. If they were Jason's size—super-soldier size—it would be two, max.

He stepped close to her, lowering to his haunches, his deep

brown eyes studying every inch of her face. "Hey, Court. How you doing?"

Oh, boy. Even in the midst of terror, she could get lost in those eyes. "I've been better."

The side of his mouth tugged up, showing off one of his ridiculously gorgeous dimples.

Grace sounded through the phone. "Jason?"

"Yep. I've got it from here."

She sighed. "Good. Call me if you need me."

"Will do."

Grace hung up but Courtney continued to sit there, frozen, like one of those statues of a woman holding an urn, but her urn was a phone.

Jason reached out, gently sliding the cell from her hand. His fingers grazed hers, and for a moment, she was pulled out of her haze, pinged by a wave of electricity cascading down her arm.

She sucked in a quick breath.

Jason tilted his head to the side. "You want to get out of here?"

Heck, yes, she did. "I do. But... we're not moving."

This time, both sides of his mouth lifted, and good golly, but there was a rush of something magical in her belly.

"We aren't. But if you want, I can lift us both through that hole up there." He pointed up. "I already pried open the doors on the sixth floor. I would open these doors, but we're between floors right now."

Lift her? To the top of an elevator? It was an effort not to squeak like a scared mouse at his suggestion. She knew he was all kinds of strong, so much stronger than most men, and capable of things he shouldn't be capable of. But the idea of trading this terrifying small space for another, darker one...

She opened her mouth to say yes, but the word caught.

He studied her for another beat, then, instead of urging her to stand, he sat beside her, so close that his heat penetrated her side. "How'd the interview go?"

Interview...? So, they were dropping the scale-the-elevator idea in exchange for chitchat?

"Good." She wet her lips. "I spoke about my mugs."

His deep chuckle skirted through her belly, causing little vibrations. Her lips almost tilted up.

"Did they ask which was your favorite?"

Had he shifted closer? Because he felt closer. "Yes. I said it would be like asking a mother to choose her favorite child. Impossible."

Jason laughed again. Yep, another belly flip. She snuck a peek at him from below her lashes. "If they'd asked me, I would have said your 'Bob' mug."

This time, it was Courtney who chuckled. The mug said *This is Bob. Bob has no arms.* There was a stick figure picture of Bob, then below, *Knock, Knock. Who's there? It isn't Bob.*

"You're right. That's a good one."

There was a pause, and even though she was no longer looking at him, she could feel his eyes on her, like hot beams melting her insides.

"I like the new streaks in your hair," he said quietly.

She absently touched the side of her head. There had been two streaks of bright pink in the blond the last time he'd seen her. Last night, she'd felt like a change and dyed the streaks purple. Mostly because she thought they'd match her new purple sneakers for work.

"Thank you. I felt like a change."

"Good choice. You look beautiful."

Okay. This time, it wasn't just her stomach that vibrated at his words. It was all of her.

CHAPTER 2

*J*ason talked as the tension eased from Courtney's body. The muscles in her arms, which hugged her legs, had visibly loosened. The lines around her eyes had smoothed out just a fraction.

He watched as she chatted a bit about her coffee shop. She'd never been able to speak to him without stress jumbling or stealing her words. He liked this side of her. It was like the fear of the elevator distracted her from how nervous he made her.

Her lips curled up when she started a story about a particular customer. His heart gave a little thump against his ribs. The passion this woman had for her business was damn sexy. *She* was damn sexy.

And then there were her eyes. Two different shades, one green, one the lightest brown. Her eyes were as unique as the rest of her.

The customer story led into a spider story. Her eyes turned wide. "I *hate* spiders. Like, if-I-see-one-I-freak-the-heck-out kind of hate." There was a small pause as she looked around. "I guess I can add small spaces to my hate list, too."

The smile began to slip from her mouth.

"What made you open your shop?" He was a desperate man. Desperate to see more of those smiles. Desperate to see the light wash over her face rather than the fear.

Her smile faded completely. Jeez, did he ask the wrong question?

"It was an idea my cousin and I had together. We dreamed about opening this colorful coffee shop in a small town." Courtney touched her necklace. "She, um, died a couple years ago."

Jason's muscles tensed. "I'm sorry."

"Thank you. We were really close growing up, but then she moved away for work. Even though we weren't as close when she died, losing her was still hard."

"Of course." He wanted to touch her. Her knee. Her thigh. Offer some sort of comfort. He didn't, having no idea how she would react. "What did you both do for work back then?"

"She moved to Richmond and worked as a nurse while I stayed in Jacksonville and worked as an architect. My dad's an architect and runs his own business. It was almost a foregone conclusion while I was growing up that I would join him and take over the company one day."

Her thumb rubbed in circles on the gem at the bottom of the necklace.

He couldn't imagine this woman being an architect. She had too much energy to sit at a drafting table or computer all day.

"And I did work with him for a while. But then Jessica died, and I guess you could say it woke me up. Made me acknowledge that life isn't forever, and you never know which day will be your last. I was doing what was expected of me, rather than what I wanted. So I left my family in Jacksonville, chose the town with the cutest name I could find, and used all my savings to open The Grind. I turned the dream that Jessica and I had into a reality."

So the woman was brave as well as beautiful.

Jason knew better than anyone that uprooting your entire life was anything but easy. "I know the feeling. I left the Army after five years to pursue a science degree."

Her head shot up. "Really?"

"Yeah. I got this itch, like there was something else I needed to do. When I graduated from pharmaceutical science at MIT, I got a job with the government, working on performance-enhancing drugs."

Surprise flickered over her face. "Were they the drugs..."

"That were used on me and my team while we were held hostage? Yep."

It didn't take long for him to realize the drugs they were working on did more than they should. All it had taken was one conversation with his boss, and that night, he'd been taken. Held hostage for years. Drugged. Forced to train.

"I'm not angry, though. I'm a strong believer in everything happening for a reason. I was supposed to learn about Project Arma so I could help destroy it. I was supposed to meet my team-mates, now my best friends and business partners. And I was supposed to be what I am now, so that I can help people."

Courtney's hand went to his forearm, and damn if he didn't feel her touch deep, like she'd singed him with fire. "You're amazing."

No. He'd just learned how to survive what had been thrown his way. "How did your cousin die?"

She sighed, her hand falling from his arm. He missed her touch immediately.

"Home invasion. She was, ah... beaten to death."

Every part of him tensed at that. Fuck, he hated lowlife scumbags who preyed on those weaker than them.

She shook her head. "What were you doing when Grace called?"

He wanted to ask more about her cousin. About her life. Hell, he wanted to learn everything there was to know about this woman. He didn't. "I went to buy some stuff for the reception desk at Blue Halo. We just hired a receptionist, and I think she was less than impressed with the supplies."

"But more than impressed by the muscle?" For a second her eyes widened, like she couldn't believe the words had come out of her mouth.

Jason only just held back a grin.

Suddenly, the elevator lurched.

Courtney leaned forward, grabbing his wrist in a tight hold. "Sweet Jesus, what was that?"

Taking her hand in his, Jason stood, tugging her up with him. He scanned the hatch he'd opened at the top of the car. "I think it might be time we got—"

Before he could finish, the elevator started moving again. Fortunately, it wasn't a lurch this time, but a normal pace.

Had someone finally fixed it?

Courtney just about sagged into his side, the tense fingers that had wrapped around his own in a death grip finally easing.

"Oh, good. It's working again. We're not going to die. Not today."

"No one's dying today, honey." His voice was light, just to keep her at ease, but in reality, he'd been moments away from throwing the woman over his shoulder and jumping through the top of the elevator.

They'd barely begun moving when the car stopped again. Peering up, he found the fourth-floor light glowing. When the doors opened, he expected to see someone waiting to get in.

He didn't. They were greeted by a large office space. Empty desks were scattered about the place. A few chairs and the odd bookcase.

What the hell?

Stepping forward, Jason pressed the button to close the doors. They waited a few seconds. Then a few more. The doors remained open, elevator unmoving.

"Let's just get out of here," Courtney said quietly, a sliver of unease in her voice. "Maybe the stairs are available again."

She slipped her hand from his and stepped out. The second her feet hit the fourth floor, she sighed so loudly it echoed off the walls. But her sigh wasn't the only thing Jason heard.

Voices. So quiet he almost missed them. *Would* have missed them if it wasn't for his enhanced hearing.

He swung his gaze to one side of the huge space, spotting an open door. Three men suddenly stepped out of what appeared to be a supply closet, each of them wearing a janitor's uniform. They looked to be around mid-thirties, all with dark hair and fit physiques.

The guy in front studied Courtney with interest before eyeing Jason. Then he almost looked angry.

Out of instinct, Jason took a half-step in front of her.

The guy's gaze narrowed. "What are you doing here?"

Jason tilted his head, trying to work out why these guys had his protective instincts pounding to the forefront. "There's a problem with the elevator. It delivered us here."

The guy sucked in a sharp breath. "I recognize you."

Of course he did. It had only been a few short months since his entire team had been plastered all over the Internet on every news report and social media platform.

The guy's eyes widened. "You're one of the soldiers who escaped that project. Had those experimental drugs used on him." He scanned Jason from head to toe, like he was looking for a second head to pop out or something.

"I am."

Now the guy looked nervous. Why? Because Jason was powerful? Strong?

The man nearest him started to move forward, but the front guy held out his arm, stopping him.

A voice, from what had to be an earpiece, pricked Jason's ears.

It was quiet, even for him, designed only for anyone wearing the device to hear. The voice was too muffled to understand.

The one man who had yet to move or speak angled his body away from them, responding to the voice by saying low and quiet, "No."

One word. *No to what?*

"Well, I think you should be going now," said the man who had done all the talking so far. "We have a lot of work to do here."

Jason remained where he was for a second. Then Courtney's hand grazed his arm, tugging at his attention.

"Jason. Let's go."

He nodded as the three men continued to watch them closely. Placing a hand on the small of Courtney's back, he walked her toward the door at the other end of the large room with an exit sign above the frame.

Eyes pierced his back the entire time. He listened for the slightest movement from the men. Even the rustling of clothing. There was only silence.

Jason had almost reached the door when he turned. "Does it always take three men to clean an unoccupied office?"

Something flashed in Front Guy's eyes. It was so fleeting, Jason couldn't quite identify it before it disappeared. "We're just doing the job we were asked to do."

Jason could spot a lie. People gave themselves away with shifts in breathing patterns. Hesitation in voices. This guy was telling the truth.

Turning, Jason followed Courtney down the last three flights of stairs. He continued to listen to everything around them. There was something about those guys that felt... off.

As they stepped outside, Courtney closed her eyes. "Fresh air has never felt so good." When her phone started to ring, she dug it out of her bag.

He listened in as she spoke to someone from the radio station. The woman was apologizing for missing her call. She then apologized again for their "glitchy" elevator. Apparently, this wasn't the first time it had stopped working. In fact, it had been happening for a couple of weeks.

"No, really, it's okay. I'm out. I'm fine." Jason looked up at the building as she ended the call. "They said this has been happening a bit over the—" She stopped, shaking her head. "What am I doing? I know you heard every word."

He lifted a shoulder, turning back to her. "That's okay."

She fiddled with the strap on her bag, taking a small step back. "Okay, well, thank you for coming. For, uh, keeping me company while I tried not to lose my mind. I really appreciate your help."

Her gaze flicked around the parking lot.

"Where are you parked?" he asked gently.

"Nowhere. I mean, *somewhere*, obviously, but you don't need to come with me. Not that you offered to walk me." She started walking backward as she rambled, and he almost laughed at her awkwardness. Now that the danger was over, she was nervous around him again. It was cute. "Since I'm no longer six floors up in a tiny deathtrap, I'm okay."

He stepped forward. The curb was right behind her. "Ah, Courtney—"

"No, really. You've done so much, I don't—"

She yelped a second before she tumbled backward. Jason reached her side before she hit the ground, tugging her back up, her chest so close to his that they almost touched.

Her lips parted on a small gasp. Heat washed over his abdomen. Every part of him wanted to take those lips with his own. See what this woman felt like. Tasted like. He bet she was sweet.

Her gaze shot to his mouth. His entire body hardened, his fingers around her arm tightening.

Then he gave himself a quick shake. They were in a parking

lot. Not exactly the place for a first kiss. Not with a woman like Courtney. She deserved more. Flowers. Dinner. Romance.

He forced himself to step back. Look away and take a breath in a weak attempt to calm himself.

Something crossed over her face. Disappointment maybe?

"Courtney—"

"Thank you. I, uh… yeah, thank you." Then she was gone. Turning and walking quickly across the road.

CHAPTER 3

*C*ourtney groaned as she rolled over onto her back. Okay, that dream had been way too real. *Jason* had been way too real. All six-feet-four of him.

Were you supposed to feel a person's breath on your skin in a dream? Or taste them when they kissed you? No. *Hell no.* Because then you just woke up hot, bothered, and disappointed, like she was right now.

She scrubbed her face, trying and failing to scour the dream away.

Jason had been standing right there in front of her outside that radio station, just like yesterday. Only in her dream, instead of him stepping back when she'd glanced at his mouth, he'd stepped *forward*, planting those beautiful lips on hers and all but devouring her.

Her heart pounded against her ribs at the memory.

Argh, dreams sucked.

No. Reality sucked. And not just the him-not-kissing-her part.

She cringed at the memory of what she'd done after the not-kiss. If turning into a nervous, bumbling mess wasn't enough, she'd then walked off in the complete opposite direction of her car. And, of course, she hadn't turned around like a normal person when sense had finally found her. No, she'd had to do a full lap around a random block just to save face.

Lun-a-tic.

Reaching across the bed, she grabbed a pillow and shoved it over her face. He had to know she'd wanted him to kiss her. But he hadn't. Spoke volumes, didn't it?

Gah. Throwing the pillow to the side, she pushed up onto her elbows. Eddie stretched beside her, meowing loudly as she rubbed his belly.

"How was your sleep, Eddie? Better than mine?" Did cats dream? Surely. And their dreams probably didn't torture them with stolen moments that would never become reality.

Okay. Time to get up. She needed to be at The Grind by nine. What was the time?

Stretching toward the side table, she'd just grabbed her phone when a knock came at her apartment door.

She jumped, a screech leaving her lips as she tumbled off the bed, hitting the floor with a thud.

God dang it. This was not her day. Heck, this was not her *week*.

She knew who it was, who it always was... Helen Ellis from the apartment next to hers. The woman was always at her door. Usually talking about her dog, Bernie. She treated him like he was a king among men. Home-cooked food—all organic, of course—a bedroom all to himself, outfits... the list went on.

She stood, leaning over and giving a startled Eddie one last pat. "Sorry, buddy. You're just an ordinary pet in this household."

He purred, leaning into her hand.

Yeah, you don't mind.

Another knock echoed through the apartment, this time louder. "Yeah, yeah, I'm coming, old woman."

Courtney reached the door, talking before the thing was even open. "Helen, I'm really not—"

She looked up, almost choking on her words before slamming the door shut again. *Not* Helen. Not even a small, minuscule crumb of a resemblance to the older woman.

"Courtney?" Jason's deep, rumbly voice had all the fine hairs on her arms standing on end.

Taking a step back, she looked at the mirror across the room. Oh, sweet Jesus.

A mess. A total and complete mess. Her naturally wavy blond hair was akin to a bird's nest. Her pink sleep top with cute bunnies on the front was crooked and wrinkled. And was that a handprint on the side of her face?

"Are you okay?"

She took another step back at the deep timbre of his voice. It took three seconds for her shocked vocals to produce anything. "Uh, yes." Okay, she'd definitely just croaked those words.

"Can I come in?"

Her gaze darted around the living room. Her cozy, lived-in apartment suddenly seemed cluttered and even smaller. "No."

He chuckled. "Why not, honey?"

"Because my apartment's a mess and I look like a bridge troll."

Another sexy laugh that had her feminine parts tingling. "I already saw you. You look beautiful."

Beautiful?

"And I brought coffee."

She frowned. "I own a coffee shop."

"I know. I made this one at my place."

He made her coffee? No one ever made her coffee. *She* was the coffee maker. Argh, now she *had* to let him in, didn't she? "Okay, uh, hang on."

Running to her bathroom, she rummaged through a drawer.

Bingo. A hair tie that might just save her.

She pulled the tangled mess into a bun on top of her head and inspected herself in the mirror. Not great, but not terrible. Now at least it looked like an intentional bird's nest. Rushing back to the bedroom, she threw on a pair of jeans and T-shirt before returning to the door.

Okay, deep breath.

When she opened it, Jason's mouth lifted on one side, showing that dimple she loved so much. Yep, the man was stunning, even at crazy early hours of the morning.

"Come in." She stepped back.

He moved into the room, dwarfing the small space in much the same way he had the elevator yesterday. "I don't see the mess you were talking about. Your place looks great."

Her cheeks heated at the compliment. Closing the door, she turned to face him, and the second she did, every single English word that she'd ever learned disappeared from her frazzled mind. So she went with a smile.

"Did I hear a thud before you came to the door?"

Crap. Yes, and he would have heard the screech, and the muttered words under her breath to Eddie and about Helen.

She headed to the kitchen, swallowing and forcing her brain to produce words. "I fell out of bed."

His brows rose as he scanned her body. "Are you okay?"

"Yes." It was just her pride that was wounded. She tugged the fridge door open, more to hide herself than anything else. "Have you eaten? I can scramble up some eggs on toast?" Wait, did she have bread? And if she did, was it edible?

Eating a lot of meals at The Grind sometimes meant the food she kept at home was minimal. And when she said sometimes, she meant every dang day.

"No, that's okay. I just came to check on you."

Phew. She was pretty sure eggs were all she had to offer, and really, who wanted eggs with a side of eggs?

She closed the door, almost jumping out of her skin when Jason was right there. Like, literally standing where the fridge door had just been.

The coffees were now sitting on the island counter.

Suddenly, images from her dream bombarded her. Of Jason bending down. His breath brushing her lips. His mouth pressing against hers.

Her belly flopped. Jeez, she needed to get out of her head. Taking three big steps back, she hit the counter. "Check on me? Oh, after yesterday? Yeah, I'm okay. I just... I'm struggling with small spaces at the moment."

Struggling, scared out of her mind... They were the same thing, right?

"The other week, when you couldn't walk into the freezer at The Grind, I thought it was just that space, because that's where you'd been locked in."

Holy Moses, she'd almost forgotten about Jason walking into the back room at The Grind to find her standing there like a stunned mullet, unable to move. The second he'd offered to go into the freezer and grab the cakes for her, she'd almost fallen into his arms in gratitude.

"No. Not just the freezer, although yes, that thing terrifies me now. Joey's been moving what we need each day into the smaller freezers I just bought."

Joey was her second-in-charge at the coffee shop. Her right-hand man. Her life jacket in the stormy sea of running a cafe.

Worry skittered over Jason's features. "Have you thought about talking to Grace about what happened?"

Yes. But each time she considered it, she also gave herself a reason not to. Like she was busy. Or Grace wouldn't have time. Or it was strange asking her friend to put her therapist hat on for a formal appointment.

And the reason she'd come up with all those excuses was because she was sure Grace would make her relive the experience. That was how therapy worked, wasn't it? You had to talk about what happened. What you felt.

No, thank you. Not right now, at least.

"I'm okay. It's Grace we should be worried about. Logan and

her father were almost murdered before her eyes. Not to mention the way she had to run for her life and almost froze to death."

Jason lifted a coffee from the island. Taking slow steps toward her, he handed her the drink. Her skin tingled where it brushed his, the tingle rushing from her hand right up her arm.

"Her experience doesn't diminish yours," he said quietly.

Where had this man come from? A factory of men who had twelve-packs and said perfect things? She'd never dated a guy like him. Heck, she'd never *met* a guy like him until moving to Cradle Mountain.

All the guys she'd ever dated had been douchebags. The kind who squeezed your ass when you were close and thought two words was the extent of conversation required for the day.

"I know. And I appreciate you checking on me. And for coming and helping me yesterday." *Saving me.* She lifted the coffee, taking a sip. "Mm, it's good."

He lifted his own. "But not as good as yours?"

"Rule number one of business, believe in your product. I can't go telling people their homemade coffee is better than my coffee shop coffee. I'd go out of business."

One of his massive shoulders lifted. "You could just tell me. I can keep a secret."

She chuckled. "Good try, buddy, not happening. My lips are sealed." Particularly because his coffee was damn good. What beans did he use?

He took a small step closer. She breathed him in. Nature and coffee. It was a scent she could easily become addicted to.

"I like that sound."

Her breath tried to catch in her throat, but she greedily sucked in air. "What sound?"

"That beautiful laugh of yours."

Her limbs suddenly felt lethargic. "That's the second time you've said beautiful in reference to me today."

Another step forward. Oh, God, she might pass out on the spot if he got any closer. As it was, her heart was crashing against her ribs like a swinging punching bag. When he lifted a hand and placed it on her upper arm, a small squeak nearly escaped her lips.

"Because you are."

Words left her head once more. She almost looked down at his mouth again. Almost.

Giving herself a quick mental shake, Courtney stepped to the side before moving around the island, not entirely certain she wasn't running away from him.

Okay, she was definitely running away from him and one hundred percent hiding from his touch.

"Thank you for stopping by." She almost wanted to pat herself on the back for speaking actual words. "I should get ready for work. Joey hates it when I'm late. Sometimes you'd wonder who's the boss, him or me."

A ghost of a smile tugged at Jason's lips. Too. Damn. Sexy.

Turning, she headed for the door, tugging it open. "And thank you for the coffee."

And the visit. And the smiles. And calling me beautiful so many times my insides turn molten.

He followed and stopped in front of her. Her eyes hit his big chest like it was the most interesting thing she'd ever seen... which wasn't far from the truth.

"I'm glad you're okay." Then his hand went to her upper arm again. He gave her a gentle squeeze before walking away. And she was left standing there, feeling branded—burned—by his touch.

CHAPTER 4

"*S*omeone's happy."

Jason swung his head around at the sound of his friend and business partner, Tyler. Tyler was the youngest on the team, but you'd never be able to tell. He was just as big and strong as the rest of them. And equally dangerous.

Closing his car door, Jason nodded. "Always happy to be at work."

But more than that, happy to start his day off with a bit of Courtney.

Tyler gave him a knowing smile. "Nah, it's something else."

Damn, the guy saw right through him.

They headed across the parking lot. "It wouldn't be our new blue-eyed receptionist, would it?"

Amy? Jason almost laughed out loud. The woman was pretty, and he was sure most men would fall all over themselves for her. But she wasn't the one who plagued his mind morning, noon, and night.

Amy had been a late applicant for the receptionist job, but the guys had still decided to interview her, and she'd blown the other applicants out of the water. She'd been by far the most confident, with the most experience behind her. And because they'd handled the interviewing and selection process, he'd offered to take the lead on training the woman.

"Barely even registered she had blue eyes."

The door was midway open when Tyler froze. "You're serious? You've spent the last week training her and didn't notice how stunning she is? How on earth is that—" He stopped, understanding lighting his eyes.

Ah, crap.

"Courtney."

Jason shook his head, walking past Tyler and onto the stairs. His entire team had probably seen the way he looked at the woman. It was hard to miss. "If you think Amy's stunning, ask her out. I'm pretty sure she's single."

Actually, he knew she was. The woman had told him on her first day at Blue Halo. He'd responded with what he'd hoped was a polite smile.

Tyler chuckled, following him up the stairs. "Maybe I will. And maybe you should ask Courtney out."

That was an idea he could get behind. And something he'd already thought about... a lot.

Stopping at Courtney's place this morning had been a last-minute decision. Best damn decision he'd made all week. The idea of dating her, kissing her... yeah, he liked it.

"Maybe."

Before his friend could respond, Jason pushed open the door to Blue Halo. Amy immediately stood from her position behind the desk.

"Good morning." Her smile was wide, teeth so white they were almost blinding.

The woman *was* pretty in a perfectly polished and understated kind of way. Not Jason's type. He liked color. Vibrancy. An effortless, natural beauty.

"Good morning." He stopped in front of the desk, tapping the surface with his hand. "You're here early."

She'd only been with the company for a week, but so far, she'd impressed the hell out of him and everyone else on the team. She was efficient, hardworking, and quick to pick things up.

She lifted a shoulder. "I'm an early bird. Should I make some coffee? Or I could run down to the coffee shop and grab some for everyone?"

"Not for me, thanks." Jason had barely finished his cup before arriving.

Tyler stepped up beside him. "Me either."

She nodded, eyes darting to the computer. She bent over, clicking on something with the mouse. "Jason, I was wondering if you could help me. I was having trouble with the calendars."

"Sure thing." Heading around the desk, he didn't miss the way Tyler nudged his shoulder, or the way he lifted his brows suggestively as he walked down the hall.

Get lost, buddy.

"I'll open Tyler's calendar to show you." She clicked into it. "See, there's this blacked-out section that wasn't there yesterday. And usually when I click on an item, it gives me details, but when I click on the blacked-out days, I just get 'unavailable'."

Jason nodded. The blacked-out periods were days when the team would be occupied with off-the-books missions, assigned to them by their FBI liaison, Steve. That was a part of the business that Amy knew very little about—and would continue to know little about, until she'd been working for them a lot longer.

"Remember when I told you there were certain parts of the business we couldn't share just yet? That's one of them."

"Oh." She glanced at the screen, and then back to him, recovering quickly. "Okay, no problem. So, I'll just consider those blacked-out periods as someone being completely unavailable?"

He gave a quick nod. "Yep."

She touched his arm, giving it a light squeeze. "That's a relief.

For a moment I thought I was going crazy, accidentally messing up huge chunks of the calendar or something."

When her touch fell away, Jason almost felt relieved.

Yeah. He was definitely taken by another woman.

He was about to walk away when Amy stepped closer. Again, she touched his arm. "Don't run away. There were a couple of messages for you overnight. I was going to email them, but now that you're here, I can just tell you."

Reaching behind her, she grabbed a piece of paper. "Steve called and wants someone to call him back. Your eleven o'clock appointment asked to reschedule, and the superintendent from the building on Greenby Street called, claiming he was returning your call."

Good. He'd been waiting for that guy to get back to him. He took the paper from Amy's outstretched hand.

"The superintendent said he's free anytime today if you want to call him back."

It was like the woman read his mind. This is why she'd become an asset to the office. "Great. Thanks, Amy."

She gave him one of her huge smiles before winking. "You got it."

Jason headed into his own office, then sat behind the desk and immediately dialed the number.

"Andrew speaking."

He leaned back. "Andrew, this is Jason Porter, sorry I missed your call."

"Jason, yes, and I'm sorry I missed your call too, from yesterday. What can I do for you?"

He tapped his fingers on the desk. "A friend and I got stuck in your elevator yesterday. I was wondering if that happens a lot?"

The guy sighed. "Yeah, sorry, it's happened a couple of times over the last few weeks. I got an electrician out, but he couldn't find anything wrong. I guess I can get someone else out to have a second look. The thing is old though, just like the building, not really a surprise it's acting up."

Surprising or not, it wasn't okay. The problem needed to be identified and people taking the elevator warned. "Do you keep any video surveillance in the building?"

"Surveillance? No. Why would I? These are offices and a radio station. Cradle Mountain isn't exactly a place of high crime."

No, it wasn't. He scrubbed a hand down his face. "Okay. Thanks. One more thing... we ran into some janitors on the fourth floor. Do they work for you?"

"Kid, I source my janitors from Ketchum Janitorial Services. I don't keep on top of exactly who they send, all I care about is whether they get the job done. Which they do. Why? Was there a problem? Because I've never had a problem with them in the past."

The guy's voice was starting to get defensive. Jason already knew he wasn't getting anything else from him.

He remained calm as he thanked the building manager and hung up.

Leaning back, he took a moment to digest the information. Maybe he was overthinking what happened yesterday. It was looking like the incident had been nothing more than a faulty elevator.

COURTNEY SLID another coffee across the counter. It had to be the hundredth she'd personally served today, or some equally crazy number. Usually, she rotated between making drinks and working the floor, but the server she had on was young and not confident in making coffee, and Joey looked... tired.

Even though he was only twenty-one, a good ten years her junior, she loved the guy. He was more of a friend than an employee. And usually the quickest person in the place. Today, though, he looked exhausted. She cast another glance at him from beneath her lashes.

The second his gaze clashed with hers, she looked away. *Dang it.*

The next second, he was beside her. "Courtney, I told you, I'm fine."

"I know." She busied herself with starting the next order, keeping her eyes off him. Truth be told, he had a right to be annoyed. It was nearing closing time, and she'd probably studied him a gazillion times.

"Then why is it I keep catching you looking at me like I'm a drowning rat that needs saving?"

She spun around, hands on her hips, voice low. "Maybe because you have rings under your eyes that look like they've been drawn on with permanent marker. Did you sleep last night?"

He rolled his eyes. He was the only person who worked for her who would do such a thing. And the only person she didn't mind doing it. "Of course. Courtney, I'm a young guy. I went out last night, it's what we do. I'm sorry if it's affected my work today—"

"It hasn't. I was just worried."

Both statements were true. Even though he looked tired, he'd pulled his weight. Still, she'd insisted he be on the lighter table-bussing duty.

Some of the strain eased from his face. "I appreciate that you're concerned, but you don't need to be. I should be the one pestering *you* about how flushed you look every time a certain *someone* enters the shop."

Ah, crap. She was so dang obvious, wasn't she? And if Joey noticed, there was no way Jason hadn't.

Even though he'd dropped by her apartment with coffee yesterday morning, he'd also come to The Grind for lunch a few hours later. She tried not to read too much into it. It wasn't unusual for him to visit the shop at some point during the day. She loved it and hated it at the same time. Hated it because her words got jumbled on a daily basis in her own workplace. Loved it because, well, it was Jason.

"No pestering required, Joey." Heck, she pestered herself enough.

When the doorbell dinged, Courtney looked up to see a man in a suit walk inside. She touched Joey's arm. "I've got it."

He muttered something under his breath that sounded like, "Of course you do."

She chuckled, walking over to the tall stranger at the end of the counter. He wasn't looking back—instead, he scanned the shop before his gaze landed on a framed magazine article on the side wall.

Courtney's smile widened. It was the *Living in Idaho Today* two-page spread of the shop. It included a big writeup as well as a collage of pictures. The picture in the middle, the biggest, was of Courtney, smiling behind the counter.

How many copies of the magazine had she bought? Probably a dozen. And the only reason she hadn't bought more was because she wanted *some* other people to have a chance to read it.

It was evidence of her hard work. Of her success. She wished Jessica was here to celebrate with her but knew her cousin would be looking down at her, proud as punch.

With a mental shake of her head, she smiled at the man. "Hi! I'm Courtney, can I grab you a coffee?"

The man was clearly an out-of-towner, which hadn't been out of the ordinary for Cradle Mountain lately. Not just because of her article in the magazine, but also because the men from Blue Halo—the illegal experiments they'd endured—had been exposed.

The man turned, studying her in much the same way as he'd studied the article. When his gaze lowered to her chest—and *remained* on her chest for a good thirty seconds—her smile faltered.

Okay, this suit had quickly turned into a sleazebag.

"We're actually closing in a few minutes," she said quickly. And then, only because she felt compelled out of politeness, added, "I can get you something to go."

He gave a curt nod. "A coffee to go would be good."

Accent. Figures. He looked like a *rich* sleazebag, from somewhere far away.

This time, her smile was tight as she turned and started on the coffee. She made sure her back was firmly facing the guy as she worked. And if he stared at her ass, she didn't want to know.

"You are the owner?"

She nodded without turning. "I am. Been running this baby for almost two years now. She's my pride and joy."

"And before?"

"Before I lived in Cradle Mountain?" So now the chest-starer wanted information on her? Uh, that was a solid no. "I moved around a bit." Lie. "I lived in at least a dozen towns before I settled on this one."

Big. Fat. Lie. If he read the article, he'd know that, but she doubted a guy like him would bother.

"Do you have a boyfriend?"

For a second, she paused in what she was doing. Okay, she might have just thrown up a bit in her mouth. "Yep. I do." The lies were just rolling off her tongue now. "He's former military. Very big and strong and we're totally infatuated with each other. Barely apart." Barely apart *in her dreams*.

She finished the coffee quickly, fitting the lid before turning and handing it to the guy. "Here you go."

He handed over a bill. "Keep the change."

She looked down, and her eyes almost bugged out of her head. A hundred-dollar bill? "Are you sure?"

This could buy him twenty coffees, with a healthy side of donuts.

"It was nice to meet you, Courtney."

She was still standing there, mouth so far open it was almost touching her chest, when Joey came to stand beside her. "Holy shit, did he give you a hundred? For a coffee?"

"It would appear so." It should make her like him more, shouldn't it? But it didn't. In fact, she wanted nothing more than to get rid of the bill from the guy who'd checked her out like she was a piece of meat.

She handed it to Joey.

This time, *his* eyes almost bugged out of his head. "You're giving it to me?"

The dirty money? Yeah. "You deserve it. Consider it a tip because I'd be lost without you." Like, completely lost. She had other workers, but they didn't come close to having his work ethic, availability, or skills. She pushed it into his hand. "And you can go now if you want. I'll do the close."

There was one customer left in a booth, and Courtney could already see the woman grabbing her bag to go.

"Okay, who are you and what have you done with hard-ass Courtney?"

She chuckled, pushing him away. "Go."

"Seriously though, are you sure?" He held up the hundred.

"Yes! Now get your ass out of here before I physically remove you."

He chuckled, and boy was it good to see a smile on his face, probably the first of the day. "Okay. Thank you. For the tip and the early finish."

"Don't thank me. Thank Mr. Suit." Aka, Mr. Chest-Starer.

He shook his head, already moving toward the door.

Once Joey and the last customer had left, Courtney cleaned the coffee machine then mopped the floors. Half an hour later, she was leaving as well. Her apartment was right in the center of

Cradle Mountain, so she rarely ever drove to work. Locking the doors, she headed across the street.

Takeout was on the menu for tonight. And lots of Eddie cuddles on the couch. She smiled, already dreaming about her lazy night.

When something sounded behind her—footsteps—Courtney paused, turning her head.

There was no one there.

She frowned. Was she going so loopy that she was hearing things now? Hearing people that didn't exist? Giving herself a mental shake, she kept walking.

Mr. Suit had probably affected her. That, and her experience of having a knife pressed against her throat and being locked in her freezer with a dead body. God, she really *did* need to book a session with Grace. She knew she should. Heck, she was sure Grace would make any space available that she needed.

But if Courtney was good at anything, it was putting off hard stuff that she didn't want to do. Why else would she have gone into an architecture career that she never wanted? Or dated men who were so wrong for her and treated her like crap?

It was easier to avoid hard conversations.

Grow some courage, woman.

When the noise behind her sounded again, Courtney didn't stop this time, instead sneaking a peek over her shoulder as she turned a corner.

She only just faced forward in time to see a huge body in front of her.

God Almighty!

Her hands flew to a hard chest, while bigger hands grabbed her upper arms.

CHAPTER 5

*J*ason grabbed Courtney's arms to steady her. Her small, warm hands flattened on his chest, awareness trilling in his veins.

She yanked them back. He almost chuckled at her wide eyes. "Are you okay?" he asked.

"I'm sorry! Yes, I'm okay, I was just"—she glanced over her shoulder for a beat then looked back at him—"distracted."

When she didn't offer anything more in the way of explanation, Jason followed her gaze. He didn't see anything but an empty street. "Distracted by what?"

She gave a small shake of her head. "It's nothing. My imagination has been way too overactive since... well, you know. What happened with Kieran." Jason's hands tightened a fraction at the mention of that asshole's name. "Plus, I just had Mr. Suit come into the shop and stare at my chest for a solid thirty seconds. *That* was a bit off-putting."

This time, it wasn't just Jason's hands that tightened. "Someone came in and stared at your chest?" Who was this scumbag and where could Jason find him to knock his damn teeth out?

"Yes, but he didn't stay long. Not after I told him we were closing. Don't worry, if he had, I would have thrown some coffee into his lap or something, you know, as an accident."

Good. He was almost tempted to tell Courtney to let him know if the jerk returned, but only just stopped himself. They weren't dating, so he couldn't really ask her to do that. Not yet. "Did you walk to work?"

"Yep." A thread of blond hair escaped her ponytail, and Jason's hand twitched to reach out and brush it back. To graze that delicate skin of hers. Instead, he stepped to her side. "I'll walk you home."

For a second, she looked like she was going to argue. Her mouth opened, and those green and brown eyes shot from him to the path behind them and back.

"Really?"

Actually, he wanted to do more than that. But everything else would have to wait. "Yes. If that's okay. I was walking to the shop and hoping to catch you."

For a moment she looked like a deer caught in headlights. God, the woman was cute. "Catch me?"

Yeah, sounded kind of creepy like that, didn't it? "Just to chat, Courtney."

Her mouth formed a small 'O'. She remained like that for another few seconds. Jason almost chuckled.

Then the word he was waiting for slipped from her lips. "Okay."

His smile widened. As they started to walk, he matched his steps to hers. Even though they weren't touching, her heat—her energy—bounced from her body to his. "Any grand plans for your Wednesday night?"

She scoffed. "If ordering takeout and eating it on the couch with Eddie counts as grand plans, then sure."

Ah, maybe one day he would get an invite to a night like that.

It would certainly be grand for him. "What kind of takeout does Eddie like?"

Her lips twitched. "Ha-ha. As much as I love Eddie, there's no way I'd share my dumplings and pizza with him."

"Dumplings *and* pizza?"

"Yeah." She glanced up at him, a twinkle in her eyes. "I order a pepperoni pizza from Pizza Malloy, and some Asian greens and prawn dumplings from Popshaw. That factors in my vegetables, my carbs, and my protein. And *sometimes*, when I'm feeling extra indulgent, I also get some chocolate mousse from Perry's Desserts."

Jason's eyebrows flew up. How the heck did the woman stay so tiny? "Three different deliveries?"

She nodded. "Yup."

"And Perry will deliver you a single serving of mousse?"

"Perry loves me. The first time she came into The Grind, she asked me to put an extra spoon of sugar into her coffee. Then she told me that she'd never ask again because if she didn't know about it, it didn't exist." She lifted a shoulder. "So, I've been putting that extra spoon in ever since. I also give her a free cookie. Which she doesn't ask for but also ordered the first time she came in."

He chuckled. Was that woman-logic or something? "Okay. But ever thought about getting Asian one night, pizza another, and just stopping for your dessert on the way home?"

She paused mid-step. "Jason, have you tried Popshaw's dumplings? They're *a-mazing*. And don't even get me started on the pepperoni pizza. Also, if Perry doesn't mind delivering the cups of fluffy heaven that melt on your tongue, then why make an unnecessary detour?"

He'd tried the mousse. It was good, but heaven that melts on your tongue? Nope. Kissing Courtney, on the other hand...

"I prefer Perry's homemade hazelnut ice cream." His voice was too gruff, but dammit, he couldn't help it.

"Hm, I haven't tried it."

"Maybe it's time to try something new." He lifted a shoulder. "Life's short. You don't want to miss out on something that might be a game changer."

For a second her gaze heated, then just as quickly, she faced forward and her feet started moving again.

Another chuckle he barely held in.

Were her thoughts in line with his? That *they* could be a game changer? Because he was almost certain of it.

Conversation remained light for the rest of the walk. And even though Courtney had insisted there had been nothing behind her, he kept his gaze peeled, constantly watching in case of any threats.

When they reached her apartment stairwell—bypassing the elevator, of course—he held the door open for her, trailing up behind. The apartment building was fairly new, but it didn't have nearly the level of security that Jason would have preferred. As it was, the door Courtney had just opened at street level remained unlocked during the day. And the complete lack of any alarm system, even at night, left her prey to intruders.

At her door, Courtney turned to face him, fiddling with the key in both hands. "Thank you for walking me. It was lovely to have the company."

Some of her earlier confidence seeped away.

He took a small step closer, her scent of coffee and gardenias washing over him. "Courtney, I wanted to say something."

She became completely still. The hall was silent, bar the pitter-patter of her heart.

"Sometimes," *a lot of the time*, "I feel your nervous energy around me."

Another slight increase in her heart rate, this time accompanied with a shift in her breathing. "You make me nervous," she said quietly. So quietly, her words barely met his ears.

"Why?"

She almost looked like she was going to laugh. "Have you seen yourself? You look like you belong on a magazine cover and you have these dimples in your cheeks when you smile that make my tummy do this weird flippy thing."

Okay, now the woman was just pumping his ego. "So... I make you nervous because you like me?" He already knew the answer, but he wanted her to confirm it. He needed the words.

Her multicolored eyes remained glued to his. Intense. Watching. "Yes."

Good. It meant he wouldn't feel like an overstepping creep when he did this...

Another small step forward. Her eyes widened. Then he bent and pressed a kiss on her cheek, right beside her ear. He was tempted to take her lips, so damn tempted, but that would come.

His lips lingered as her heart pounded loudly.

When he finally lifted his mouth, it was only a fraction, and only so that he could whisper into her ear, "I like you too, Courtney Davies."

COURTNEY PUSHED the door to her apartment closed, narrowly stopping herself from sinking to the floor.

Okay, it hadn't been a kiss on the lips, but holy smokes, she swore she felt his lips all over her.

Every. Single. Limb.

And then his warm breath against her ear... Argh, could a brain short circuit from a kiss? Because it sure felt like it.

A low meow at her feet pulled Courtney out of her thoughts. Sighing, she bent down, patting Eddie's head. "Sorry, buddy, I know you're hungry. Mommy's a bit distracted."

Very distracted.

Straightening, she pulled out her phone and made the three

separate calls for dinner before feeding Eddie. Then she headed to the shower, thoughts of Jason—of his touches, his kiss—skittering through her mind like a TV show on replay. Lord, she was obsessed.

She'd just thrown on her sleep clothes when her dumplings, pizza, and ice cream arrived, almost at once. And yes, she'd taken a chance and gone with the ice cream.

She studied the tub. *I'm trusting you, Jason. This better be good.*

Ha, even if it wasn't, just looking at the stuff would make her think about him... so totally worth it.

Popping the ice cream into the freezer, she grabbed some food before dropping onto the couch with the remote.

Time to become a couch potato.

She flicked through the channels, trying to find something to hold her attention. Trying and failing. Damn Jason and his too-sexy-for-his-own-good lips. The man was robbing her of her nightly entertainment. Even *The Office*, a show which never failed her—because really, who didn't love a bit of Dwight in their life? —almost felt like watching paint dry.

It was official. The man was ruining her.

Taking a bite of pizza, she pulled out her phone and texted Grace.

Courtney: I need something to watch. Something super interesting.

Grace's response was almost immediate.

Grace: Hm, Logan and I just finished a season of You. That was good.

Was that the show about the cute "normal" guy who turned out to be a homicidal psychopath? Eh, no.

Courtney: Anything else? Anything less homicidal?

Grace: Lol. The Office?

Courtney almost laughed. Her friend shared her love for the show, but where Courtney loved Dwight, the dorky, intense paper salesman, Grace loved the budding romance between two of the main characters, Jim and Pam. To be fair, the way Jim treated Pam on the show was what dreams were made of. It definitely far exceeded anything Courtney had experienced in real life.

Courtney: Yeah. I might just watch that. Are you coming to the shop tomorrow?

Grace came in most days, and Courtney loved it. Twice a day probably wouldn't be enough. The woman was so damn calm that it almost evened out Courtney's crazy.

Grace: Yes! I'll pop in late morning. Is that okay?

Courtney: Girl, if you don't, I'll be hunting you down. I have a lot to tell you.

Okay, maybe not a lot in normal-person speak, but a kiss from Jason, even if it was just on the cheek, was a lot for Courtney. Especially when, on an average day, she struggled to even talk to the guy.

Grace: Now I'm looking forward to catching up even more. Enjoy The Office. X

Courtney: See you tomorrow. xox

She took another bite of her pizza, putting her phone down on the coffee table. She was two slices, three dumplings, and four episodes into *The Office* when she finally decided it was time to call it a night. She hadn't gotten to the ice cream yet, but it could wait until tomorrow. She was stuffed.

Courtney had just packed up everything and gone to her room when her cell buzzed. She plucked it from the bedside table. When she looked at the screen, the phone almost tumbled from her fingers.

Holy Jesus...

Hey! It's Jason. Did you end up going with the ice cream or the mousse?

How did the guy even have her number? Not that she was surprised he did. He was in the security business. They could get their hands on entire background checks within minutes, couldn't they?

Courtney perched herself on the edge of the bed for a solid five minutes, just looking at the screen. She started typing a few messages, only to quickly delete the words.

Don't overthink it, Courtney. Just message the guy.

Her fingers returned to the keys.

Courtney: Hey! You might be pleased to discover that I trusted your judgment and went with the ice cream. Although, it's still untouched in my freezer because I went a bit too hard on the dumplings and pizza.

The second she hit send, she scrunched her eyes shut. Stuffing your face with takeout was hardly a turn-on.

Jason: Maybe I'll have to join you when you start on the ice cream.

The fine hairs on her arms stood on end.

Courtney: How did you get my number?

Jason: I may have asked a certain friend of yours for it.

So, Grace. Not surprising. Not when Grace knew how infatuated she was with the guy. Permission wasn't needed.

Jason: Is that okay?

Okay? Heck, she would have personally jogged it over to Blue Halo if she'd known he wanted it.

Courtney: Yes.

Jason: Good, so you're not sick of me yet.

Could a woman get sick of a man like Jason? Ha. No.

Courtney: Not yet. And I guess you texting means you're not sick of me either.

Jason: Impossible.

She smiled, despite knowing that wasn't true. Not even a little bit. Not if her history with guys said anything. Cheating meant you were sick of someone, didn't it? But then, something told her that Jason wouldn't do that. Call it a gut instinct.

Eddie jumped onto the bed, sidling up beside her. She patted his smooth golden mane, considering how to respond. A second later, another message came through.

Jason: I'm glad we were able to clear the air on how we feel about each other.

Her hand paused mid-stroke, eyes temporarily shuttering, remembering the kiss.

Courtney: Me too.

Rising from the bed, she walked over to the window, about to pull down the blinds... but before she did, her gaze caught something on the lawn below her apartment.

Was that a person beside the tree?

Her phone dinged in her hand, but instead of looking at it, she squinted through the glass. Definitely a person. And for a second, she thought they were looking up at her. But now they were walking away...

She quickly gave herself a shake. She lived in an apartment building in the middle of town. Of course there were people around the place.

She shut the blinds and slid beneath the sheets, then looked back to her phone. Her heart immediately gave a little kick.

Jason: I'm really looking forward to getting to know you better, Courtney.

Jeez, there went her heartbeat taking off again.

Courtney: I'm not very interesting.

Jason: I doubt that.

Courtney: And I'll try not to freeze up on you.

Or talk like a rambling idiot.

Jason: You're perfect either way.

Oh, sweet Jesus. First he'd called her beautiful, and now perfect. So different from any other guy who'd been in her life.

Courtney: You should stop saying such sweet things to me. I don't know if my heart can take it.

In fact, she was almost certain it couldn't.

Jason: I can't promise you that. Sleep well, honey.

She closed her eyes, elation filtering through her limbs.

Courtney: You too, Jason. X

She swore under her breath at the accidental kiss. Dang it. But then the next message from Jason came through.

Jason: Xox

Oh, Lord. She was in trouble.

CHAPTER 6

"*T*ickets are all booked, and we'll be up Friday."

Jason leaned back in his seat, grinning with excitement to see his twin sister. She and her partner Mason didn't get to visit nearly enough, especially with him living in Cradle Mountain and her in Marble Falls. The only reason he was okay with her being so far away was because he knew how capable Mason from Marble Protection was of looking after her.

His fingers brushed against the wooden desk in his office. "Logan and I will have all the camping gear ready to go for Saturday night. Remember, it's cold here, so pack warm clothes."

Weather in Idaho was far different from the weather in Texas. Luckily, Jason didn't get affected by the cold too much. Sage did, though, so he hoped she packed well for her trip.

They were camping on some land owned by Flynn, which was right here in Idaho, only an hour out of Cradle Mountain.

"I'm so excited. Both to see you and to camp for a night. I haven't camped since... gosh, it would have to be since we were kids."

With it being so cold, they were only going for one night, but hell, a night camping with his sister was better than nothing.

He chuckled. "Don't worry, the overwhelming smell of smoke, pine trees, and hot cocoa will come back to you."

"And s'mores. We can't forget the s'mores."

Shuffling noises sounded in the background seconds before his sister chuckled.

Mason. It had to be.

And that was his cue. "I'm going to get going, sis. I'll see you next weekend."

She chuckled again, clearly distracted now. "Okay. I love you."

"Love you, too."

Hanging up, he placed his phone down and clicked into his emails.

God, he loved his sister. They'd been close growing up. Being twins, it was impossible not to be. Same classes, same friends... even as adults they'd remained close. Then Project Arma had happened. It had affected his sister more than it should have.

His muscles clenched at the memory. The men who had taken Jason had taken her too. Only for a day, but that was all it took for her to almost die.

To almost die at *his* hands.

A sick nausea welled in his gut. The same nausea that rolled in every time he thought about it. He'd been drugged. Forced into a murderous rage, while she'd been right there in the cage with him.

He ground his teeth, his grip on the mouse tightening.

Never again would he be someone else's victim. A pawn in someone else's game.

A knock on the door tugged him out of his thoughts, sending his gaze up.

"You got a sec?" Logan asked.

"For you, always."

His friend folded his big body into the seat on the other side of Jason's desk. "I spoke to Grace about the camping trip. She's looking forward to it." There was an edge to Logan's voice.

"But...?"

Logan sighed. "She's a bit anxious about spending time with Sage and Mason after talking to the reporter."

That was understandable. Grace had been working as a therapist for two of the women in Marble Falls. She'd then broken patient/therapist confidentiality by speaking to a reporter. Exposing Project Arma for all involved.

"Did you tell her that Sage and Mason specifically asked for her to come? That they know why Grace did what she did, and they want to tell her in person that no one is holding a grudge?"

With Grace's permission, Logan had told the team in Texas everything. That she was threatened by the reporter. Told that if she didn't share what she knew, he'd expose her own dark past, thereby putting her life—and her father's—in jeopardy. It was an impossible situation to be placed in.

"Yes, I did. And I also suggested something else."

Jason arched a brow. "Should I be nervous?"

Something lit Logan's eyes. Amusement? "I suggested she invite Courtney." A beat of silence passed as Logan watched him closely.

"Courtney?"

Logan lifted a shoulder. "I know you have a thing for her, so if you'd prefer she didn't come, I'll message Grace."

A thing for her? Is that what the guys were calling it? It felt like a hell of a lot more than that.

"I don't mind."

Probably not correct. He did mind, but in the best way. There was only one downside—that his sister would see what he felt for Courtney. There was no way Sage wouldn't. And the woman would harass the hell out of him.

He frowned at the thought. Yeah, that part wasn't great.

"Want me to message Grace and tell her not to ask?"

"Nope. It's fine." His sister's teasing was worth the time he'd gain with Courtney. So damn worth it. "My sister will be subtle with Courtney then won't let me hear the end of it. I'll survive."

"Okay, good, because Grace is asking her this morning." Logan looked down at his watch. "Now, actually. And her big vulnerable eyes will probably convince the woman."

Jason was counting on it. "You know what, all this talk about Courtney has made me twitchy for a coffee." Aka, Courtney. "Want me to bring one back for you?"

Logan stood too. "Coffee would be great."

When he stepped into the reception area, Amy immediately looked up, her mouth stretching into a wide smile. "Hey!"

"Hey, Amy. I'm just popping over to The Grind to grab some coffee. Want one?"

"Actually, I was just about to go on my break." She clicked a few keys on the laptop, fiddled with the phone, then stood. "Mind if I join you? I could use some coffee and fresh air."

Jason dipped his head. "Don't mind at all."

He waited for Amy to come around the desk and trailed behind her as they made their way down the stairs and pushed outside.

"Jeez, it's cold here." She wrapped her arms around her waist. "The cold of Cradle Mountain just smacks you right in the face like a bag of ice."

Her thin blazer and pencil skirt probably weren't helping the matter. "You don't have a jacket you can grab?"

"I'm okay. I'll just stick close to you. Your body lets off enough heat that you're like a big furnace."

He wasn't sure if that was true, considering they weren't touching, but if the woman said she was fine... "Glad to help."

He sped up his pace, hoping that would warm the woman a bit. The Grind was only a street away yet still, he often wished it was closer. Right beside Blue Halo wouldn't be so bad. Hell, in the building.

"I've been meaning to say thank you," she said softly.

"For what?"

"You've been so helpful in showing me the ropes around the office. You've made the transition to Cradle Mountain super easy. And your team is just so lovely."

He lifted a shoulder, crossing the road. "It's been no problem. You've picked everything up really quickly." A lot quicker than he'd expected.

Her chuckle was light and airy. "You're too kind. I was a bit nervous moving here. You know, not knowing anyone, not having a job. It's been so much easier than I anticipated."

"What made you decide to move here?"

She'd already answered this question with his team in the interview process, but it seemed polite to ask himself.

"There was just something about Cradle Mountain that pulled me in. When I saw your job advertised, I thought it was fate."

That was it? He hadn't heard of many people moving to a new place based on a town "pulling them in". Or maybe he was out of touch and it was more common than he thought.

"Had you been here before?"

She shook her head. "Nope."

Interesting.

He stopped as they arrived at The Grind. "Well, we're lucky you saw the ad."

He held the door open, and Amy stepped inside. He followed—but came to an abrupt halt as she stopped in front of him, turning and touching his arm. "*I'm* the lucky one. Thank you."

"OKAY, so I have fifteen minutes. Tell me your stuff and I'll tell you mine. But first"—Courtney slid a mug onto the table—"like your mug?"

Grace peered down, reading the mug out loud. "How are men

like coffee? The best ones are rich, hot, and can keep you up all night." She chuckled. "Is this new?"

"Yeah, I saw it online the other week and *poof*, a week later it arrived." Along with about a dozen others. To say the cupboards at The Grind were overflowing was an understatement. "Now, news?"

Grace wrapped her fingers around the mug. "Okay, so, I wanted to tell you about a camping trip that Logan and I are going on this Saturday night."

"Ooh, camping, how romantic."

"Hm, not that romantic. Jason, his sister, and his sister's partner will be there."

Okay, that might kill the romance a bit.

A tinge of jealousy coursed through her. The woman got to go camping with Jason? Lord, how had she managed that? "Maybe not super romantic, but fun. His sister and her boyfriend are from Marble Falls, right?"

"Yep."

Courtney didn't miss the way her friend's eyes pinched at the corners.

Oh, the poor thing. She was nervous. After everything that had happened with that reporter, she didn't blame her. Grace had told her the entire terrible story.

"I'm sure now that they know the danger you would have been in if you didn't talk, they'll understand. Not to mention, your father would have been put in prison. Heck, if Logan and his entire team can forgive you, I'm sure they will."

"But the guys here trust Logan, so when he forgave me, so did they. Also, Sage and Mason haven't spent as much time with me as everyone here in Cradle Mountain."

Courtney leaned forward. "I think you'll be okay, but if you're that nervous, you could always skip it."

"Sage and Mason specifically asked for me to come, so I kind of feel like I have to." Grace took a sip of her coffee, seeming to consider her next words. "But I was wondering if maybe you'd come too? I know I'll have Logan, but having a girlfriend there would make it just a bit easier."

A little flutter tickled her belly. Okay, not a little flutter, a huge, gigantic, you-want-me-to-go-camping-with-who? flutter. "Really?"

"Only if you want. I'd love you to be there, but if you'd prefer not to, that's completely fine."

She was halfway between flinging herself across the table at her friend in gratitude and flat-out refusing. Camping involved peeing behind trees, right? And no access to showers?

"You can always think about it," Grace said softly.

Damn, Grace and her puppy dog eyes. The woman could probably convince Courtney to be Thelma to her Louise. "This Saturday happens to be my weekend off. And usually, I try to move as little as possible. Like literally, just enough so that people don't think I'm dead."

Grace's chuckle told her she thought Courtney was joking. She really wasn't.

"I can make an exception this weekend though. I'll come."

The second the words slipped from her lips, her skin began to tingle in anticipation. Two days of Jason. An entire night sleeping in a tent beside him.

Grace sighed, relief washing over her features. Yeah, it had been important to the woman. "Thank you. Logan said the guys have a spare tent and stuff you can borrow."

"Good. Because the last time I went camping was probably a good five or so years ago. I have nothing. Zilch."

She remembered that trip well. She'd gone with her douchebag boyfriend of the time. He'd gotten drunk and thrown up in the tent before passing out. Whole lot of fun that was.

"Don't worry, it's been even longer for me." Grace swirled her coffee. "So, how has it been with Jason?"

"If you mean is the guy still a dreamboat who makes my lady

parts flutter, then the answer is yes. And I think my conversational skills are improving around him. I'd almost say I can talk like an adult."

Grace's smile widened. "I'm so glad."

"There's something else." She bit her lip. "He kissed me on the cheek last night. I know, a kiss on the cheek isn't much, but—"

Grace reached over, grabbing Courtney's hand in a firm grip. "What? He kissed you?"

This was why she was friends with this woman. "Yep. And let me tell you, his lips are soft as a cloud. And the way his mouth lingered..."

Ah, hell, she was getting hot and flustered just thinking about it.

Grace gave a little squeak that had Courtney chuckling.

"What about you and Logan? Still the perfect couple?"

Over their coffees, Courtney listened as Grace told her every little perfect thing about her relationship. Her friend was happy, and Courtney was so incredibly happy *for* her. She'd been through a lot, been hurt in the most traumatic way. For a while, Grace had thought she wasn't ever going to be able to have a romantic relationship with a man again. All that changed with Logan.

Way too soon, it was time for Grace to leave.

Courtney returned behind the counter. She'd just given a customer their coffee when the door to the shop swung open.

Courtney grinned, her belly warming at the sight of Jason. Her smile faltered, though, when the woman in front of him—the freaking gorgeous runway-model-looking woman—put her hand on his arm, leaning into him.

Jason didn't pull away. And when he looked down at her, his eyes warmed, his dimples on full display as he smiled.

Courtney's breath caught, and not in a good way. Her gaze remained glued to them until he looked up.

She jolted, forcing herself to look away. Grabbing a cloth, she began madly scrubbing the counter like it was the dirtiest thing she'd ever seen.

Even though her gaze was down, she felt their presence as they stopped on the other side of the counter. Courtney took her time looking up. The moment she did, she almost wished she hadn't. The woman was even prettier up close. Bright blue eyes. Lush red lips. She wore a tight shirt under a blazer that gave Courtney a perfect view of a generous chest that just about jumped out of the top.

Stunning.

Courtney turned to Jason, forcing a smile onto her face that was about as fake as the woman's boobs. "Hi. What can I get for you both today?"

The brunette turned her loved-up eyes on Jason, and another burst of jealousy shot through Courtney.

Stop, she chided herself. *You're not dating the man. If this stunning creature wants to touch him, it's fine.*

"Have you tried their iced lattes? They're divine," the woman said.

At least she was a fan of the product. Although, Courtney was a bit surprised she'd been here before. Joey or one of the girls must have served her, because there was no way Courtney would forget a face and body like hers.

When Courtney flicked her gaze across to Jason, she noticed that instead of looking at his companion, he was looking at her. Closely. Intensely.

The smile on Courtney's face almost slipped. Why was he looking at *her* and not the walking boobs beside him?

"Everything's divine here."

Was he... talking about *her?* A small light flicked back on in her chest.

"I'll have my usual," he said softly. "And one of Logan's usuals, as well."

She gave a small nod, words somehow failing her right now.

Dragging her gaze away, she looked back to the woman—whose smile was tighter now.

"I'll have an iced latte."

"Coming right up."

While she made the drinks, she tried not to look at them, she really did. But often, *too often*, and without her permission, her gaze slid over.

Argh. The woman was now leaning into him, saying something while laughing. Fortunately, Jason wasn't looking at her. And it really was fortunate because if he had been, she had no doubt he would get a big shot of breasts.

It wasn't until the third time she looked at them from beneath her lashes that Jason's gaze clashed with her own. He winked at her.

Holy crap on a cracker. Was he actually seeing her? Even with that stunning woman beside him? Her history of shitty boyfriends had just about trained her to believe that when a beautiful woman walked into the room, she became invisible.

Finishing the drinks, she slid them across the counter.

"Thanks, Courtney." He gave her his card, and when she gave it back, his entire hand slid over the back of hers in the process.

There was no way that wasn't intentional.

He winked at her a second time before turning toward the door.

The woman gave her a look that was chillier than the tip of Cradle Mountain, and it had Courtney pausing. Who was she? Where was she from? And what was she to Jason?

CHAPTER 7

*C*ourtney stood in the back kitchen of The Grind, her fingers flying over the keys on her phone.

Courtney: I've taken my bag out.

And that was the extent of her packing. They were camping for one night. How long would it take?

Jason: Ah, we leave tomorrow...

She chuckled, leaning her hip against the wall.

She shouldn't be hiding in the back, not when Joey was out front cleaning, but really, what was the point of being the boss if you couldn't sneakily escape from cleanup duty?

Courtney: Yes, I realize. But I've been busy.

Yeah, busy watching reruns of *The Office* with Eddie.

Jason: Busy with what?

Crap, the man was onto her.

Courtney: Well, I changed the colors of the streaks in my hair.

She'd thought Jason would pop in today and see them, but the man had been oddly missing. Oddly, because it was the first day in weeks that she hadn't seen him.

Was it sad that she actually missed their usual ten-minute chat?

Maybe that was why she was being a slacker and letting Joey do all the work tonight. Because she was desperate for some Jason time, even if it was over text. The man had probably spent the day with Sage and Mason. The couple had arrived that morning, so she should have expected his absence.

Jason: No more purple?

Courtney: No more purple.

Jason: What color did you go with?

Courtney: You'll just have to wait and see.

She grinned at the broken heart emoji she got in response. When she texted the guy, it was just so... easy. She could be fully and unapologetically herself.

"So, I'm doing the cleanup myself, am I?"

Courtney squeaked, the phone almost slipping from her fingers at Joey's sudden voice. "God, Joey, you walk like a cat."

He lifted a brow. "No, I walk like a man trying to sneak up on the person hiding in the kitchen."

Sheesh, everyone was onto her tonight.

Tucking the phone into her pocket, she moved out front. "Sorry. I've been distracted."

"I know. It's okay, it's a perk of being the boss. Everything's done, we just need to give the floors a quick mop." He headed over to the two buckets he'd already prepared, mops poking out of the top, and handed her one.

She didn't deserve the guy. "Where would I be without you?"

"Oh, you'd be right here, not realizing what you were missing."

It would be funny if it wasn't so true.

"So, who were you messaging?" he asked as he started at one end of the room and she went to work at the other.

"Jason."

Like he didn't know. He'd caught her messaging him on numerous occasions already that week, most of which she'd also sent while hiding in the back. She was terrible.

"Are you guys dating?"

Her heart skidded in her chest. Ah, wasn't that the dream? "We're just friends."

"Ha. I give it a week."

"Well, if that happens, you'll see me walking around here with a deliriously big smile on my face."

"Yeah, I'm expecting it."

They were just finishing the floors when Joey yawned. Okay, that was like the tenth time she'd caught him yawning that day. Not to mention the shadows under his eyes that were still there, dark as ever.

Once they'd cleaned their mops and buckets in the back room, they headed out of the kitchen. Courtney stopped in front of him. "Joey, I just wanted to check that everything is really okay with you? You've seemed a bit... off the last few shifts. Tired." Exhausted, actually.

He ran a hand through his hair. "Sorry, I'll do better."

Courtney stepped closer. "No, I don't mean it as a criticism. You know that I think you're the bee's knees when it comes to this place. And I don't see that changing. I'm worried about *you*."

"I..." He paused. It was like he wanted to say something but couldn't. "I'm fine."

Fine? No. He was not fine. "Are you sure? Because if something's wrong, I might be able to help. I *want* to help. Or I could at least be an ear to listen."

Another beat of silence. "I was actually going to ask..." For a moment he looked uncomfortable. His jaw clenched, eyes darting away then back at her. "Would it be possible for me to get an advance on my next pay?"

Courtney was careful to keep her expression clear. "You need money?"

"I'm just a bit behind on my rent right now."

The guy lived alone in an apartment building not far from hers. He'd been living there since he started working at The

Grind. He'd never mentioned being behind on rent or having money issues before...

"If that's not okay—"

"No." She touched his arm. "It is. I was just surprised. Of course you can have an advance on your next paycheck. I'll organize it now, before I leave."

He sighed, his chest deflating as relief came off him in waves. How bad exactly was his situation?

"Thank you."

"If you want to talk about anything..."

Joey had not only been her first employee at The Grind, he'd also been her first friend in Cradle Mountain, the ten-year age gap never posing a problem to their friendship. If he needed help, then she wanted to do whatever she could for him.

"I'm okay."

She gave a small nod. "Okay."

She'd just turned when she felt his hand on her arm. "Actually, Courtney—"

The front door suddenly opened. Courtney looked over her shoulder to see Jason stepping inside.

Immediately, Joey's hand dropped. He stepped back.

Jason went still, his gaze moving from the part of her arm Joey had just touched, to Joey, then across to her. "Everything okay here?"

～

JASON FROWNED at what he'd walked into. It wasn't just Joey touching Courtney, or their closeness that had him pausing, it was the thickness of the air around them.

Courtney took a step away from her employee. "Of course."

There was definitely something wrong with Joey. Not only did he look a lot more tired than usual, but stress all but bounced off him.

What had he just walked into?

"I'm going to go." Joey headed across the room, walking past Jason and out the door.

When the door closed, he took slow steps across to Courtney. "I feel like I interrupted something." Actually, he *knew* he'd interrupted something. He just didn't know what.

As he stopped in front of her, she tilted her head back to look at him. "It's okay. He was going to tell me something. Whatever it was, he can tell me another time."

But there was a note of hesitation in Courtney's voice. Maybe she wasn't sure Joey *would* tell her another time.

"What are you doing here?" she asked, a soft smile playing at her lips.

"I'm an impatient man."

Funnily enough, he didn't used to be. That impatience had only come about since meeting Courtney. Since he had to teach himself to wait whatever period of time was necessary before he could see her face again. Hear her voice.

He lifted a hand, fingers grazing the soft strand of dyed hair at the side of her head before cupping her cheek. That same awareness he usually felt when he touched her rippled from his hand right down his arm. "Sky blue. I like it."

She swallowed, pausing before responding. "I'm glad."

There was a lot he liked about this woman. "I think I would like any color on you, though."

Any color. Any hairdo. Anything.

He slid his hand from her cheek to the back of her neck, his thumb grazing over the skin. So damn soft. When her eyes dropped to his lips, parts of him hardened that had no business hardening right now.

"You kill me when you do that," he said quietly. It was literal death. "It makes it really hard not to kiss you." Especially now, when no one else was around and he had nowhere else to be.

"Kiss me?"

His lips tilted up. "Yeah, honey, kiss you."

Her gaze swung down to his lips a second time.

He almost growled out loud. "Courtney." It was definitely a warning.

Her hands went to his chest, her head tilting farther back. "Maybe you should."

Fuck.

His hand tightened on her neck. Then, in a swift move, he lowered his head, taking her lips with his own. She made a soft noise, a little between a sigh and a whimper, and something fierce and primal awoke in his chest.

Her lips were plush and warm and swiped across his slowly. His other hand grabbed her waist, tugging her closer, pressing her softness into his hard.

The pounding of her heart was like a beat in the background that crashed through the silence.

When her lips separated, she entered his mouth, tangling her tongue with his.

Another flicker in his chest.

So. Damn. Sweet.

It would be easy to take this further. To get lost in the woman in his arms. To make love to every part of her. That's why he had to stop.

Slowly—painfully—Jason lifted his head. Her small groan of protest rivaled the one battling the slim tendrils of his self-restraint.

"I could get used to kissing you."

Her hands went to his biceps. Clenching. Steadying herself. "And I could easily become addicted to you doing that."

Oh, he knew all about addiction. How often did he think about her? Crave her?

"Let me walk you home."

The sigh that released from her lips, the small step away, told him he wouldn't be getting more time with Courtney. Not tonight.

"I need to stay for a bit and put an employee's pay through. I thought I'd do a couple other paperwork things while I'm at it." When she looked up, she bit her bottom lip, and damn if it didn't take all his strength to *not* take that lip between his own teeth.

Jason tightened his hands on her hips, loving the way she sank into him. "But I'll see you tomorrow?" He was driving his sister and Mason, while Courtney was going with Grace and Logan.

"I'll see you tomorrow." Her words were quiet.

He pressed a last kiss to her lips. Last for now... certainly not for long.

CHAPTER 8

$\mathcal{C}$ ourtney was still smiling as she walked up the stairs to her apartment. Now she really had something to talk to Grace about. Not a small kiss on the cheek, or a heated breath near her ear. No. Now she could tell Grace that she'd kissed the man smack-dab on the lips.

She absently touched her necklace. And Lord, but she could have sworn she'd been about to combust right there and then.

Courtney had almost reached her floor when the cell in her pocket started to vibrate. Tugging it out, she looked at the screen, almost groaning out loud when she saw who it was.

Helen. She'd asked her neighbor to pop over and feed Eddie while she was away tomorrow night, and the woman hadn't stopped calling since. Literally, a call an hour. About Eddie's food, did he require pats, medication... it was endless.

She pressed the phone to her ear. "Hi, Helen."

"Courtney. Where are you?"

Why was the woman whispering? "I'm just walking up the stairs. Is everything okay?"

Courtney stepped onto her floor.

"There are men in suits outside your apartment."

She stopped when she saw them. Her apartment was halfway down the hall. Three men. All looking equally serious.

"I'm here. Thank you for the warning."

Helen huffed. "I don't like strangers standing in our hall. Who are they?"

She rolled her eyes. Trust the older woman to be dramatic. "I don't know, but I'll find out."

She hung up before her neighbor could say anything else, tucking her phone into her pocket and only stopping when she neared the men.

"Courtney Davies?" It was a blond man who spoke. He stood an inch taller than the other two and had an air of authority about him.

"Yes."

He reached out his hand. The guy wasn't as big as Jason, but he was still tall at probably a bit over six feet. Courtney slipped her hand into his larger one.

"I'm Special Agent David Peters from the FBI, and these are two of my guys." His hand released hers, slipping into his pocket and pulling out a badge that looked all kinds of official. "Do you have a few minutes? I'd like to ask you a few questions."

The FBI? Sweet mother of God. Even though he'd said her name, this had to be a case of mistaken identity. Was there another Courtney Davies close by? Because she certainly couldn't be involved in any criminal activity. That was what the FBI did, wasn't it?

"Err, what is this in regard to?"

"Could we talk inside your apartment, Miss Davies? What I have to talk to you about is classified."

She shot a quick glance at her door, trepidation crawling up her spine.

It wasn't that she didn't think he was the real deal—he probably was. But IDs could be faked, couldn't they? And her trust in people was running a bit low these days after the freezer fiasco.

"There's a couch downstairs." A small couch to one side of the large foyer, but it was better than her apartment or the hallway. "Do you mind if we go there instead? It's private."

"That's fine."

She gave a small nod, turning and heading back down the stairs. Her spine was ramrod straight and the back of her neck tingled from the guys walking behind her.

When they reached the seating area, he sat first, looking ridiculously official.

"Isn't it a bit late for a house call?" she asked, lowering beside him while trying and failing not to fiddle with her phone in her lap. She'd pulled it out as they headed down the stairs, feeling safer with it between her fingers.

"We know the hours of your business. We timed our visit according to your schedule."

That wasn't creepy at all. "What is this about?"

The agent didn't break eye contact. "I'll get right to it, Miss Davies. The FBI has been monitoring an Italian Mafia organization called the Bonvicin Family for a while now. They're based in Philadelphia. Six months ago, the head of the organization died, and we've been trying to establish who the new boss is ever since."

A Mafia group? So, yep. Wrong person. There was no two ways about it.

"Establishing who the boss is, and learning the complex layers of their business, will ultimately help us set up a sting to bring them down," he continued.

"Okay."

"Over the last couple of weeks, we've tracked a few of the members to Cradle Mountain."

Her jaw dropped.

The agent studied her closely, his eyes penetrating. Searching. "During surveillance, we've seen them in or around The Grind on numerous occasions."

A chill skittered up her spine. Still, she just nodded, as if what he said made sense when really it didn't.

"We decided to look into you and your employees, looking for any connection between any of you and the Bonvicin family. And we found something interesting."

Oh, Lord, did she even want to know?

No. No, she didn't. Not when he said it like he had information that would have her cuffed and put away within minutes.

"Do you know a Ryan Calo, Miss Davies?"

Her eyes widened, a trickle of unease crawling up her spine. Ryan Calo, as in…

"We believe Calo was dating and living with your cousin, a Jessica Quinton, two years ago, prior to her death."

Even though shock and confusion coursed through her body, her heart still ached at the mention of Jess being dead.

She shook her head. "I'm sorry, how does Ryan fit into this?"

"Two years ago, Calo was being inducted into the family before he was murdered."

She gasped. First of all, she hadn't known Ryan was dead, let alone murdered. And second of all… "You mean while he was with Jess? He was being inducted into the Mafia while he was with my cousin?" No. That didn't make sense. Jessica would never be with a man who was part of the mob or hoping to *become* part of the mob.

"Yes." Peters didn't hesitate or flinch when he answered. "Did Jessica ever talk to you about their involvement with the Bonvicin family?"

Their? "No. Jessica would never involve herself in criminal activity." No way. No how. "She was a nurse, living and working in Virginia. She was kind and empathetic and generous in nature. People connected to the Mafia aren't those things."

They were cruel and sadistic and lived in multi-million-dollar penthouse apartments and had collections of guns and knives, didn't they? Hit men at their beck and call…

"Even if she wasn't involved with the group, Ryan certainly was. I have little doubt she would have known about it. She didn't mention anything to you? We have it on record that she flew from Virginia to Florida a couple of times while she lived with Calo. Once for your birthday, another time for your grandmother's funeral."

Her throat closed at the reminder. Their grandmother had basically been Jessica's mother, raising her after her own parents had died when she was a baby. "She didn't mention anything about a Mafia group."

"Was she acting any differently on those visits?"

Courtney tried not to squirm in her seat. If she was honest with herself, she didn't like to think about the year before Jessica died.

"She was a bit different after she started dating Ryan." Because Ryan was an ass. "More closed off and reserved. I never got a good feeling around him. After they started dating, her phone calls became less frequent. And when I did see her, she just... smiled less." She ran her thumb over the edge of her phone. "At first, I put it down to the death of our grandmother. Then the last time I saw her, there were, um, bruises on her arms. I tried to ask about them but she didn't want to discuss it."

In fact, she'd threatened to leave that night, any time Courtney brought up the bruises.

Courtney swallowed. "How... how did he die?"

"A few months after Jessica's death, his body was found floating in James River in Virginia, with a bullet wound to the head and obvious signs of abuse."

Her breath thudded to a stop in her throat. A bullet to the head? "What kind of abuse?"

"He'd been tortured, Miss Davies."

The fine hairs on her arms stood on end. She was pretty sure she was close to experiencing a brain overload. Mafia. Murder. Torture. Those were words that belonged in Hollywood movies.

"You think these Mafia people killed him?" she asked quietly.

"Yes. We now believe so."

"Do you think they killed *her*?" Courtney was told it was a home invasion and Jessica had been beaten to death. But maybe...

"It's possible."

That's all he said—possible. It made her heart ache.

"Miss Davies, do you have any idea why the Bonvicin family may be in Cradle Mountain right now?"

"No." That was probably the quickest she'd ever answered any question in her life. "I'd never heard of them before you got here. I don't think they're here for me though. I'm not connected to them at all. Jessica and Ryan are dead..."

No. It was one big fat coincidence, and she was sticking to that assumption.

She wasn't sure if he believed her, but he gave a small nod and stood. Pulling a card from his pocket, he told her, "If anything comes back to you, I would love for you to give me a call. In the meantime, I'll have some of my guys patrolling your shop and the apartment building."

She nodded as she stood and took the card. "I'm going away this weekend, so you don't need anyone on until Monday."

"Are you going with anyone?"

"Some friends from Blue Halo Security. I'll be safe with them."

He dipped his head, clearly already knowing who she was talking about. He was about to walk away when she stopped him with a final question.

"Do you know why they would have killed Ryan?"

When his gaze returned to Courtney's, his eyes were harder. "The Mafia needs very little reason to kill someone. One screw-up and you're gone. We don't know what Ryan's screw-up was, but it wouldn't have taken much."

She swallowed in an attempt to wet her dry throat.

"Thank you for your time, Miss Davies."

And then they were gone, disappearing out the door and into

the early evening, leaving Courtney standing there, no doubt looking as confused as she felt.

Thoughts ran wild through her head as she made her way back up the stairs. Had Jessica known about Ryan's activities? If so, why had she stayed with him? Could Courtney have helped her?

When she returned to her apartment, Helen stepped into the hall. The woman was mid-seventies, with graying hair and lines wrinkling her face. Her dog, Bernie, was in her arms. "Everything okay?"

Was it? She'd just found out her late cousin and best friend had been dating a guy who was in bed with the Mafia.

"Everything's fine, Helen." Not really, but she wasn't about to tell the entire morbid story to the old woman. She'd probably have a heart attack.

She opened her door, but before she could close it, she heard Helen's quick footsteps nearing. "Are you expecting any more visitors like them?"

Good God, she hoped not. There was only so much Mafia talk she could take before her brain exploded. "No."

The older woman watched her for a beat before nodding and turning back to her apartment.

The second Courtney's door was closed, she pressed her forehead against the wood.

Oh, Jessica, what did you get yourself into?

CHAPTER 9

*V*oices *hummed around Courtney. Voices of family, of elderly friends of her grandmother, of strangers she'd never met before. She wouldn't say there had been a lot of people at the funeral and burial, but definitely more than she'd expected for a ninety-five-year-old woman who'd spent a large chunk of her final years at home. And almost everyone had come to the afternoon tea.*

She searched for her parents. Her father was taking the passing of his mother well, but then, everyone had been expecting it to be soon, what with the woman's age and everything.

For a moment, she wondered if it brought back memories of his sister's funeral... Jessica's mother. Courtney had been too young to remember that day, but it had to have been tough.

Her dad caught her gaze, smiling at her. She returned the smile before flicking her attention to the front door. Where was Jessica? She'd expected her cousin to be the first person here.

Courtney fiddled with a button on her dress. She hated the distance that had grown between them the last couple of years. It didn't feel like that long ago when they'd been inseparable. Growing up in each other's backyards. Always in the same classes at school. Always at each other's houses.

Guilt heated her cheeks. The distance made it hard. Richmond was an eight-hour drive from Jacksonville, and with the long hours they both worked, it made visits rare.

Courtney's eyes were still on her late grandmother's front door when it opened, and Jessica walked in. Her bloodshot eyes were red-rimmed, bottom lip slightly trembling. And behind her was the man Courtney had only been introduced to that morning. The man she hadn't even known her cousin was dating. Ryan.

Tattoos spidered along his arms. A jewel pierced his bottom lip. It wasn't the tattoos or the piercing that had Courtney feeling wary of him though. To be honest, she wasn't entirely sure what it was. There was just something about him that made her... uncomfortable. Like if he was there, she didn't want to be.

It shouldn't have surprised Courtney. Both she and Jessica had always had terrible taste in men, their relationships never ending well.

Courtney moved across the room to her cousin, wrapping her arms around her shoulders.

"How are you doing?" she whispered. She'd stood beside her at the funeral. Held her hand at the burial. But there hadn't been enough words spoken. Not really.

Jessica's breath shuddered out of her chest. "I'm okay."

Courtney leaned back but kept her face close and her voice low. "You don't need to pretend with me, Jess."

"Okay. I'm shit. I feel like I just lost the parent who raised me. Like I lost the only woman who fully understood me."

She leaned closer, forehead almost touching Jess's. "That's because you did lose the parent who raised you." Technically, she was a grandmother, but in every important way, she was definitely a mother. "But she wasn't the only person who understood you, Jess. I do."

And it killed her that her friend was going through this pain. Courtney was devastated too, but it couldn't be anywhere near what Jessica was feeling.

"If it's too hard being here, you're allowed to leave. You don't owe anyone anything." Courtney had no idea what Jessica would prefer, but

if it was to get out of her childhood home, she should do it. And Courtney would follow.

Jessica looked around. Her bottom lip continued to tremble, new tears shone in her dark eyes. Jessica opened her mouth, but before any words were spoken, a tattooed arm wrapped around her waist.

"Come on, Jess, let's get a drink."

Courtney's gaze clashed with Ryan's, and an immediate chill swept over her skin. His eyes were hard. Like he'd seen things that others hadn't. Bad things. Or maybe he lacked basic empathy.

He tugged Jessica the other way, completely disregarding Courtney.

Courtney placed a hand on her elbow. "Jess—"

Jessica stopped for a second, then she leaned down, talking quietly into Courtney's ear. "Don't. You're too late. You didn't save me. So leave me alone."

~

Courtney shot up in bed, the pounding on her front door almost in sync with the pounding of her own heartbeat. Grabbing her phone, she saw it was already past eight in the morning.

The dream had been a memory, almost exactly how her grandmother's funeral had really gone. Except the ending, of course.

Thoughts scurried through Courtney's mind. Peters had said it was possible that Jessica had been murdered at the hands of the Mafia. But what if it hadn't been a random home invasion *or* the Mafia? What if it had been Ryan?

Courtney dropped her head into her hands, the sweat that had beaded her forehead slicking her palms.

She'd known he was no good. Felt it as strongly as she'd felt anything. Yet she hadn't forced her cousin away from the guy. Why?

The rational side of her brain knew that you couldn't force someone to leave their partner, no matter how close you were.

But she could have done more, couldn't she? She could have visited her cousin in Richmond. Checked in more.

More banging. "Courtney, are you awake?"

Helen.

Courtney pulled herself out of bed and walked to the door slowly, shaking her head to rid herself of the dream that tangled in her mind, threatened her conscience.

The second the door was open, Helen was stepping inside her apartment, holding Bernie tightly in her arms. "Dear, I've been thinking about your visitors, and I think you need to tell me who those men were. I can't have felons coming into this building."

Courtney closed the door, rubbing her eyes. She was way too tired for this. "Felons?"

"The men were either felons or cops. I could tell."

Hm, the woman might be wiser than Courtney gave her credit for. "They were cops, okay?" Kind of. They were in law enforcement. "They just needed to ask me about someone I knew. I'm not in danger, and you're certainly not in danger. I don't anticipate them returning."

The older woman seemed to digest that information before giving a curt nod. "Good. Do you have the key?"

Walking to an accent table, Courtney pulled open the drawer and grabbed the spare apartment key. After handing it to the other women, she went into the kitchen, lifting the instructions she'd prepared. "I wrote down everything. When to feed him, how much he eats, and where to find the food."

She handed the note to Helen before heading to the cupboard. Helen followed closely behind, watching as Courtney grabbed a bag of dry cat food and pointed out the cans.

She heard the murmurs of disapproval. "Hm. My Bernie only has the premium meat from Ruben's Pet Food Store."

Courtney almost groaned out loud, knowing what was coming next. She had way too much on her mind to hear—

"Feeding your pet higher-quality food will lead to better

health for them. They're family members, after all. It's a small price to pay to keep them in your life for as long as possible."

Lord, *she* didn't even eat organic food.

Courtney scooped some dry food into Eddie's bowl, giving him a stroke as he came over to eat, all while Helen continued to talk.

"Well, at least think about what I've said."

Courtney nodded. "I most definitely will." *Not.* "Thank you so much for looking after Eddie while I'm gone." This time, she was genuine. She was grateful for the help, even if the woman ground her gears sometimes.

Helen huffed again, already heading back to the door. "I can't pet him. You know that, don't you? Bernie gets very jealous."

"It's only one night. He'll survive."

Eddie was extremely low maintenance. In fact, usually *she* was demanding cuddles from *him.*

Helen stopped at the door, clearly waiting for Courtney to open it. She almost laughed as she reached around the woman and pulled it open.

Her neighbor stepped into the hall and turned. "You're sure you won't be getting any more visitors this weekend? I really don't want to talk to any strangers and explain that you've gone away."

"No. There will be no more visitors."

"Hm. Well. Have a nice weekend, dear. Please don't be late getting back."

Courtney nodded as she closed the door. Eddie immediately pressed against her legs. She lifted him into her arms, pressing her face into his fur. "Sorry, buddy. It was her or the old man who lives across the hall, and he smells like fish."

Putting Eddie back down, she stepped into the bedroom. Her backpack *still* wasn't packed yet. Not even a little bit. And she one hundred percent blamed her visitors from the night before. There was no way she'd felt like packing after they'd left. Instead, she'd sat on the couch, on her phone, going through old pictures of her and Jessica while stuffing her face with hazelnut ice cream, which Jason had been right about. The stuff was amazing.

Sighing, she went to the bathroom, stripping then stepping into the shower.

She hadn't dreamed about Jessica in a long time. Agent Peters had brought everything back to the surface. The regret that she hadn't spent more time with the woman. The weight of her loss. The soul-crushing "what ifs".

She was just stepping out of the shower when the doorbell rang. Ah, hell. That had to be Grace and Logan. She'd never checked the time. And she still wasn't packed...

She was throwing clothes on her damp body when Grace's voice called, "Courtney?"

"I told you, she's in there," Logan said.

Crap, crap, crap.

She ran to the door and tugged it open. "Come in. Make yourself comfortable. I'll be five minutes."

Or ten.

She barely looked at them. But she heard the chuckle from behind as she ran back to the bedroom.

CHAPTER 10

"So, tell us about this woman."

Jason smiled at Sage's question. She sat in the back of his vehicle, with Mason in the passenger seat beside him. They were halfway to the property where they were camping and his sister had already asked a hundred and one questions about his life in Cradle Mountain. He had a feeling they were just going to keep coming, right up until she left.

"Her name is Courtney and she runs the local coffee shop, The Grind. She's vibrant and funny and dyes streaks in her hair." *And she's goddamn beautiful.*

"How often do you see her?"

Lately? Every day, and it still didn't feel like enough. "Often. I get coffee from her shop regularly."

Sage leaned forward. "You like her, don't you?"

"Sage..." Mason growled her name, but there was an air of amusement to it.

"What? I just want to get as much information as possible before we meet the woman. So I understand."

Jason cracked a half smile. His sister was inquisitive by

nature, probably why she'd become a doctor, but when it came to him, she was a damn bloodhound. The woman didn't stop. "I do."

Sage clapped her hands. "This trip just keeps getting better."

This time, Mason chuckled. "Good luck, brother." He muttered the words under his breath, just loud enough for Jason's ears.

"We're not dating." They'd kissed. Once. But if Jason had his way, it would be the first of many.

"Why not?"

Mason sighed. "Sage, maybe we should just leave it."

"Because we're still new," Jason said quietly, spotting their next turnoff ahead.

"So maybe soon." She sounded hopeful.

"Maybe." *Definitely.* He turned off the highway. "We're about half an hour away."

Sage sat back in her seat. "So, this is your friend Flynn's property?"

Jason almost sagged in relief. Although he liked to think about Courtney, talking about her to his very perceptive sister, when he hardly knew where they stood himself, wasn't his idea of fun. "Yep. The property has been in his family for years. It's huge, and even has a river that goes through the forest with a small waterfall."

She sighed. "Oh, dang it, I didn't bring my swimsuit."

Mason shook his head. "Sweetheart, the water is freezing. You'd turn into a block of ice."

"But then you'd warm me back up again."

He turned and gave her one of his exasperated smiles. There was also a hint of something else in his face. Heat.

And this was why, even though Jason missed his sister like hell, there were moments he wasn't so sad about the distance.

～

STUPID DANG NO-GOOD INSTRUCTIONS.

Courtney was following the directions on the page exactly. Like, to-the-T exactly. But nothing seemed to be working for her. Nothing! It had taken her a solid twenty minutes to fit all the tent poles together, and now she was struggling to fit those poles into the right sections of the cover.

Who had written this thing? Clearly not a woman, because a woman would have color-coded everything. Wasn't that the logical thing to do?

Letting out a huff, she lifted the page for the hundredth time. Why the heck were there no pictures on this thing? Didn't whoever wrote the instructions know that, like, sixty-five percent of the population were visual learners?

She felt Logan and Grace's gazes on her again. They'd come over a dozen times already to ask if she needed help, but she'd refused each time. Because she could do it. She was a modern, independent, hands-on, learn-new-skills type of woman.

Smoothing her features, she lifted one of the poles. She *would not* let this tent beat her.

Courtney was just reading the instructions yet again when a hand pressed to her shoulder.

"Logan, I told you, I've got this. It's just taking me a bit longer than I anti—" She stopped abruptly when she looked over her shoulder. "You're not Logan."

Jason grinned. "I'm not. I'll never have his bone structure."

Ha. If Jason's bone structure were any more perfect, he'd have been sculpted by a master. "Did you, ah, just arrive?"

"I did. With my—"

"Hi!" Suddenly, a short blond woman who looked nothing like Jason stood beside him. "I'm the twin sister, Sage."

Okay, was someone punking Courtney? This woman couldn't be his twin. She was short and delicate and fair, whereas Jason... wasn't. "You guys look nothing alike."

Sage chuckled, the sound light and lyrical. "I know. I got my dad's fair features and Mom's height, while he took after Mom in everything *but* height."

A man approached Sage, wrapping an arm around her waist. He had intense black eyes and was just as tall and muscular as Jason and his teammates. Holy heck, where did all these big, dangerous men come from?

"Hi, I'm Mason."

She smiled. "Courtney."

He pressed a kiss to Sage's temple. Cute!

"I'm so looking forward to spending the weekend with you," Sage said, before glancing toward Grace and Logan. "I'll catch up with you again after we've put up our tent."

"Sounds good." Courtney frowned at Jason once his sister was gone. "Are you sure she's your twin?"

"Unless there was a switch up at the hospital, I'm absolutely sure." He shot a look over her head. "Need some help?"

Yes, dammit, she did. "These instructions are setting me up to fail, but you should get yours up first, and if I'm still a bumbling mess of tent poles and curse words when you're done, I might ask for your help." With her luck, she'd be in exactly the same position then as she was now.

"Or here's another idea. I help you, then you help me."

That was almost comical. "I can't even put my *own* tent up, Jason, what help could I offer you?"

"Four hands are better than two." He reached out, covering her hand with his own.

Her skin tingled, a light tremor rocking her spine. "Okay." To be honest, any words could have come out of her mouth just then. His touch turned her brain to mush.

He gave her hand a gentle squeeze before releasing it and taking the sheet from her other fingers.

"There are no pictures, in case you're as utterly clueless with written instructions as I am..." Her words trailed off when she saw his lips twitch.

He winked as he started attaching a pole to the body of the tent. The guy looked like he'd done it a hundred times before. Now she just felt incompetent.

Over the next few minutes, Jason took the lead on the tent construction. He was good at giving directions. Calm. Patient. Two things a lot of people would *not* have been, had they been working with Courtney and her slow-to-process brain.

He glanced over at her. "You doing okay? You seem a bit distracted today."

Was it that obvious? She opened her mouth to tell him about her visit from the FBI agents last night, but quickly closed it again. She hadn't told Grace or Logan either. She didn't really know why. Maybe because she couldn't stop thinking about her dream. About the possibility that Jessica's death had been at the hands of her no-good boyfriend... and Courtney had done nothing to prevent it.

Besides, did it really matter if she told them? It wasn't like she was going to see the agent again.

"I'm fine. Just not a practiced camper like you." She reached for the gem hanging from her necklace. Touching it always made her feel closer to them. Closer to Jessica.

Jason pushed a peg into the dirt. "I wouldn't call myself practiced, but I've definitely slept in worse places."

Courtney attempted to push her peg into the dirt. It moved about an inch, maybe less. "Oh yeah, like where?" She tried again, this time putting more of her body weight into it.

"Aircrafts, on the beach. Hell, during field training, I slept outside in sub-freezing temperatures."

Maybe that was why she'd never considered enlisting. Ha. Along with about a dozen other reasons. "The beach doesn't sound so bad." More weight on the peg. It didn't budge. Not even a little bit.

"Trust me, it sounds more comfortable than it is. Especially when you compare it to a warm bed."

She chuckled. "Nothing beats a warm bed. Especially your own."

Suddenly, heat pressed against her side moments before he was bending down beside her. She hadn't even heard the man rise.

His hand slid over hers, pushing the peg into the ground. When he looked at her, his eyes were... darker. Deeper. "I'd have to agree with you."

Courtney forgot what she'd said. Every thought slipped out of her mind except thoughts of him. Jason touching her. His mouth, his lips, so close to hers.

"Even though you're not a practiced camper, I'm glad you agreed to come," he said quietly.

Every word he spoke had more hot breath slipping through his lips and brushing against her own. Sweet Jesus, but the man was affecting her.

She nodded because any words would probably be simple and stuttered. For a moment, she wondered if he was going to kiss her again. And if he did, would it be as earth-shattering as their kiss last night?

Her heart gave a little kick at the thought. Her lips separated in anticipation.

"Jason, can you—" Sage stopped mid-sentence. "Oh, sorry!"

The moment was lost.

A long breath whooshed out of Courtney's chest as she cast her gaze down. Jason stood slowly, but his hand went to her elbow, helping her up with him.

His lips moved to her ear, his words barely a whisper. "Next time."

CHAPTER 11

*C*ourtney stepped over another tree root. The tweeting of birds overhead and whistle of wind through the trees pierced her ears as she headed to Logan's truck. She'd left her phone-charging cord for her portable charger in there, having plugged her phone in on the way to the site.

Grace and Sage walked behind her, their voices hushed as they spoke.

"No one is angry at you," Sage said gently. "Logan told us why you did what you did, and the position that reporter put you in. You were scared and did what you thought you needed to do to protect yourself from Kieran and your father from jail."

"Are you sure?" Courtney almost smiled when she heard the relief and emotion in Grace's voice. "Because I kind of just threw everyone into the deep end then apologized without giving a reason for my actions."

"You didn't tell us because you were scared, and you didn't know who to trust. And you left to apologize to Logan's team."

Courtney paused when she heard the women stop. She cast a look over her shoulder in time to see Sage pulling Grace into her arms. This was exactly what Grace needed—confirmation that no one blamed her.

She breathed a sigh of relief for her friend.

When they separated, all three of them continued to Logan's truck. It was parked about a ten-minute walk from where they'd set up camp. They'd tasked the men to start the fire while they were gone.

Courtney stepped over another tree root. "I swear it didn't feel this far when we were walking to the campsite." And on the way, they'd been holding all their camping gear. Actually, to be fair, Logan had carried most of it in his gorilla-sized arms. "Maybe we're heading in the wrong direction."

"Is that it?"

Courtney looked to where Grace pointed through the trees. Sure enough, there was a hint of Logan's white truck ahead.

"Ah, see? Who needs men?"

They stepped out of the clearing, and Grace lifted the key to unlock the doors. Courtney got into the front seat, climbing onto her knees and stretching to tug the cord from the back of the center console where it was connected.

She was just about to climb out when she felt something on her hand. Something *crawling* on her hand. She looked down.

Was that... a black widow spider?

A screech that could have raised the dead came from her lips. Her entire body jerked so hard that she fell flat on her stomach over the console.

No, no, no. This was not happening.

"Courtney...?"

She didn't know who that was, she was too busy shaking her arm like a mad woman, almost like she was trying to disconnect the thing from her body.

She had no idea if it was gone yet when she tried pushing up. Her shirt caught on something, tugging her back down. She jerked back, finally released, and all but fell backward, out of the truck and right onto Grace and Sage, throwing them all to the ground.

"Are you okay?" It was Grace who asked, but when Courtney rolled off them and stared at the women, Sage looked equally panicked.

Courtney scanned her hand and arm. No spider. She closed her eyes, lying flat on her back for a moment, then a laugh bubbled to the surface. It was clearly her body's way of coping with near death. Her breaths were still whooshing in and out of her chest, but at least she wasn't in the truck, aka the death-mobile.

"I think I just almost died."

Both women frowned, glancing from her to the vehicle and back.

"I'm not a hundred percent sure, but I think there's a black widow spider in there."

Grace gasped while Sage stood and peered into the open door.

"Don't get too close! Its bite is venomous," Courtney warned. The other woman was a doctor, she'd probably know that... but then, what the heck was she doing?

Sage turned, shaking her head. "It's a hobo."

"A what?" Courtney pushed to her feet, taking very small, tentative steps forward before peeking over Sage's shoulder.

And there it was again. She almost cringed at the sight of the spider on the passenger seat. The thing wasn't scared at all, just sitting there calmly for all the world to see. But now that she was giving the spider a proper look, she realized it was a lighter color than she'd originally thought.

"Are hobo spider bites dangerous?" Courtney asked.

Sage shook her head. "Not at all. In fact, quite often you don't even feel the bite and won't have any reaction."

An image of the little creature's teeth latching onto her skin came to mind.

Yuck.

Sage looked around, grabbing a large leaf before returning to the truck and placing it next to the spider.

Courtney cringed. It may not be dangerous, but it was still a *spider*.

Sage had just placed the leaf and the spider on the ground when Grace's unsteady voice sounded. "Um, guys, I think we might have bigger troubles."

Courtney blew out a long breath. "No, I just overreacted." Although, if she was honest, she'd probably overreact every time a spider was so close.

"Turn around," Grace whispered.

Courtney turned. And another scream attempted to crawl up her throat. Trickles of terror slid up her spine.

"A bison," Sage said quietly.

Grace took a step backward. "A mother and her calf."

"Which is worse, right?" Courtney said quietly. "Because bison can become aggressive when protecting their babies, can't they?"

Heck, they could get aggressive when people just got too close. She'd watched a documentary about them once. Risk of maternal aggression. And the bison certainly looked aggressive right now. She was pawing the ground, bobbing her head, and raising her tail.

Suddenly, a loud snort sounded through the trees. Out of instinct, all three women stumbled back three steps.

Courtney realized their mistake immediately, as the bison shifted closer to the car. They could probably still dive inside, but it would be a risk, especially for the last woman.

"I think we should stay very still," Sage said. "If she sees that we pose no threat, she might leave us alone."

They remained as they were for long seconds. Those seconds ticked into minutes.

Suddenly, the bison stepped forward. Then she stepped forward again.

Oh God, she looked moments away from charging. This wasn't working.

Courtney took a step to the side, hearing Grace's sharp intake of breath.

"What are you doing?"

"I'm going to walk this way and see if the mother follows. If she does, you both run back to the guys." She took another step.

"Courtney!" Grace's whisper was sharp and panicked.

Courtney took a third step. Her limbs shook, eyes glued to the bison. Finally, on her fourth step, the bison switched her attention from Grace and Sage to her. "Walk around the car so she doesn't think you're heading toward her calf. I'll use the trees as protection."

"Courtney, *no.*" This time it was Sage. "It's too dangerous."

Another step away. Another step from the bison. The calf trailed behind its mother, just like Courtney suspected it would.

"*Go.* The longer you stay there, the longer it will take the guys to get here." They could take on a fully grown bison, right? Not hurt it, just... detain it. Remove it from the area.

Courtney took her gaze off the bison for a second, holding Grace's. "Please go get them."

Her friend frowned, clearly unhappy with the situation, but when the bison took another step away from them, the other women finally started to move.

Courtney continued to take small, slow steps into the trees, the female bison following. She just prayed it wouldn't charge.

THE CRUNCH of leaves under Jason's feet was loud in the quiet forest. So too were Logan and Mason's steps behind him. They moved quickly, jumping over tree roots, negotiating their way around the vegetation.

The women had gone to get something from Logan's truck,

but not only had they been gone for a while, he'd just heard a screech through the forest. He was almost certain it had been Courtney.

They were probably fine, but the guys weren't taking any chances.

Jason tuned into the forest around him, listening for anything that sounded even remotely like people. That's when he heard it. Heavy footsteps of people moving toward them. Running. And they were close.

He increased his pace. So did the men behind him. A second later, Sage and Grace came into view.

Unease stalled his breath. Where was Courtney?

Grace stopped short, almost tumbling into Logan's arms. "Bison! A mother and a calf. They approached us when we were at the truck and the mother looked to be on the verge of becoming aggressive."

Sage grabbed Mason's arms and his hands went to her waist. "Courtney led them away so we could come get you."

"She *what*?" Jason didn't even stick around to hear the rest.

He moved through the forest faster than before, trees flashing by as he listened and searched for the woman. Footsteps sounded behind him. He wasn't sure if it was Logan or Mason, and he didn't stop to check.

It was another few seconds before he spotted her, slowly walking backwards, the huge bison maybe a dozen yards away, bobbing her head and pawing the ground like she was preparing to attack.

Fuck.

With her next step, Courtney tripped on something, stumbling, and landing on her behind. She quickly scrambled to her knees.

The bison charged.

Jason pushed his body to move faster than ever before, racing forward and swiping Courtney from the ground seconds before the animal reached her.

He didn't stop. He kept moving, Courtney secure in his arms. He could hear Logan behind him, talking to the bison, trying to soothe the animal. He knew his friend would take care of it. His focus remained on Courtney.

Her side was pressed to his chest as his arm bracketed her back and legs, her limbs trembling against him.

When he'd put enough distance between them and the threat, he slowed his pace to a walk, scanning her body from head to toe. Her eyes were wide, her face a mask of fear.

"Are you okay?" His voice was clipped with barely concealed rage, but dammit, he couldn't help it. He'd just almost watched her get trampled by a wild animal roughly ten times her weight. It could have easily killed her.

His jaw ticked, frustration filling his gut like acid.

"I'm okay." But her voice shook. She pressed a hand against his chest and wiggled her hips. "I can walk."

I don't think so, darlin'.

"No."

He continued to move, refusing to slow. He wanted to run again, but the wind was picking up and it would be too chilly if he went too fast.

"Are you angry?" Her voice had evened out now, the fear of a few seconds ago easing from her features.

Angry? Yeah. He could say that. There were also a dozen other words he could use. "You directed an aggressive mother bison's attention toward you and walked into the forest unprotected. Yeah, I'm angry."

"What else was I supposed to do? We tried remaining still, and it didn't help."

"Did you try jumping into the truck? Crawling *under* the truck and calling for us?" Surely anything would have been more logical than what she'd done.

"It would have been a risk, especially for Grace who was the furthest from the car."

When a gust of wind blew, she snuggled tighter into his chest.

"What you did wasn't smart, Courtney."

He could almost feel her spine straightening. Her muscles tensing. "Not that it's any of your business, but I wasn't trying to be smart. I was trying to save my friends."

"Like hell it's not my business." He muttered the words under his breath.

"What was that?"

"Nothing." He saw the set of her jaw moments before she started to wriggle in earnest. "Cut it out, Courtney."

"Put me down. *Now.*"

When he didn't, she fought harder. Cursing under his breath, he lowered her to her feet, not wanting her to fall and hurt herself.

She started walking—or more accurately, marching—ahead. He followed.

"You think I'm wrong?"

She spun around, her slim finger slamming into his chest. "You do *not* get to tell me whether I'm being smart or dumb, especially when you weren't there!"

He stalked forward a step and gave her a small smile. "Really?"

She frowned, eyes darting to his feet before she took a step back. "Yes." Her response was quieter than her last, some of the bravado gone.

Another short step forward. "Why not?" He could hear the soft pitter-patter of her heartbeat speeding up in her chest.

"Because we're not... *anything.*"

When she stepped back, her heel hit a rock and she started going down, just like she had when the bison attacked. For the second time that day, he swiped her off her feet seconds before she hit the dirt. Lifting her into his arms, he pivoted, pressing her back against a tree.

A soft gasp flew from her lips, even as her legs wrapped around him.

"Yet." The heat from her core pressed against his stomach, setting his blood roaring between his ears.

Her little frown was cute. "W-what?"

He inched forward. He could nearly taste her breath. "We're not anything *yet*." But soon...

He'd never wanted a woman like he wanted Courtney. The need tipped his blood from warm to blazing hot. It was something he'd never felt before but wasn't about to question.

He put his hand on the back of her neck, inching up, slipping into her hair.

"You don't want to date me," she said quietly.

He lifted a brow. He was pretty sure he did. In fact, there was little else he was as certain about. But she'd piqued his interest.

"Why not?"

"Because... my cat sleeps on the bed with me and takes up all the room. I'm insecure at the best of times. I'm a grump in the morning and I've been known on occasion to respond to text messages in my head, and not *actually* respond for a good week."

None of those were deal breakers. Not even a little. "Your cat can sleep on top of me for all I care. I'll work damn hard to prove you're the only woman I want. I'll put a smile on your face in the morning with a single kiss, and if you don't respond to my texts, I'll search you out, hunt you down, until I have my response."

She was silent, mouth dropping open just a fraction.

He lowered his head. "Don't do anything dangerous or self-sacrificing again. Okay?"

Her breaths were short and shallow. Her voice quiet. "Okay."

Then he couldn't help it—he took her lips, firm and unrelenting. The fear of losing her began to subside as he touched her. Tasted her.

He inched closer, and a deep whimper from Courtney sent shards of fire through his limbs.

God, he ached for the woman.

She moaned, pressing her breasts against his chest. Unable to stop himself, he cradled a breast in his hand. Even though there were layers of clothing between his palm and her skin, he could feel her pebbled nipple, hungry for attention. She gasped as he massaged her, and he took advantage, diving into her warm mouth.

Their tongues rubbed together. She arched, her breast pressing into his hand, hips grinding against him. The woman had every part of his body yearning. Craving. Burning.

He swiped and licked, brushing his thumb over her nipple once, twice, until slowly, reluctantly, he lifted his head. Courtney's next whimper was one of disappointment, and it almost had him chuckling.

He pressed his forehead to hers. "I can't get enough of you."

And he had a feeling he never would.

A protective instinct grew in his chest, wrapping around the woman in his arms. Seeing her almost injured today had him wanting to hold her tightly and never let go.

CHAPTER 12

*C*ourtney took a sip of her drink, the sweet flavor heating her blood. Voices buzzed around her and a pleasant haze had settled in her mind.

She glanced down at the pink bottle that someone had slipped into her hand. What was it... her third? Honestly, she couldn't remember, but she was starting to think they were deceptively high in alcohol. Although, to be fair, she was a lightweight.

She watched as the fire crackled, lighting and heating the area. The guys had placed logs around it. After they'd taken care of the bison situation, of course. She didn't even know how they'd taken care of it, but Logan assured her the animals were gone.

Good. So, no more bison. And no more heated kisses against trees.

She smiled at the memory and looked up. Jason's gaze immediately caught hers. Or maybe his eyes had already been on her, she wasn't sure. He winked, dimples flashing at her through the fire.

Sober Courtney would probably look away. Drunk Courtney

was a bit more fearless. She gave him a big, tipsy, I-think-you're-cute-and-could-get-lost-in-those-brown-eyes kind of smile.

She watched his chest move slightly with a quiet chuckle. His gigantic, muscular chest. Her gaze lowered to the long, strong fingers wrapped around his beer. Fingers that just a few hours ago had been wrapped around her breast while her core had pressed against his hard stomach.

Desire crashed through her lower abdomen, making her toes curl in her shoes.

Reluctantly, she dragged her glazed eyes away, trying to focus on whatever Mason was saying. People were laughing, so it had to be something funny. He had his arm wrapped around Sage's shoulders, his fingers drawing circles on her upper arm. On another log, Grace leaned into Logan's side, the expression on her face a perfect mix of happy and sleepy.

So much love in the air.

Courtney reached up to touch her necklace, frowning when her fingers found nothing but clothes. She tucked her hand inside her jacket, searching, but could only feel skin.

What the heck? Had she taken it off?

No. She never took it off.

Placing the half-empty bottle on the ground, Courtney rose to her feet and headed to her tent. Could it have fallen off in there? She lifted scattered clothes, checking every inch of her bag and the floor of the tent.

Nope. No necklace.

She was mildly aware that she should be more anxious than she was, especially given how precious the jewelry was to her, but the effects of the alcohol were keeping her nice and calm.

Where had she gone that afternoon? Her sluggish brain struggled to backtrack. The only thing she was really sure of was Jason. Lifting her up. Kissing her like he was starved for her.

Maybe that's where she'd lost it? Against that tree. Either that or during their pre-dinner walk to the waterfall.

Leaving the tent, Courtney headed into the trees. They all kind of looked the same, but she'd be able to find the right one. Surely there'd be something akin to a big sign that read "This is it! The place he set your blood soaring", right?

Well, it made sense in her mind. *A mind that you probably shouldn't trust right now, Courtney.*

She ignored the whisper in her head, touching the trees as she walked, leaning just a tad too heavily on each one. Every few steps, she stumbled but never fell. Which was probably a win considering the darkness.

"Where are you going?"

The deep voice broke through the silence. Courtney spun around and raised her hands like she was going to kung fu the stranger.

Her gaze fell on deep brown eyes. Not a stranger. And not someone she had any hope of karate chopping.

"Jason..." She almost sighed his name. This was good. Maybe she could lean on him instead of the trees. Or she could just convince him to carry her. "I think that's the closest I've ever come to a heart attack. Unless you can have a half-heart attack? If so, I think I had one of those."

The dim light of the moon through the trees cast shadows over his face. It didn't take away from how good-looking he was. If anything, it just made him look... more. More dangerous. More mysterious.

He took a small step forward, hands going to her arms, chafing them. "You shouldn't be out here alone. It's dark, you're drunk, and you'll freeze."

She glanced down at her arms. Where had her jacket gone? She'd been wearing it over her sweatshirt all night. Strange. She must have taken it off in the tent. "I'm okay."

In fact, the alcohol had heated her blood nicely.

"Hm."

There was a hint of disapproval woven into his tone.

Reaching up, she touched the crease between his brows. "You shouldn't frown. I like your smile." The frown slowly vanished, a small smile tugging at his lips. "That's better."

Don't get her wrong, the man looked sexy any and every way. But when he smiled, it was like his lips were speaking straight to her lady parts.

"What are you doing out here, Courtney?"

She watched his lips move, wondering if they'd kiss her again tonight. He didn't strike her as the kind of person to kiss a drunk woman, but maybe she could convince him—

"*Courtney.*"

She frowned, dragging her gaze back to his eyes. "Yes?"

Another heart-stopping smile. "What are you doing out here?"

Good question. What *was* she doing out here? She scanned the trees around her, trying to grab onto her last memory.

COURTNEY'S NOSE wrinkled as she frowned. Her eyes were just a bit glazed over.

So, the woman was cute even while drunk.

"I was looking for something." She glanced around, like the answer was in the trees and the moonlight.

Jason continued to chafe her arms, keeping her warm. He tilted his head to the side. "What's that?"

She bit her bottom lip, gnawing at it as she looked back at him. It drew his attention to her pretty pink mouth like a moth to a flame.

"When I'm with you," she said softly, "I forget things."

His smile widened. "I think that's the alcohol, darlin'."

She shook her head. "No. It's not just now. Although right now, I do feel very... muddy. When I'm with you, my brain turns to mush and I forget how to think. That's never happened with anyone else before."

When she started to gnaw on her bottom lip again, he raised a hand to her chin, tugging the lip out and stroking it with his thumb. "Anyone else?"

She leaned into his touch, and he swore he heard the softest hum from her chest. "You don't need to worry about them. My exes were all lying, cheating buttholes."

His body tensed, an angry burst skittering through his veins. "Your ex-boyfriends cheated on you?"

"Oh yeah. And not just one, but a few. One of them I even caught in my bed doing the deed. Talk about assholery, right? Jess never dated good guys either. I started to wonder if all men were lowlife scumbags, or if I'm just not someone who can hold a man's attention."

Motherfuckers.

He stepped closer, hands going to her cheeks. "We're not all scumbags." He grazed his lips across her cheek. "And you command every little bit of my attention. When you're around"—and even when she wasn't—"other women don't exist."

She sucked in a deep breath, that sexy lip between her teeth again. "I'm not that special."

Oh, how Jason wished he could meet the men who'd made her believe that. Teach them a fucking lesson. "You are." So damn special. And he'd make sure that soon, she realized how much. "Do you want to go back?"

Her nose wrinkled again. When she shook her head, little tendrils of blond hair mixed with blue highlights slipped onto her face.

"What would you like to do, sweetheart?"

When her cheekbones turned a rosy-pink shade, visible to his enhanced eyesight even in the dark, yearning churned his gut. He almost groaned out loud.

Shut it down, Jason. The woman's drunk.

Sliding his hand down her arm, he tangled his fingers through hers. "How about we go for a walk?" Maybe he could help her walk off the alcohol, then he could kiss her without feeling like he was taking advantage.

They walked for a while in silence, the sound of the waterfall growing steadily louder.

He negotiated their way through the trees, watching her steps more than his own, conscious of the way her feet moved unsteadily over the dirt.

"You seemed distracted today, Courtney."

It probably wasn't fair, him bringing this up while she was drunk and more likely to tell him things that sober Courtney wouldn't. But he'd seen her face in the little moments when she thought no one was watching. The pulling together of her brows. The faraway look in her eye. Like something was on her mind, rolling through her head and snatching her attention.

"I've started to think that maybe my cousin Jessica didn't die from a random home invasion."

His fingers tightened around hers. Hearing about her cousin's death, a woman who had once been close to her, made him want to hold her close. Another example of the fragility of life. How easy it was to lose someone.

She stumbled, but he kept her on her feet easily.

"What makes you think that?" he asked softly.

"A part of me suspected before yesterday." *Yesterday?* "But I didn't want to believe it. Because then I played a part in her death, didn't I? If I had this gut feeling that she wasn't safe in her relationship, and I didn't force her to leave, and she died because of him... it's partly my fault."

He stopped at the river. The top of the waterfall was now loud and just yards away. "It's not your fault. Not even a little bit."

She frowned. And even though she'd had a few drinks, he could see how deeply she was entrenched in her thoughts.

He pushed a strand of hair behind her ear, grazing her soft skin. "How do you know she wasn't safe?"

Her eyes were on his, but he could see that her mind was far away. "I knew while she was alive. I only met him the one time. But it was the way he touched her. It was possessive. Rough. And the way he spoke to her. More demanding than anything. And when she came to visit me on my birthday, I saw bruises on her arms."

The breath Courtney sucked in was shaky.

"Did you try to talk to her about it?" he asked softly.

"Yes. But it was like Jessica knew what I was going to say before I said it, and she kept changing the subject. Shutting me down. She didn't want to talk about it."

His hands rose, rubbing warmth into her arms again. God, he wished he had a jacket he could give her. "As hard as it sounds, you can't save someone who doesn't want to be saved. All you can do is try. Be there. Listen. And I'm sure you did all of that."

She gave a small nod before rocking forward and back. He wasn't sure if she was rocking from the wind or the alcohol, but he held her steady.

"What made you think about this?" he asked.

Her gaze lifted to his. "I had a dream." She sighed. "I dream a lot though..." Some of the tension eased from her features. "Sometimes about you."

Well, that wasn't a terrible confession. "You dream about me?"

Her hands rose to his head, fingers sifting through his hair and tugging him down. Her lips were close. Whispers of her heated breath brushed against skin before she spoke softly into his ear. "You kissed me in my dreams before I ever felt your lips for real."

His blood turned molten, red-hot need clawing at him. For a moment, his breathing was choppy, but he worked hard to control it.

She moved back, that damn lip captured by her teeth again.

Then she pulled away, taking a step toward the waterfall. Immediately, he tugged her back with a hand on her arm, giving her no leeway. Maybe she was drunker than he thought.

"I don't think so."

"I was just going to sit."

In her current state? "I think here is close enough."

"Are you doubting your ability to keep me safe?"

"Never." He'd keep this woman safe in a tornado.

The smile dropped from her lips. Then she sat, crossing her legs beneath her. Jason lowered to her side.

"I wish Jessica could have met you. She would have loved you." Courtney looked at the water. "She probably would have told me to lock this down."

"This?"

"You. Us."

Sounds like he would have liked Jessica, too.

She lifted her hand, touching his face, tracing the contours slowly. "You're the most perfect man I've ever met."

He almost laughed. "I'm far from perfect."

She shook her head. "Not true."

Every time her finger grazed his cheekbone, it was like a brand. Her touch soft but searing. Then she rose to her knees, slowly crawling onto his lap, straddling his hips. He steeled himself, forcing himself to remain still.

When her head lowered, he spoke her name as a warning. "Courtney..."

"Just one kiss."

One kiss under the moonlight with the girl who made his skin burn and his heart soar. He shouldn't. He knew he shouldn't. But, dammit, he was a weak man where Courtney was concerned, so when her mouth touched his, he didn't pull away.

She brushed and nipped at his lips.

A few seconds. That was as long as he lasted before a deep growl reverberated through his chest. He gripped the back of her neck, holding her while he made love to her mouth.

Minutes passed, dozens of them, neither of them coming up

for air. The sound of her heart pounding in her chest rivaled the crashing of waves at the bottom of the waterfall.

She finally lifted her head, her deep breathing all he could hear.

"Kissing you is like magic," she whispered.

He pressed his forehead to hers, closing his eyes and inhaling the sweet scent of the woman stealing his heart. "It's out of this world."

CHAPTER 13

Courtney waved goodbye to Grace and Logan with a smile. They'd tried to walk her up, but she'd refused. It was coming into the evening, she was tired, and everyone had bags to unpack and dinner to prepare.

The tiredness didn't stop her smile though. She'd smiled the entire drive home. It was a huge, cheesy grin, really, that creased the corners of her eyes and had her heart fluttering.

The second she stepped out of her tent that morning, she'd seen him. Felt him. His presence big and intense and powerful. The entire day, she'd received those spine-tingling touches from Jason. Hard gazes. Even a few more earth-shattering kisses when the others hadn't been around.

Yeah. It was a good weekend. And it was making her reconsider her earlier subtle dislike of camping.

She entered her building and started up the stairs. Even though it had been a great time, she was still looking forward to getting home to Eddie. Fortunately, even though Helen wasn't always the easiest person to be around, Courtney knew the woman would have taken good care of her cat.

She was halfway to the fourth floor when her phone vibrated.

Pulling it from her pocket, she looked down and her smile widened.

Jason: Get home safe, honey?

Her skin tingled. Sheesh, if the man could do that with just a message, imagine when they got deeper into their relationship.

Courtney: Yep. Just walking up the stairs now. Fantasizing about my hot shower. You?

Jason: Bag's unpacked, shower done, and dinner on the stove.

No way. She knew he was superhuman, but really? What did he do, speed all the way home? And how the heck was he so organized? She didn't plan to unpack her bag until way into tomorrow. Like late evening.

Courtney laughed. What was she thinking? The bag was more likely to remain packed for the next few days.

And cooking? No. No, no, no. Ordering in would work just fine.

Courtney: What's for dinner?

Jason: Just curry chicken.

So, the man was beautiful and he could cook.

She reached her floor, her quiet steps drumming through the otherwise silent hall.

Courtney: I was thinking of curry too.

Prepared and delivered to her door by the trusty Mumbai Indian restaurant deliveryman.

Courtney reached her apartment, quickly turning the key in the door and pushing it open. She'd only taken a single step inside when her feet slammed to a sudden stop. Her eyes widened, heart crashing against her ribs.

The phone in her hand vibrated with another message, but it barely pierced her mind.

Someone had been in her apartment. Searched the place. Trashed it.

Cushions from her couch lay scattered along the carpet. Photo frames, which had been carefully placed on various shelves and counters, now lay shattered on the formerly tidy floor. Every cupboard in her kitchen was open, the contents broken and messy.

Her phone buzzed again.

She turned her head, scanning her cozy little bedroom through the open door.

The same. The drawers to her bedside tables were open, the contents tossed on the bed and floor.

Ice skittered through her blood. Who had been here? When had they been here? Why?

With trembling fingers, she lifted the phone, not even reading the messages Jason had just sent before typing her own.

Courtney: Someone's been in my apartment.

His response was instant.

Jason: Get out. Now.

A mewl came from the bedroom.

Eddie.

She almost fell over her own feet racing into the room, her heart catapulting into her throat at what she saw.

Eddie lay on his side, his small stomach heaving up and down much too quickly, eyes closed.

Oh God! She dropped to her knees, reaching out to touch him before swiftly pulling her hand away. He lay at an odd angle, like someone had thrown or kicked him.

Her breaths sawed in and out of her chest.

Her phone started to buzz, and she quickly hit answer and put it on speaker.

"Eddie's barely breathing!" Her voice was desperate and shrill.

"Courtney, I'm driving to you now. Did you get out?"

"I...I can't! Eddie—"

"We'll get Eddie to the vet," he interrupted. "But right now, I need you to get out of that apartment, go to your car, lock the doors and drive away."

The warning in Jason's voice had her rising to her feet. She took a small step away from Eddie when the sound of a door opening down the hall penetrated the quiet. The door to Helen's apartment.

Footsteps sounded in the hallway. Heavy footsteps. Too heavy to belong to the older woman.

"Someone's coming!" she whispered.

Jason cursed. His next words were quiet. "Run to the bathroom, lock the door."

She did as he said, her legs almost jelly, barely holding her up. The last thing she saw before slamming the door was a man entering her apartment. He was tall, wearing a dark suit, the gun at his waist visible beneath an open jacket.

A whisper in her subconscious mind said he looked familiar, but her ability to think right now, to connect the past to her present, was nonexistent.

The lock clicked and she took three hurried steps back, hip colliding with the vanity. The handle immediately jiggled, and she tried to push back farther. Fear stole her breath, and her hands shook, icy.

The loud sound of an engine revved over the phone. "Courtney, talk to me. Are you okay?"

She scanned the small bathroom for a weapon, but somehow doubted squirting shampoo and conditioner into the guy's eyes would stop him. "He's trying to open the door!" Terror coated her voice, and her hand clutched the phone so tightly that, had she been stronger, she was sure it would have shattered.

Jason's voice held the calmness she lacked. "Courtney, I want you to turn up the phone as loud as it goes and place it close to the door."

That involved moving forward. Toward the man with the gun and the black eyes.

She could do that. A door separated them. She'd be okay.

She took a step forward. Then another.

"I'm at the door," she whispered.

"Hey, asshole." Jason's voice was loud, causing her to jolt and almost drop the cell. "I'm only two minutes away, and so are five other deadly soldiers. We were in Project Arma—heard of that? The experiment that made us ten times faster and stronger than a normal man? If you touch a hair on her head, a fucking strand, I'm going to tear you apart limb from limb."

The doorknob stilled. Silence settled, thick and heavy, and her heartbeat drummed in her ears.

Then retreating footsteps.

She took two giant steps back, dropping to the floor and hugging her knees. He was gone. Would he come back?

"Courtney?"

She managed something that sounded remotely like a yes. Then dropped her head to her knees. A minute passed. Then another.

When the doorknob jiggled again, she gasped, her head shooting up. This time there had been no footsteps in warning.

"Courtney?"

The air whooshed out of her lungs. It wasn't Jason, but it was one of his teammates. Aidan, maybe?

"Court, I'm coming in. Okay?"

She nodded, knowing full well he couldn't see her.

A second later, the lock broke, the knob turning. Then Aidan stood there, looking tall and fierce, ready for action. He took slow steps toward her before crouching.

"Are you okay?" His voice was low and gentle, but still held a hard edge.

She nodded. It seemed nodding was all she could manage at this very moment in time.

He reached his hand out. He didn't touch her, just held it open in front of her, offering her help if she wanted to rise. She slid her fingers into his large, warm palm and let him tug her to her feet.

"You're safe," he said quietly.

Another nod.

A second later, Jason appeared behind him. He stepped around Aidan, tugging her into his arms.

Courtney melted against him, finally feeling safe.

~

JASON KEPT his arm firmly around Courtney's shoulders as she recounted her version of the evening to the police officer. The officer's notepad was open, and he was taking notes, but Christ, he looked young. Too young. So did the other officers walking around her place. All of them were kids.

Grace and Sage sat on the other side of Courtney, while Aidan, Blake, Logan, and Mason were scattered around the room. Helen, Courtney's neighbor, had just been wheeled off to the hospital with suspected broken ribs and a concussion.

The guy had been hiding out in her apartment, waiting for Courtney to get home.

The older woman's dog had received similar treatment to Eddie. Flynn had taken both to the local veterinary hospital. Courtney had wanted to go, too, but that wasn't possible. Not with the police needing information.

Jason listened as Courtney described the man, committing every detail to memory.

"Do you know why someone would want to break into your apartment, Miss Davies? Do you have any enemies? Exes who were up to no good?"

Courtney was silent for a beat. When the silence stretched, Jason studied her closely. She *did* suspect someone.

Who?

"No."

Lie. He heard it clear as day. By the slight hitch in her voice, the small alteration in her breathing…

The officer closed his notebook, promising he'd look into the break-in before talking to her about safety precautions like new locks and not going out alone.

Jason barely heard him. He just wanted the guy out so he could question her. Find out exactly what it was she hadn't told the officer. And why.

The second he closed the door behind the last cop, Jason took a seat beside her again. Fiery need pummeled through his veins. Need to know what she was hiding. Who the guy was who could have so easily taken her. Hurt her.

"Who do you think was in your apartment?"

She didn't look surprised by his question. She'd probably been expecting it, knowing that each of them could detect a lie.

"The only reason I didn't say anything was because the agent told me the information was classified. I wasn't sure if I was allowed to talk to local law enforcement."

His muscles tensed. Agent? Classified information? What the hell? "Tell us, Courtney."

She wet her lips, fingers smoothing the little wrinkles in her pants. "Two nights ago, I returned home to guys waiting outside my apartment."

Two nights ago? That would mean the night he'd visited her at the coffee shop.

"They were FBI agents."

A wave of unease slithered along his spine. They also worked with the FBI. To take down the meanest sons of bitches around. "What did they want?"

Courtney took a breath, then slowly started to describe her visit with the agents. Every word she spoke had the dread and unease in his gut growing.

Mafia, torture...

"So, the only alleged connection to you is your relationship with your late cousin, Jessica, but members of the family have been spotted outside The Grind?" Aidan confirmed.

She nodded. "I saw her a couple of times that final year. Agent

Peters wanted to know if she ever said anything about Ryan's involvement with the Mafia family."

"But she never did?" Jason asked quietly.

"No. I'd like to think that she didn't know anything about it, but to be honest, she wasn't herself those last two years. I think she'd gotten herself into a bad relationship that she couldn't leave." Courtney shook her head. "Or didn't feel like she could leave."

He heard the guilt lacing each of Courtney's words. And maybe even a bit of shame. His hand lay on her leg and he gave her a little squeeze of reassurance.

"If the man who was here tonight was Mafia"—Jason's blood cooled at his own words—"what was he after?" Because he was definitely after something. His destruction of her apartment hadn't been for the hell of it. He'd been looking for something specific. What?

"I don't know. And if it has something to do with Jessica and Ryan, I don't understand why they would suddenly come after me, years after Jessica and Ryan are dead."

Jason looked around at the guys, communicating without words, before looking back to Courtney. "We have a contact in the FBI, Steve. He works in Intelligence and gives us some off-the-books work every so often." Missions that normal soldiers could seldom complete. "We'll make contact with him. See if he can talk to this Agent Peters tomorrow."

Truth be told, Jason was pissed that Courtney had received a visit from some agent and Steve hadn't notified them. It was possible Steve hadn't known, but then, the town was small. It seemed a visit from any FBI agent was something he should know about, especially when there was no field office in Idaho.

Blake straightened. "We can arrange for new locks and a security system on your door tomorrow."

"I'll stay here tonight," Jason added. He actually intended to stay longer than a night, or take her to his place… but that was a conversation for another time. Tonight, she was too rattled.

Courtney didn't even try to hide the relieved sigh escaping her lips. "Thank you."

The team spent the next hour putting the rooms back together. In that time, Grace ordered food for everyone and Flynn returned with a bag of clothes for Jason. Courtney took a moment away to call the vet hospital and check on Eddie who was stable and doing well.

By the time they were all filtering out, it was late, and exhaustion was visible on Courtney's features.

When the door closed, she turned, leaning on the wood. "What a mess."

He walked up to her slowly, her gaze following his movements the entire way. Then he took her face into his hands, holding her. "Why didn't you tell me?"

Her gaze skittered between his eyes, frowning. "Because I couldn't wrap my head around the Mafia being here for *me*. So I convinced myself they weren't. Because I don't like to think about Ryan, and I didn't want to make the weekend about that. Because you and I are just starting out and our relationship should be light and fun."

"Oh, honey, we're so much more than light and fun."

He and Courtney were going to be everything. The deep. The intense. The meaningful. She just didn't know it yet.

CHAPTER 14

*A*gent Peters's fingers tapped against the keyboard of his laptop. Three of his men sat around him at the Blue Halo conference table. There was something about the guy that had Jason disliking him on sight. It wasn't just because it had taken twenty goddamn minutes to convince the guy to allow Jason to be in the room with Courtney, half of that spent with Steve on the phone.

No, it was something else. Like an intuitively bad gut feeling.

Jason stroked the back of Courtney's hand under the table. He'd slept on her couch last night, and he planned to do it again tonight, even with the new security system. He wasn't taking any chances.

Her hand tensed beneath his as Peters spoke. "We have photos of most of the guys in the Bonvicin group. We'll show you images one by one, and you tell us if you recognize the guy from last night."

Courtney nodded, sitting a bit straighter. "I hope I remember what he looks like."

There was uncertainty there. Jason understood that. She'd

only caught a glimpse of him. And fear did funny things to the memory. Muddied it. Altered it.

"This organization is small compared to other Mafia families," Peters continued. "Even though the boss died six months ago, and we're not sure who's taken over, the muscle should all be the same."

Peters connected his laptop to the projector and a second later, a man with dark brown hair and hard black eyes stared back at them.

Courtney shook her head. Peters flicked to the next man. Same thing.

It was on the sixth photo that Courtney's breath hitched. Her heart rate changed, starting to race.

But she wasn't the only one who reacted to the man's image.

Jason leaned forward, a silent curse whispering through his head. He felt Courtney's eyes on him. When he looked at her, it was to see confusion and shock swirling through the green and brown depths of her gaze.

"Do you know him?" Peters asked.

Courtney looked back to the agent. "A couple weeks ago, I had an interview at the local Cradle Mountain radio station. There was a problem with the elevator, it got stuck, and Jason came to help me. When the elevator started working again, it stopped on the fourth floor. That man was one of three janitors on the floor."

Peters didn't react. In fact, his features remained perfectly blank.

"It was a setup," Courtney said quietly, looking at Jason. "They did something to the elevator, making sure I stopped on the fourth floor."

The *deserted* fourth floor. Deserted other than those three men.

"But they recognized you," she continued, still speaking to

Jason. "They knew what you were capable of. If you hadn't been with me…"

Her hand trembled beneath his. He gave it a gentle squeeze, when what he really wanted to do was surrender himself to the rage taking over his body.

"But I was."

One of Peters's men made a note on his own laptop before Peters flicked to the next image. "Let's keep going through the photos and we'll talk about what all this means later."

Over the next couple of minutes, Jason and Courtney recognized and identified the two other janitors. No one was surprised. Peters was still flipping through photos when Courtney jolted under his hand again.

Peters must have seen it, because he asked, "Is this the man you saw in your apartment?"

She gave a small nod. "And he was in the coffee shop, too." Jason's throat tightened. "I didn't connect it until now. He came in the other week. He was staring at the magazine spread I'd framed on the wall of The Grind. Then when he looked at me…"

Her pause killed him. He wasn't a patient man right now. "What is it, honey?"

"He just creeped me out. I was happy when he left."

He suddenly recalled what she'd said that night when he had walked her home from work. About a guy leering at her chest at The Grind. His stomach twisted in anger at how close the guy had gotten to her.

"This man's name is Tommy Lima. He's the guy we suspect has taken over as head of the family. He's also one of the guys we spotted around The Grind a few times."

And that was who was after her?

Courtney shook her head. "This doesn't make sense! What do they want with me? And why now?"

"That's what we'd like to know, Miss Davies."

The way Peters said it, combined with the way he looked at

her—like he didn't believe she was as clueless as she maintained —infuriated Jason. Hell, the guy looked like he was one step away from cuffing her wrists and dragging her away.

"Are you sure Jessica never mentioned any of this to you?"

The muscles in Courtney's leg constricted under his hand.

"Yes," she said firmly.

That look never dropped from Peters's face.

Jason was about to jump to her defense when she leaned across the table, her voice hardening. "I'm telling the truth."

That's my girl.

Footsteps sounded in the hall seconds before the door opened. Peters quickly shut his computer as Amy stepped through the door behind him, a tray of coffee and tea in her hands. "Hello, I brought—"

Jason was on his feet in seconds. "This is a private meeting."

"Oh. I just thought as the receptionist, it was okay for—"

"It's not."

Her mouth opened and closed a few times before she quickly recovered. "Sorry. I'll set the tea on the reception desk for when you're done."

The second the door closed, Courtney sighed. "Are we done here for today? Because I've identified the man who was in my apartment, I've told you that I don't know what they're after. There's nothing else I can share that would be useful."

"It's just difficult to believe that you know nothing about what they might want, yet they've been trailing you, targeting you, searching through your home... and there's a connection between them and you."

"He was connected to her cousin, not Courtney," Jason said. "In fact, as far as you know, the only connection was to her cousin's boyfriend. So how about you do your job and figure out why they're now harassing an innocent woman?"

The guy's lips tightened.

Courtney lifted a hand, touching her neck—then she stiffened. Suddenly, she was on her feet. "Okay, well. If that's every-thing, I'm going to go." She was already walking to the door before she'd finished speaking.

Jason's hand went to the small of her back, but before they exited the room, Peters rose from the table. "Miss Davies..."

She paused, spine ramrod-straight as she turned.

A vein in Peters's neck popped out. He wasn't happy. "If you remember anything, figure anything out, let us know."

She gave a quick nod before moving into the hallway. She walked straight past Amy at the reception desk and out the door. He followed her all the way down the stairs. It wasn't until she hit the sidewalk that he finally took her hand. "Courtney, where are you going?"

"I lost it!" Her voice was almost frantic.

"You lost what, honey?"

"My necklace!"

The one she never took off. "So, let's go look for it."

"WE'VE SEARCHED every inch of this place, Jason. I think I just need to accept it's gone." Even though the thought felt like razor blades running over her heart.

They'd searched Flynn's property, paying particular attention to their camping grounds and the section of forest where she'd run from the bison. And now they'd ended up here, at the top of the magnificent waterfall, the very place she'd been sitting with Jason two nights ago.

"We'll find it," Jason said quietly. "Maybe not today, but we'll find it."

She was glad he was confident because she certainly wasn't. Not wearing it meant she felt naked. She'd had it around her neck for over two years, rarely taking it off.

She walked over to the rushing water, crouching to feel the

icy cascade against her hand. "Thank you for coming out and looking with me. And for staying while the FBI agent questioned me this morning. And staying over last night."

Heck, the guy was basically her superhero, he was just missing a cape.

"Of course."

She looked up to see him studying the dirt, rocks, and rubble. They'd already searched the area. But boy, she was grateful for his perseverance.

She was just about to rise when something tickled her hand where it rested on a large rock beside the water. A screech so loud it was probably heard for miles escaped her throat when she saw yet another spider. A spider that looked scarily similar to the one in Logan's truck the other day.

She tried to shake it off, but the thing ran beneath her jacket and right up her arm.

Oh, baby Jesus, if her worst nightmare were ever to come to life, this was it.

Courtney was on her feet in seconds, screeching and jumping, almost tipping right into the water. A strong hand grabbed her by the shoulder, pulling her back just before she fell in sideways.

She didn't stop. She flailed her limbs like she was being attacked. The spider swiftly crawling over her shoulder and onto her chest had bile rising into her throat.

"Baby, calm down! What's wrong?"

Jason's hands were grabbing at her, latching on to her wrists, restraining.

She tried to tug herself away, screamed again. Christ Almighty, it was on her stomach. "It's under my shirt! Get it off! *Get it off!*"

She barely registered Jason's confused face. The second his hands released her, she wrenched the shirt off, flinging it away along with her jacket.

The huge-ass spider ran across her stomach like she was his own personal playground.

Hell no!

She was trying to shimmy the thing off when Jason reached out, curling his hand around the arachnid. He gave a slight chuckle as he lifted it off her.

Her mouth dropped open, nausea now rolling around in her gut. He was voluntarily *holding* it?

He walked off into the bushes, disappearing for a moment before returning.

Courtney's breaths were still whooshing in and out of her chest. The urge to scrub every inch of skin the spider had touched was intense.

That was it. She was never coming to this place again. Ever.

Jason's hands went to her shoulders. "Are you okay?"

Was that... amusement in his eyes?

Some of the panic began to recede, something akin to irritation taking its place. "Are you *smiling*?"

His lips pursed, but she was almost certain the man was biting the inside of his cheek. "No. The spider was tiny and harmless, but I can see how it would have been scary."

Okay, now he was just placating her.

Her eyes narrowed, hands going to his chest and giving him a huge shove. Fortunately, he stepped back, making her effort seem worthwhile, because there was no way she'd actually be able to move him an inch by herself.

"It *was* scary! Arachnophobia—which is the fear of spiders—is a very real thing! Your smiling does not help the situation. And don't think I didn't hear your chuckle when I was in the middle of experiencing some very real terror!"

Oh, she'd heard the laugh. And she was only just letting herself feel the anger of it now.

She scanned the ground, spotting her top and jacket, and marched over to them.

"Courtney—"

Leaning down, she lifted her clothes. "I think we should go."

She headed for the trees, making it only a few steps before a large body suddenly appeared in front of her. She took a step to the side. He mirrored her.

"Can you put your clothes back on first, please?"

Put her clothes on? Oh, the gall of the man... laughing at her terror one minute and telling her what to do the next.

"I told you the last time we were here, you don't tell me what to do."

The truth was, she was freaking freezing. The wind against her bare skin felt like pins prickling her arms. Her chest. But no way was she admitting that.

He took a step closer, his voice lowering. "Courtney."

And now he was using his deep, I'm-warning-you voice.

She took a small step toward him. "What? Are you going to carry me again? Shove me against a tree and kiss my brains out?"

At the darkening of his eyes, she almost stepped back. Almost.

"You sure you want to play this game?"

Some of the frustration of moments ago eased from her body, and a smile flirted at her lips. She was starting to understand that when it came to safety, the man liked to be listened to.

Well, she liked it when people didn't laugh at her panic.

She took a half step forward, rising to her toes, and slid her fingers into his hair. Tugging him down, she nipped his bottom lip—hard—before whispering against his mouth, "What I want is for you to stop telling me what to do."

Another small chuckle. Like a breath of warning against her chilled face.

His mouth went to her neck, the tingling of breath and the brushing of lips like shots of awareness shooting across her skin.

"And I don't like watching your skin turn blue from the cold."

Suddenly, he shifted her. A tree once again touched her back, but this time her feet remained on the ground. His hands slid down her arms, grabbing her wrists and tugging them above her head. He switched both to one hand, lowering the other and gliding it over her bare side.

A delicious shudder raced up her spine.

His mouth returned to her neck, first kissing her gently. Then alternating between sucking and nipping, her entire body jolting with each rough touch.

She was vaguely aware of the hand on her side grazing across her stomach, her ribs, before landing over her bra.

Her throat constricted. Then his hand slipped inside the bra, cupping her, thumb pressing against her pebbled nipple.

White-hot bursts of lava spread through her.

"If you don't protect yourself, then I can't protect you either. And that means we have a problem." His words were soft, deceptively so.

His thumb flicked her hard nipple. A cry escaped her throat. She tugged at her hands but there was no give.

His head rose, lips hovering over hers. He lightly pinched her nipple with his thumb and forefinger. More fire flickered from her chest to her core.

Courtney arched, her mouth slipping open. Jason thrust his tongue inside, massaging, sipping, while continuing to work her peak. Every flick of his thumb was torture. Every pinch caused new bursts of pleasure to thrum through her body.

Soon it wasn't enough, a throbbing need from deep inside pushing her to the edge. Craving more. She wriggled her hips, moaning into his mouth.

Like he read her mind, his hand lowered, skimmed over her skin before pushing inside her jeans and the thin lace covering her sex.

Her heart stopped. Then it took off again, hitting against her ribs hard, threatening to break free.

His mouth lifted but his forehead pressed against hers. A single finger brushed against her clit. She flinched. Rocked forward as shock waves of awareness ripped through her. His mouth crashed back down, tongue dueling and dancing with her own.

She arched and cried as his finger continued to brush and press against her sensitive bud. Pulling at her hands, she once again met impenetrable resistance.

His finger left her clit, and she almost cried out loud.

Then there was a finger at her entrance, pausing.

Oh Lord, she would die right here and now if he didn't move.

He touched her lips again before his breath brushed against her with his words. "Will you let me protect you?"

Protect her? She whimpered, moving her hips, desperately seeking relief.

"Courtney." His finger pressed inside her, but only a fraction. Then he pulled it out again. Her moan vibrated her entire body.

"Will you let me protect you?" he repeated.

"How?" The words were wrenched from somewhere deep inside her.

The finger at her entrance began to draw little circles. They were circles of torture. "Follow my instructions when I need you to do something. Like put your damn shirt and jacket back on."

He trailed his mouth up her cheek, nipping her earlobe.

She nodded before a single word left her lips. "Yes."

Then his finger pushed inside her, filling her. Her mouth opened, but nothing came out. No words. No breath.

He sucked on her neck, pulling his finger all the way out of her before pushing back in, rubbing something exquisite inside her. His thumb pressed against her clit.

Suddenly her body shook, nails digging into her palms as a violent orgasm took her. Claimed her. Shattered her.

CHAPTER 15

*C*ourtney placed an iced coffee and an egg and bacon bagel beside Blake's laptop.

He blinked. "Ah, I didn't—"

"Order this? I know. But I hate that you're having to sit here and watch me work all day."

Watch. Protect. Stop an Italian Mafia family from coming in and snatching her. Same- same.

Blake leaned back, eyes softening. "You don't need to do that. I'm only here as a precaution. I don't think they'll attack in the middle of the day while the store is busy. And I'm doing the same work here as I'd be doing in my office, so I'm not losing time."

"Hm, so now that you have a bagel and iced coffee, you could say that working here is *better* than working at the office. Or at least has more perks."

He shook his head, smiling, before she continued.

"I should have become a target for the mob earlier." She chuckled, whereas the smile slipped from Blake's lips.

"Not funny, Courtney."

She held out her thumb and forefinger so they were almost touching. "A little bit funny."

The smallest hint of a smile cracked his stony face. "Thank you for the coffee and bagel."

"You're welcome."

He shut the laptop, pushing it to the side without taking his eyes from her. "You doing okay with all this?"

"Sure. I'm just covering up my terror with a poor attempt at humor." He tilted his head. She lifted a shoulder. "I'm okay. Jason slept on my couch again last night. He makes me feel safe. So do you and the rest of your team."

Several days had passed since the break-in, and she'd offered Jason her bed every night. Each time he flat-out refused. She'd almost suggested they *share* the bed, but then scaredy-cat Courtney had come out and sealed her lips shut.

"It's okay to not be okay," he said softly. "Fear is a normal reaction to what's going on right now."

Oh dang, how was she supposed to be brave when he came out and said things like that? "I know. But seriously, I'm so grateful to have all of you looking out for me."

For changing her locks. Protecting her every minute of the day. Even using whatever resources they had to track down this Mafia family.

He dipped his head. "Wouldn't have it any other way."

Yeah, these guys were awesome. "Is Mila popping in today?"

His smile widened. The guy was utterly infatuated with his daughter. It melted Courtney's heart. "Willow's bringing her in after preschool. It'll just be a quick drop-off because Aidan will take over from me. She might twist my arm and ask for a milkshake before she leaves, though."

Courtney chuckled. "Of course! I love that the kid loves my shakes."

Not love. Obsession.

He shook his head. "She'll kiss your feet."

She would take all the kisses the kid wanted to shell out. She was adorable. "Give me a shout if you need anything else."

She headed back to the counter. One of her servers, Nicole, was running the floor, while Joey was in the back room. She headed back to see him. He had his head in the coffee bean cupboard and was pulling out a huge bag.

She stopped beside him. "Hey! You look a bit better rested today."

Joey placed the bag on the counter, cracking a smile. "Well, that would be because I feel better, boss."

Good. She hadn't seen that smile for weeks, and she wasn't going to lie, it had started to worry her. "Anything in particular help with the change?"

Something crossed his face. An anxious, almost worried look. But as fast as it had appeared, it was gone. He reached for the next bag. "The advance on my pay helped. Thanks."

She stepped closer. "You never did tell me why you needed that money."

If he didn't want to share, that was fine. But if he needed someone to talk to, she really hoped it could be her. She wanted to help and support the guy in whatever way she could.

Joey sighed, placing the bag of coffee down before turning and giving her his full attention. A trickle of unease snaked through her stomach at what he was going to say. Drugs? Gambling? An investment that had turned sideways and lost him a chunk of money?

"I wasn't going to tell you this because I didn't want you to worry, but... my mom, who lives in Delaware, has coronary artery disease." Courtney gasped, placing one hand to her chest and grabbing his upper arm with the other. "I send her money for her medication to manage it, but doctors have just told her it's at the point where she needs surgery."

She stepped forward, gently squeezing his arm. "I'm so sorry. You should have told me earlier. What can I do? Do you need more money?"

He shook his head quickly. "No. It's… a lot of money. That's why I was stressing. But it's fixed now."

If it was so much money, then how had circumstances changed in such a short period of time? "How did you fix it?"

His eyes lowered to the beans when he lifted the bag he'd just taken out. "An unexpected opportunity presented itself to me. Honestly, you don't need to worry."

She gave a small nod, wanting to ask more, but getting the feeling that Joey was done sharing. He took a step to walk around her, then stopped. "You're not wearing your necklace?"

She touched her chest where the gem usually sat. "I know. I lost it during the camping trip."

Saying that out loud made her heart hurt.

"Ah, I'm so sorry to hear that. Where'd you go camping? Surely it's still there."

You'd think so, wouldn't you? "Flynn has a property just outside Cradle Mountain, a bit north of the city. There's no house or anything on the land, but plenty of space to camp, and even a waterfall." Her cheeks burned at the memories she'd made at the top of that waterfall. Oh Lord, she hoped Joey didn't notice. "We went back but had no luck finding it."

She and Jason had searched every inch of that campsite, finding diddly-squat.

"Sorry, Court. Hopefully it shows up." He gently tapped her shoulder with his own before heading out.

She took a moment to digest what Joey had told her. God, she hated that he'd been going through so much and she hadn't even known. The stress of his mother being sick, the financial strain of paying her medical bills… it would have been awful to deal with alone.

Sighing, she headed back out.

Blake stood at the counter, now joined by Aidan. Both were waiting for her. Listening.

The door to the shop opened and Blake's daughter Mila

walked in, closely followed by her mother. Willow was tall, with spectacular green eyes and long brown hair that had the most magnificent waves. Courtney would kill for hair that luscious.

Blake had only taken one step toward them when Mila sprinted, barreling into him, scrawny arms wrapping around his neck as he lifted her up.

"Hey, munchkin, how was school?"

"Good! It was Alexander's birthday and his mom brought chocolate and orange cake."

Chocolate and orange? Mm, maybe she should get that combo into the shop.

"Alexander turned four." She held up four fingers. "He's the youngest in the class."

Willow stopped beside them, a pink backpack slung over her shoulder. She smiled at Courtney. "Hi, Courtney."

"Willow, hey! Are you staying? Can I get you anything?"

"A to-go coffee would be wonderful. I'm heading straight for study group and need something to keep me awake. I think Mila might want—"

"A chocolate milkshake with extra sprinkles, please," Mila interrupted.

Courtney smiled at the girl's excited grin. Sprinkles wasn't something she usually added to her milkshakes, but Mila had a fondness for them that Courtney wasn't about to deny.

Blake stepped closer to Willow, placing a hand on her elbow and leaning in to press a kiss to her cheek.

"Tutoring go okay?" he asked softly.

Courtney looked away. The moment seemed intimate. But then, it usually did with these two. They were the classic couple who were supposed to be together, but for some reason just... weren't. Like Pam and Jim for the first three seasons of *The Office*.

She smiled to herself at the thought. And just like Pam and

Jim, she had no doubt Blake and Willow would find a way to make it work.

Although Blake brought Mila in for milkshakes every week, Willow came in less often. From what she'd heard, Willow worked and studied long hours.

Courtney started on the coffee, and Blake nodded to her. "We'll just be in the booth."

"Sure. I'll get the shake to Mila when it's ready."

Mila clapped her hands excitedly as Blake carried her to the table.

"She's such a happy kid," Courtney said, setting the coffee on the counter in front of Willow.

"She is. She's adjusted to the move to Cradle Mountain so well. I'm relieved. She's my whole world."

That was beautiful. "How's your studying going?" She was training to become a teacher. Elementary school, maybe?

"Good, I can finally see the light at the end of the tunnel." Willow laughed. "Less than a year to go and I'll finally get the certificate I need to work as a teacher."

"I bet you'll be glad to not have to work and study at the same time anymore."

"Oh my gosh, I might finally have time to sit on the couch and watch trashy reality TV with my feet up."

Lord, if there was ever a period in her life when Courtney *didn't* have time for that, she might just lose her will to live. "If you ever need a friend, I'm fantastic at watching trashy TV with my feet up. I usually accompany it with a bottle of wine and some dumplings."

Willow sighed. "You speak to my heart, Courtney." She paused. "I'm sorry I haven't come in more since getting to town, or made more of an effort to get to know you, but I really hope that when I have a bit more time on my hands, we can change that."

"Oh, you don't need to apologize. And I would love that."

"Good. Now I'm going to go smoosh my daughter's face before I go."

Courtney chuckled, watching as the woman did just that, laughing at the way Mila fell back in her seat, giggling.

She made the milkshake quickly and took it to Mila, loving the beaming smile she got in return. She was just stepping behind the counter when a familiar woman entered the shop.

Amy. Aka, Miss America. Argh.

Her deep green pencil skirt went down to her knees, with an absurdly long slit running up the side of her leg. Her white shirt would have provided good coverage if her breasts weren't pushed up so dang high, straining the material.

Amy stopped in front of Courtney, her smile wide. The woman had become a regular at the shop, and each visit, she seemed faker than the last. Her smile was like something you'd see on a big-ass billboard.

But maybe that was just the insecure, jealous monster in Courtney speaking.

"Hi, Courtney. Could I grab coffees for Jason and me, please? You know our regulars."

She forced her lips to tilt up into a smile. She had a feeling it didn't quite reach her eyes. "Sure."

As Courtney started on the coffees, Amy strummed her fingers on the counter. "Did you have a good weekend away?"

She was trying to make small talk? *Oh, baby Jesus, give me strength.*

"Yes, thank you. It was wonderful. Going away with other couples allowed Jason and me to have a bit more quality time together." Was that an immature swipe? Probably. She didn't care one bit.

"Hm. It was still camping though. The lack of toilets and showers doesn't really induce romance."

You'd think not, but... She smiled to herself.

Courtney glanced over her shoulder. Amy was studying her nails.

No. She could not imagine the woman camping. She turned back to the machine. "I guess it's fortunate that Jason isn't superficial."

She was making it sound like they were dating, which they weren't. But they were pretty damn close. And hell, the man *was* sleeping on her couch.

Amy chuckled, but there was no humor there. "Darling, all men are superficial. It's the way they're designed." She straightened, smoothing her hands down her legs.

Courtney placed the coffees on the counter and Amy handed over a card.

"I'll remember that," Courtney said, the words holding just enough sarcasm that the woman would know she wasn't agreeing.

"You do that. Want me to pass on any messages to Jason?"

How about, 'your receptionist's a bit of a bitch'. Yeah, right. That message would never reach his ears.

She gave the woman the sweetest smile she could muster. "No, thanks, I'll see him tonight."

CHAPTER 16

"*I* can't keep letting you sleep on the couch."

Jason chuckled softly at Courtney's stern words as he rinsed another dish and placed it in the dishwasher. Her place was small, but he kind of liked that. It made it easy to keep her in his sight. Fewer entry and exit points.

"I told you, Court, I don't mind."

Her little huff nearly had him laughing. "It's been almost a week. Your spine must be permanently curved by now."

Five days, in fact. Helen was still in the hospital, and Bernie at the vet. They'd both probably still be there for a few more days. Eddie, however, was home and recovering well.

He shot a glance over his shoulder. She'd stopped wiping down the island and was now standing behind him, hands on hips. She reminded him of an angry pixie with her high pigtail buns and multicolored short dress.

When he grinned, the little red dots on her cheeks deepened.

"That's it. I'm sleeping on the couch and you're not stopping me."

He put the last dish into the machine, then turned to dry his hands on a tea towel. "You're not."

"Wanna bet?" She pivoted, just about marching out of the room.

Rather than follow, Jason stepped into the living room and waited. He was actually intrigued to see what she'd do. Would she just camp out on the couch and think he wasn't going to move her?

A couple of minutes passed, then she stepped back into the room, the scent of peppermint and flowers infusing the air. She wore an oversized T-shirt that almost hit her knees. The outline of her nipples pushed against the soft fabric showing that there was nothing between her breasts and the top.

Blood roared in his ears, arousal flooding his system.

She'd barely made it halfway to the couch when he was in front of her. He only just kept the rumble from his voice. "You're not sleeping there."

"I am."

She tried to step around him, but he was there, in front of her, touching distance. "You're not."

One brow lifted. "How are you going to stop me, Jason? Carry me to the bed and physically restrain me for the entire night?"

Fuck. That was not a good image to put in his head right now. And damn but her sass was making him harder.

He took a small step closer, his hand rising to her chin, thumb grazing across her bottom lip. "Courtney, could you just listen to me for once?"

Something dark, almost molten, flashed through her eyes. "I've never been a good listener."

Her words vibrated through him. Her heated breath touched his finger. His hand. Burning him. He lowered his head, lips almost touching her ear. "You're not. Sleeping. On. The couch."

Two delicate, warm hands rose, grazing his neck before running through his hair. "Well, I mean, we could *both* sleep in the bed?"

Desire, hot and intense, cascaded through his limbs, her

words like a rough caress across his skin.

When he lifted his head, he saw the slight parting of her lips. The softened eyes. The yearning. Then her tongue poked out of her mouth, wetting her lips, taunting him.

He dove, crashing his lips onto hers and lifting her against him in one fell swoop.

There was no soft and gentle. No warming up to it. The kiss was heavy and intense. It was his tongue diving into her mouth. Taking. Giving. Both of them surrendering to each other.

She wiggled her hips, rubbing her core against him, fingers tugging at his hair. His breath hissed out of his chest, his normally perfect self-restraint in tatters.

Stepping forward, he pressed her against the wall, her cry matching the internal one of his own. The sleep shirt rode up her legs and he took advantage of her exposed flesh, sliding his hand up her thigh, her waist.

He'd barely skimmed over her rib cage before he was taking one perfect mound in his hand, strumming his thumb over the pebbled nipple.

Another spine-tingling whimper hissed from her lips.

"Tell me you want this." His voice barely sounded like his own. It was too deep. Too gruff.

"I want you, Jason. And if you stop, I might kill you."

He smiled against her lips before plunging back inside, swirling his tongue around Courtney's. Wrenching his lips away, he bent slightly, yanking her shirt up and taking a taut nipple into his mouth, sucking it between his teeth and flicking it with his tongue.

Her whimpers became cries, desire evident in the pounding of her heart.

He released the nipple with a pop, switching to the other one, before he forced his head up and his legs to move. Seconds later, he was lowering her to the bed, hovering over her, pressing his hardness into her soft.

Reaching for the bottom of her top, he tugged it up. Her back arched, desperate fingers grabbing at the material along with him. Next, they worked on his own shirt and jeans. Pulling everything off.

Finally, he took each of her hands in his own, threading their fingers, pressing them beside her head to the mattress. He returned to her mouth, resting his front against hers. The heat, the spine-tingling desire, burned between them.

The woman stole his breath. His focus. His sanity. She robbed him of every little bit of restraint he possessed.

Slowly, he grazed a hand down her side, pausing at her breast, gently squeezing, before continuing down to her core. When he reached her panties, he eased beneath the material, then slipped his fingers between her folds.

The jolt from Courtney had his blood simmering.

He moved his fingers in a tight, circular motion. At first slowly. Softly. Then, he increased the pressure. Learning what she liked. What caused her back to arch and her breath to seize.

A RED HAZE clouded her vision. It was the shade of fire. Of need. Of deep-seated hunger.

Every swipe had the throbbing in her lower abdomen intensifying. Had her teetering closer to the edge.

His lips left her mouth, grazing down the column of her exposed neck, her chest, down her ribs, before hovering over the thin material covering her.

Jason's fingers grasped the edges of her panties, tugging them down her thighs, her calves. Then he was parting her legs.

Her breath stopped in her throat. For a second, cool air danced over her clit. Then his head descended, mouth covering her.

Courtney's body nearly levitated off the bed, but he weighed her down in the most delicious way. Pleasure pounded in her core. The air thickened, her mind cloudy with desire as he sucked and swiped at her.

She was just there, moments from shattering, when he rose to his feet. The air whooshed out of her chest. Her whimper was one of desperation to tug him back to her.

Jason's gaze didn't leave her as he pushed his briefs to the floor. Her gaze dropped. He stood before her bare, looking huge and fierce and dangerous.

He opened the bedside drawer she indicated, donning a condom, then crawled back onto the bed, his eyes predatory. The man looked like he was about to claim her. Body and soul.

An excited, almost nervous churning began to flutter through her stomach as he positioned himself over her, his thickness between her thighs. She widened her legs, welcoming him.

His hand rose to her cheek, holding her. "You're so damn beautiful, Courtney."

Her eyes almost shuttered at his touch. His words. She just kept them open, not daring to lose him.

Slowly, he eased inside, stretching her. Filling her.

Her world slowed. Everything around her blurred. Everything, except for him.

His gaze held her hostage, watching her with a silent ferocity. For a second they were both still. A moment of quiet in the middle of a storm. Then she tugged his head down, fusing her lips to his again.

The first thrust of his hips had her core clenching. The throbbing intensified. Then he thrust a second time. A third.

She threw her head back, panting for air that was only just reaching her lungs.

His pace increased, her cries piercing the room. They were anguished sounds, physically torn from her chest.

The throbbing in her core began to sharpen, her desperation tormenting her.

Suddenly, he withdrew, pulling out of her completely. She gave a soft cry of protest. Jason chuckled before flipping her over like she weighed nothing. Grabbing a pillow, he pushed it under her hips. Then his heat surrounded her. And he was entering her again.

Courtney gasped as he began to drive in and out of her body in deep, even strokes, hitting a new spot inside that had her toes curling and her senses on overload.

His mouth went to her neck, kissing, sucking. One of his hands found her nipple, grazing the peak.

She tried to move but was trapped beneath his large form, his strength and size dwarfing her. Caging her. When he tweaked her nipple, she teetered closer to the edge, a sharp cry breaking from her lips.

His thrusts quickened, his breaths against her skin growing heavier. The hand on her breast moved down her body, where he swiped across her clit. The orgasm slammed into her core, ripping through her system. She opened her mouth to scream but no sound left her lips.

He continued to drive into her, prolonging the orgasm, demanding everything she had until his loud growl penetrated the room. Finally, his hips slowed, his head shifting from her neck and settling against her back.

She wasn't sure how long they remained like that, unable to move. Speak. Captured within a moment of pleasure and exhaustion and deep emotion.

When Jason finally slid out of her, she almost whimpered at the loss. He dropped to the side, pulling her against him.

She curled into him, her body still coming down. Still throbbing.

"That was amazing," she whispered, exhaustion barely allowing the words out.

His arm tightened, a soft kiss pressed to her forehead as sleep began to lull her into oblivion. *"You're* amazing."

CHAPTER 17

"*I*t's possible they didn't find what they were looking for at Courtney's apartment and have left Cradle Mountain."

Even though Steve was on the phone and couldn't see him, Jason shook his head. "I don't think so. And I think it would be dangerous for us to entertain that thought."

Another quiet week had gone by. That didn't mean they weren't still here or weren't coming back. Courtney was going to remain protected by him and his team until the FBI did their goddamn job and brought this Mafia organization down.

Steve sighed. "I spoke to Agent Peters. His sources say Tommy Lima is well trusted within the family. He's also the former boss's only male relative. He's looking like the best bet for the new Don."

"And you said the Bonvicin's have interests in the drug business?"

"Cocaine mostly, in both the transportation and distribution of the drug. There are whispers though that their business is growing, and it's been getting harder for them to remain under the radar so may be looking for new income streams."

Something equally illegal and harmful to the community, no doubt. "None of it makes sense. Courtney has nothing to offer them."

"I know." Steve sounded equally frustrated. Exactly why Jason had contacted him, and not Peters. He trusted Steve.

There was tapping over the line. Steve typing on a keyboard. "Something interesting to note is that since the old boss died, there's been less of a blood trail in their wake."

That *was* interesting. But there was always the chance that this new boss was just better at keeping his kills under wraps. "Thanks for the call, Steve. I appreciate you keeping me updated."

Jason hung up, leaning back in his seat and pinching the bridge of his nose. He needed more. He needed locations. Motives. He needed these guys to get the hell out of Cradle Mountain.

Sighing, he pushed to his feet just as a light tap sounded on the door. Amy stepped inside, two cups from The Grind in hand.

She lifted the drinks. "Iced coffee?"

His brows rose. It was getting close to closing and he'd been counting down the minutes until he could see Courtney. He was just opening his mouth to decline when she spoke again.

"I thought we could use them to get through the performance review."

Her performance review... shit. That was supposed to be today. *Now*. He'd written it in his calendar but had barely looked at the thing all day.

She frowned. "If it's not a good time, we can reschedule..."

"No." He wouldn't do that to the woman. Not when he'd made a commitment. "Let's do it. Have a seat."

She placed one of the drinks in front of him, and the other on her side of the desk before sitting.

He clicked into the online document the team had used to share their feedback. "Why don't you start by telling me how the last month here has been?"

Her lips stretched into a smile. As she crossed her legs, the tight skirt slid up, exposing a fair amount of skin. Jason kept his eyes trained on her face. "I love it here. You and your team have been so welcoming. The reception area is comfortable and the work has been stimulating. The only thing is..." She paused.

Jason cocked his head to the side. "What is it?"

"I guess it's just hard when there are parts of the business that I don't get let in on. It makes organizing appointments and schedules a bit difficult. For example, I scheduled some personal security work in Oregon for Flynn and Tyler next week, and finally getting confirmation about the job, but when I told the guys, they said they weren't available. That *no one* was available."

Ah, damn. Jason had asked that everyone remain in Idaho until the Mafia family was taken down, but he'd forgotten to tell Amy.

"Sorry. It should have been communicated to you that we're not taking work outside of Cradle Mountain right now. My fault. We'll let you know when we want to restart that."

She nodded. "Thank you. I guess that's it. More communication would be great."

"We can do that." He and his team were so used to only notifying each other of changes. They needed to change that. "Anything else you'd like to discuss?"

She shook her head. "Nope, everything else is going great." Her hand went to her knee, traveling up the exposed skin on her leg before smoothing back down again.

He frowned. Was the woman doing that on purpose?

"So, what does everyone think of *me*?" she asked.

He scanned the feedback on his screen. "Rave reviews. Words like efficient and quick come up multiple times. Many comments on how you're a pleasure to work with. Callum even said we need a second Amy around the office."

She chuckled and lifted her drink, taking a sip. "That's sweet."

She reached forward to return the cup to the desk as his gaze turned back to the screen.

There was a light thud, then the sound of liquid spilling.

Amy jumped to her feet, hand over her mouth. "I am so sorry! I'll grab a bucket of water and some towels."

Jason stood as she rushed from the room. He walked around the desk to see the coffee already absorbing into the carpet. Damn. The smell would hang around for weeks.

When she returned, she dropped down to her hands and knees, pressing a damp cloth onto the coffee puddle. Jason lowered, grabbing the second cloth from the small bucket of soapy water.

"Man, talk about bad timing," she said quietly. "Tipping a drink onto the floor during my performance review. And to think I thought I could hide my klutziness."

Jason laughed. "Don't worry, I won't put a mark against your name. I'd rather someone that spills a drink once in a while but is good at her job than the other way around."

"Goodness, you are such a lovely boss, Jason." She dropped the cloth into the bucket, the smile slipping from her lips. "And I'm not just talking about now. From the moment I got here, you've been so great and made me feel so comfortable."

"It's nothing." And to be honest, he felt a bit uncomfortable with the praise.

He started to rise but stopped at her hand on his shoulder.

"It's not nothing. Thank you."

He dipped his head and stood. When she went to do the same, her ankles wobbled in her high heels. Out of instinct, Jason wrapped an arm around her waist, steadying her.

Immediately her hands went to his chest, her eyes to his lips.

～

Courtney placed another chair on the table. Okay, it was probably more of a slam than a placement. The loud bang of wood hitting wood vibrated off the walls of the shop. At least it blocked out the quiet curse words escaping her in uneven intervals.

She shot a quick glance out the window, noticing the brow lift from Aidan as he watched her from his car. Yep. He heard it from all the way outside.

She was just lifting the next chair when hands yanked the thing from her fingers, none too gently.

"Okay, I know you're the boss, but I'm calling it. You're officially off chair duty." Joey placed the chair on the table a lot more gently than she would have. "I've swept this half of the floor, you can sweep the other." He indicated the other side with his head.

"Fine," she huffed, moving across the room to the broom.

"You gonna tell me what has you in a rage?"

"I'm not in a rage." But she was certainly working her way up to one.

He lifted a brow.

"Fine. Amy came in again."

God, she couldn't even say the woman's name without sneering it.

"I saw." Joey moved to the next table. "I also saw your eyes shooting death rays into her back as she left."

Courtney swung around to him. "Do you know what she said to me?" Argh, even thinking about it had her fuming.

Joey stopped, a half-smile on his face. "Tell me. Let it all out."

"She said to expect Jason home late tonight. That they had a meeting booked and she wasn't sure how long it would go for."

His brows rose for the second time. "And?"

He was right. That didn't sound so terrible. "Okay, it wasn't what she said." Courtney's tone lowered a fraction. "It was the way she said it. She was baiting me. Trying to put ideas into my head about what she might be doing with Jason. Trying to make me question his commitment to me."

"You're right. She probably was trying to achieve all that."

Probably? There was no probably about it. The woman was a snake.

"And you fell right into her trap."

She was worse than a snake. She was a—

Wait. What?

Joey folded his arms. "You let that pathetic woman walk in here, plant seeds of doubt in your mind, while she returned to your man."

"Let?"

"Yeah. Let."

Did she? Was he on to something here?

"Okay, maybe I did. But can you blame me? The woman's gorgeous! Of course I don't like her telling me about her time with Jason."

Especially when she was subconsciously waiting for history to repeat itself. Waiting for Jason to do what the others had done to her.

He walked across the shop, stopping in front of her. "You're gorgeous too, Court." His hands went to her shoulders. "Now go get your man."

She frowned. "He's working."

"If he really *is* in a meeting with her, knock on the door, and when he answers, plant a big old kiss on his lips. Remind Amy whose bed the man is sleeping in and who he belongs to."

Courtney's cheeks tingled at the bed comment. But it was true, dammit. The man *was* sleeping in her bed. He was hers.

Joey lowered his head. "The woman's trying to step on your grass. Kick her off."

"Step on my grass?"

"Go." He stepped back, pointing to the door. "Claim him right in front of her."

Something sparked inside of her. A little shot of fire. Determination. "You're right. He's mine. And she needs to see it."

"Hell yes, she does."

"Are you okay closing?"

"Get your ass out of here right now."

She chuckled, grabbing her phone from behind the counter before heading out the door. The second she stepped outside, Aidan was beside her, his long legs only needing one stride for every two of hers.

"So, it's time to kiss Jason?"

Of course the man heard with his super hearing. She didn't even care.

"Yes." A "big old kiss" right on the lips.

Aidan chuckled. "Okay. I might head off once you hit his office. I don't need to see that."

Courtney power-walked the whole way there, moving quickly up the stairs. When she opened the door, she saw Amy wasn't at her desk. She must be in his office having the meeting right now.

Walking down the hall, she turned to step into his office—but suddenly stopped. Her heart skidded in her chest, her mouth dropping open.

One of Jason's arms was wrapped around Amy's waist, and they were gazing at each other like they were about to kiss. Like they were moments away from fusing their lips together.

Jason lifted his head, looking her way.

But she barely spared him a glance, already turning and fleeing from the building.

CHAPTER 18

*C*ourtney only made it to the reception area before a hand was on her arm, tugging her to a stop.

"Courtney—"

"Don't!" She spun around, shoving at his chest. He didn't move. Not an inch. "Don't touch me. Don't come near me." She tugged her arm again. He retained his hold on it.

She tugged harder. Every second she remained where she was, the crack in her chest widened. The familiar pain and hurt and betrayal of those before him swelled, flooding her system and stealing her breath.

Tears tried to dampen her eyes but she blinked rapidly, forcing them back. She would *not* let the tears escape in front of him. She would not let him see her drown.

"Please…" His voice was quiet, pleading, but she refused to listen.

Gritting her teeth, she forced deep breaths in and out at even intervals. "Let me go, Jason." She was proud of herself that each word was as steely as the last. No tears. No trembling.

Aidan came up behind him, a hand going to Jason's shoulder. "Let her go, man."

Slowly, his fingers released her.

She took off again, moving out of the reception area and down the stairs. Her stomach twisted and turned the entire way down, the steps in front of her blurring.

She'd barely reached the street when those same familiar fingers wrapped around her arm again.

She spun around, this time putting more force into her shove against his chest. Yet again, he didn't move. She was powerless.

Powerless to push him away. Powerless to keep him. And completely defenseless.

"Don't. Touch me." She swallowed a sob, her chest burning. Clinging to the anger and using it like a shield to hold back the sadness. The devastation. "How could you?"

"Courtney, just let me—"

"No! You don't get to hold another woman, look at her like you're about to *kiss* her, and then ask me to listen while you *explain*. I've done that before. I've been there more than once. It never ends well for me. So just… stop. Let me go."

She blinked furiously.

Do not cry, Courtney. Do not break. She needed to remain whole at least for the moment.

When he continued to hold her, his fingers like a manacle around her wrist, she looked up at his face—and saw all of it. Hurt. Torment. Indecision on what to do next.

But she also saw other things. She saw the moments that were good. Visions of his lips pressed against hers. His arm wrapped around her waist, holding her.

The pain in her chest rippled, expanding.

Aidan pushed outside just as Jason's hand dropped away. An odd combination of loss and victory crawled through her, touching her soul.

She took off again. Moving her feet as fast as they'd take her without actually running. Footsteps sounded behind her. Faint, but there.

She blinked repeatedly, trying to rid her head of that image. The one of Jason holding Amy. Of his lips mere inches from hers.

Her heart wanted to wipe it from her memory... her mind wouldn't let her.

How could this have happened? *Again?* She'd lived this nightmare before, only this time it felt worse. Jason meant more than all the others combined. He *was* more.

Another pang to the chest.

How was it possible that she'd woken up feeling like the most adored and secure person in the world, cocooned in the arms of the man she loved, only to end the day feeling like her insides had been pulled from her chest and stomped on?

And yes, she loved him. She'd loved him for a while, but the words had never made it out... and now they never would.

She turned a corner, finally giving in and glancing back. But it wasn't Jason she saw. It was Aidan. And even though she'd just told Jason to stop, demanded the man let her go, not seeing him follow made it all worse. Made the weight on her heart ten times heavier.

She moved her feet faster, grabbing on to the anger with both hands, keeping it front and center.

She was smart and kind and hardworking. She was damn deserving of love. She should be enough. And if a man couldn't see that, it wasn't on her, it was on *him.*

When she reached her apartment building, she was almost proud of herself for not letting a single tear slip down her cheek. It was only when she made it to the fourth floor and saw Jason standing at her door that the anger wavered. The cloud of hurt and sadness tried to thread its way to the forefront.

Her eyes flickered to the stairs. She could walk away. Maybe go back to The Grind? Or to Grace's?

She gave herself a mental shake. No. This was her home. And she would not be run off. If he wanted to talk, then he could talk. But that did not mean he would be granted forgiveness.

A MUSCLE TICKED in Jason's jaw. His hands were clenched so tightly his short nails bit into his palms.

He'd wanted to tell her right there in the office that it hadn't been what it looked like. That he hadn't put his arm around Amy in some attempt to hold the woman or draw her in for a kiss.

But he'd seen how close Courtney had been to losing it. The anger was a mask. A thin shield to protect her from the pain. The pain that was rooted so deeply thanks to men before him.

He'd also seen something else. Something he couldn't quite identify but had made his chest ache. Like she'd expected this to happen again.

Expected him to hurt her.

He'd decided right there and then that this was a private conversation. One between him and her. And he would not leave until she heard him. Believed what he said.

At the sight of her stepping into the hall, he pushed off the wall, straightening. His entire body sung with awareness, his eyes not lowering from hers. He saw the anger. The uncertainty. The heartache that flashed for only a second before it was hidden.

For a moment, she stopped, her gaze flicking to the stairs then back at him.

Don't do it, honey. Hear me out.

Her chest rose and fell with one deep breath, then she moved forward. Even though her expression was steely, he didn't miss the tremble in her fingers as they worked the key into the door. She left it open.

Good. At least she hadn't tried slamming it in his face. That's what he'd been expecting. Closing the door behind him, he flicked the lock.

Courtney disappeared into her bedroom while Jason went to the living room and waited. A few minutes later, she stepped out in leggings and a baggy shirt.

His gaze followed every step she took. Her silence was loud as she went straight to the kitchen, grabbing a glass from the cupboard and filling it at the tap. She took a sip before placing the almost full glass into the sink.

Jason took slow steps toward her. He'd only made it to the island before Courtney spun around, holding up a hand. "Don't."

His feet halted, his muscles tensing. "Don't what, sweetheart?"

She moved to the opposite end of the island. It sat between them like a boulder. That was her intention, though, wasn't it?

"You know what," she said. "Don't come closer."

He tilted his head. "Why?"

She swallowed, her heartbeat thrumming through the quiet, loud and clear. "Because if you touch me, I'll forget. And I can't do that."

Forgetting didn't sound so bad to Jason. Hell, all he wanted to do was wish the entire afternoon away, both in memory and reality.

He took a small step forward. "Courtney—"

"*Don't*, Jason." She swallowed hard, stepping in the opposite direction, keeping the island firmly between them. "I mean it."

"I wasn't going to kiss her. And if she had tried, I wouldn't have allowed it," he said quietly.

Her mouth opened, then quickly shut, jaw locking. He tracked her every move, including the way her trembling fingers latched onto the island, like she was relying on it to keep her upright.

"You were holding her. Her eyes were on your mouth. If I'd been a second later—"

"You would have seen me stepping back." He inched closer. She didn't move this time. Whether it was because she was distracted or she believed him, he wasn't sure.

There was something new in her eyes now. Yearning.

To believe him?

A few seconds ticked by, then she gave a small shake of her head. "Why was your arm around her waist?"

"A drink tipped onto the carpet, and we were cleaning it up." An accident that he was starting to believe was very intentional. Another inch closer. "When she went to stand, she stumbled. I grabbed her to stop her from hitting the floor."

When her silence stretched, he continued to move forward. Small steps that closed the gap between them. Soon, she stood less than a foot away. So close that if he reached out, he'd be touching her.

His hand itched to reach out.

Silence followed. He could just about hear her mind ticking, turning his words over and deciding whether to take them as truths.

Do it, honey. Believe me. Trust me.

Her knuckles whitened further, her hands now clenching the island so hard it was like she was trying to crush the thing.

He took another chance. Stepped behind her. He touched her hips lightly, holding her, cherishing. Then he lowered his head, his voice softening. "I would never cheat on you, Courtney. That would be like intentionally breaking the most precious thing in my life. *Us.*"

He heard the slight shift in her breathing. The stutter of her heart.

"I need you to believe me, Courtney. I need *you.*" He nuzzled her hair, feeling the soft shudder up her spine. "I will protect what we have with my life."

Some of the white on her knuckles lessened. Slowly, she turned, looking up into his eyes. Searching. "Really?"

The second her gaze met his, some of the air that had been stuck in his chest released. He lowered his head, touching his forehead to hers. "Really, sweetheart. I would never, *ever* intentionally hurt you."

His quiet statement had her eyes closing. Slowly, she reached up, cupping his cheeks, holding him. The tension that had been eating away at his gut since she'd stepped into his office finally eased.

"I thought you were going to kiss her. I've seen it before," she said softly. "I think part of me was even waiting for something like this to happen. For the world to tell me that I wasn't enough. Again."

He lifted her, depositing her onto the island before holding her close. "You are so much more than enough. You are so much more than any man could even begin to deserve. Especially me."

The pain, the stress, the uncertainty. It all eased from her face. Like she'd been needing someone to speak those words to her for a long time.

CHAPTER 19

*J*ason opened the door to Blue Halo the next morning, not surprised to see Amy already behind the desk. She immediately stood, wringing her hands in front of her.

"Amy, can I please see you in my office?"

He didn't wait for a response, instead moving down the hall, listening to the clicking of her heels against the floor as she followed.

He'd barely dropped behind the desk before she was talking.

"I'm so sorry." She stepped into the room, stopping on the other side of his desk. "I didn't mean to cause any trouble between you and Courtney yesterday."

Jason rubbed his forehead. He'd spoken to the rest of the guys, and they all agreed if it was best for him, it was best for the company.

"I appreciate your apology, Amy. Unfortunately, we can't have you—"

"Don't say it. Please!" The desperation in her eyes was new and unexpected. "I need this job. The drink spill and fall were intentional and completely inappropriate. I just... I like you, and it blinded me to everything else."

"You're good at your job, but I just don't see how a professional relationship between us is possible now."

He'd have to work with the woman, talk to her, walk past her every day. He owed it to Courtney to ensure that wasn't the case. Amy had seen him with Courtney on multiple occasions, so what she did spoke volumes about her morals and ethics.

"I swear nothing like that will happen again. I will remain completely professional to both you and everyone else here." She reached out, clenching the desk with a firm grip. "Please."

Okay, now he just needed to know. "Why do you need this job so badly?"

The woman was a good receptionist. He doubted she'd have a hard time getting work somewhere else. Maybe not in Cradle Mountain—the town was small and he didn't think anyone was hiring—but somewhere in Idaho.

She straightened, shifting her weight from one foot to the other. "Because I need to be here in Cradle Mountain."

Didn't really answer his question.

Her eyes darted between his. "At least give me time to find something else."

He blew out a long breath. "I'll talk to the guys." And Courtney. Mostly Courtney. He hadn't run this by her. If firing Amy was important to her, then she was gone tomorrow.

She nodded, some of the tension easing from her face. "Okay. Thank you."

He was pretty set on getting rid of the woman, but... maybe she was low on cash? Why else would she try so hard to keep a job where things between them would always be awkward?

She turned, all but fleeing the room.

The rest of the day moved fairly quickly. He spent a large chunk of it in his office writing up security plans for companies.

The only break he took was to do a workout with Tyler. He avoided Amy entirely.

When it was time to leave, he was just rising to his feet when his cell rang.

"Flynn, what's going on? You still with Courtney?" He was the one who'd been assigned to her today.

Music played loudly in the background, as well as the hum of voices. "Yeah. We're at Tucker's."

Jason paused. "Tucker's? As in Tucker's Bar?"

Why were they at a bar?

"The one and only. Grace and Logan are with us. Before you ask, it was Courtney's idea. She wanted to stop for a drink."

"I'm leaving the office now."

On the drive over, gray clouds scudded across the sun. He could almost smell the rain. Good. He loved rain. It was why he hadn't minded moving to Idaho. It beat the hell out of the Texas heat.

It took him four minutes to get to the place. He stepped into the bar, which was packed. But then, it usually was. There was a homey, comfortable feeling to the place, with its wooden interior and warm lighting.

His eyes landed on Tucker standing behind the bar. He was a big man in his fifties, also former military. Tattoos snaked down his arms in sleeves.

Looks were deceiving in his case though, because despite looking like a mean son of a bitch, he had the biggest laugh Jason had ever heard and was rarely seen without a smile on his face.

Jason gave him a nod before scanning the bar. He spotted Courtney immediately. She and Grace were the only two people on the dance floor, and they were dancing like no one was watching. Their hips moved in time with the music, pure joy on their faces.

He smiled, moving over to the booth where Flynn and Logan

sat watching, sliding in beside them with a perfect view of Courtney.

"How'd it go?" Flynn asked.

"I told her I'd talk to you guys about letting her stay just until she finds another job."

He could feel Logan's eyes on him. "Really?"

"She basically begged me. She had this desperate look on her face." He breathed out a long breath. "She promised to keep everything professional. I'm going to talk to Courtney tonight. See what her thoughts are. If she says or even *looks* like she wants Amy gone straightaway, she's gone."

The guys nodded, trusting Jason to do what needed to be done.

Jason looked across to Flynn. "You been back to your family property?"

Flynn lifted his beer to his lips, taking a sip. "Not since before you guys went up. Why?"

"We never found Courtney's necklace."

"I can drive up this weekend."

Jason lifted a shoulder. "If you're already planning to go, it would be great if you could take a quick look."

Although, Jason had searched high and low. There was no sign of it.

The light drizzle of rain sounded on the roof of the bar. No one but them would be able to hear it. Not with the music and noise drowning it out.

When Courtney's eyes met his from across the room, the green and brown shades deepened. Time to see his woman.

COURTNEY'S HEART GAVE A KICK. Jason was walking toward her. His powerful thighs stretched the denim of his jeans, his biceps threatening to split the material of his shirt.

Grace gave her a little shoulder nudge before heading to the booth where Logan sat.

Jason stopped in front of her, his powerful arm sweeping around her waist, head lowering, mouth grazing her cheek.

"You're too sexy, woman."

His breath was like whispers of fire lacing her cheek. Her hands went to his shoulders and they began to sway slowly.

His head lifted. "Any reason you chose to come here?"

Did you need a reason to dance in a bar? "Grace was free, and I felt like dancing. I'm sick of working and hiding out in my apartment. And maybe I was hopeful that someone would come dance with me." The man had played right into her hands.

He smiled, but it didn't last long. "I have something I need to tell you."

Sweet mother of Jesus. What now? Tonight was about dancing and fun and not thinking about the hard stuff. And whatever he was about to say was definitely hard stuff. She could tell by the look on his face. The regret coating his words.

Dread knotted her stomach. "Okay."

"I didn't fire Amy today."

She paused mid-sway, brows pulling together. "Were you supposed to?"

His gaze flicked between her eyes. "Yes."

"For you or for me?" she asked softly.

"For us."

Sweet. But unnecessary. "Jason, I never wanted or expected you to fire her for me. Do I like her? No. Do I like that she clearly wanted to kiss you? *Hell* no. But can I see why she did it? Heck yes. Who wouldn't make a move on you?" The guy was all sex and power. "If you fire her, do it for you. Because she set you up and put you in a compromising position."

Jason looked almost shocked. "Really?"

"Really. Just last night you told me I had nothing to worry about. So... I believe you. I trust you." She gave him a small smile.

"I'm thinking about letting her stay only until she finds other work. Along with giving her a formal written warning."

Courtney gave a slow nod, considering his words. "Do you think she'll do anything like that again?"

His head shake was immediate. "No."

"Then that's fine with me." Her hands went to his chest, sliding over the hard ridges. Good Lord, the man was all muscle.

His grip tightened around her waist. "You're amazing."

"Hm. Maybe you should take me to my place and show me just *how* amazing I am." Even though she'd been the one to suggest it, her lady parts fluttered at the thought.

"I was thinking you might like to stay at mine tonight." She paused at his words. "I could make some pasta. Put the fire on."

"You have a fireplace?" That didn't sound terrible.

She hadn't been to his place yet, but that was only because she had Eddie. He hadn't been at the vet for long, but with his fractured rib, she hadn't wanted to leave him. "Maybe we could drop by my apartment to check on and feed Eddie on the way?"

"Done." His hands grazed over her arms, leaving a trail of goose bumps in their wake. "I might have to give you my jacket, it's a bit wet outside."

"It's raining?" She turned to look through a window, and sure enough, she saw the rush of raindrops against the window.

"Yeah, and I think it's raining pretty heavily now."

Her eyes shuttered. "I love the rain. Jessica and I used to dream about—"

He frowned. "About what?"

Her cheeks heated. Then she leaned up on her toes, whispering against his lips. "Instead of telling you, I'll show you when we get to your place." She pressed a quick kiss to his lips before turning and tugging him toward the door.

"You're really not gonna tell me?"

"Nope. You could use some good surprises in your life."

They stopped quickly at her house, where she gave Eddie

some love and put his dinner out. Every time she saw him, she breathed a sigh of relief that he was doing so well. Helen and Bernie were both finally due to return home tomorrow, and Courtney was already planning on baking for the older woman every chance she had.

She packed an overnight bag and they drove to Jason's. They were almost there when a text came in from Joey.

Hey, did you ever find your necklace?

She frowned. Poor Joey had enough stuff to worry about. It was kind of him to ask about the necklace, though a little odd. He saw her without it every day at work.

No. Why?

"Who's messaging?"

When no response came through, Courtney put her phone down on her lap. "Joey. He's just checking in."

Jason nodded, pulling into a garage attached to a large, modern-looking townhouse.

"Ooh, this is nice." And it sure beat her miniscule one-bedroom apartment.

He squeezed her leg with his hand.

After parking the car, he walked around to open her door, taking her hand as he led her inside. The place was just as modern on the inside as it was on the outside. The kitchen was large and all the appliances were crazy high-end. The couch in the living room was big and looked ridiculously comfy, and the TV... well, it was exactly what every man dreamed of. Huge.

Jason led her up the stairs and down a hall, opening the door to the master bedroom.

She walked around the space, inspecting the black bed sheets and gray walls. "So, this is your bachelor pad."

It was as far removed from her fluorescent, multicolored walls and bedding as you could get.

He chuckled. "I wouldn't call it a bachelor pad, but it's been home since moving here."

"It's beautiful, Jason." In a very masculine way.

Hands curved around her waist from behind. A second ago, the man had been across the room. "*You're* beautiful."

She smiled, watching the rain hit the window. The moment felt about as perfect as one could get. She turned, fingers threading behind his head. "Can I see the backyard?"

Confusion marred his brows. "Uh, sure."

She chuckled, liking that he didn't question her. They moved down the stairs and through the kitchen to the backyard. When they stepped outside, under the veranda, the rain was loud.

Courtney tugged her phone from her pocket, placing it on the outdoor table before toeing off her shoes.

Jason watched her closely. He was cute when he was confused. "Courtney..."

"Yes?" Her hands went to the top of her jeans, popping the button then pushing the zipper down.

His eyes heated about twenty degrees. "What are you doing?"

"Jessica and I used to talk about our perfect moment with a guy. What it would look like. Feel like. The emotions that would imprint those seconds into our memories forever."

He tilted his head to the side. "Did yours involve hypothermia?"

"Ha ha."

Just as he said it, a gust of wind rushed past them, causing her skin to pebble with goose bumps. Okay, he was right. It was freaking cold. But she ignored it, wriggling her hips as she pushed the jeans down to her knees, then her feet.

Then she grabbed the base of her sweatshirt, tugging it over her head. "We decided it had to involve rain, because every romantic movie we'd ever watched to that point had the peak romantic moment in the rain. It also needed to be under the cover of moonlight."

And it needed *him*. She hadn't known when she'd been a fifteen-year-old girl, dreaming with her best friend, but now she did. Her perfect moment was with Jason. Every perfect moment from here on out would be, if she had her way.

The second the material dropped to the ground, Jason was in front of her, hands going to her arms, halting her before she could unsnap her bra. "It's too cold."

"So, we'll go back inside and have a hot shower after. Drink some cocoa." His jaw ticked. "Come on, Jason. Be crazy with me for a second. Make a memory we can take with us into the future."

His touch sent waves of heat up her arm. Finally, he let go, hands going to the bottom of his top, tugging both his shirt and sweatshirt over his head. "We're only staying out there for a second."

She paused at the sight of his impressive chest. Watched the muscles ripple as he removed every scrap of clothing he wore until he stood completely bare in front of her.

She sucked in a deep breath, removing her bra and panties.

This time it was Jason's turn to breathe deeply, his gaze roaming her body from head to toe. God, his eyes on her made her feel beautiful and confident and feminine.

Taking his hand, she tugged him into the rain. The water hit her hard, feeling like tiny pinpricks all over her skin. But it also felt good. A thin connection to Jessica.

Closing her eyes, she turned her head up to the sky.

For you, Jessica. To making memories.

Her eyes shot open as Jason lifted her against him. Holding her. Warming her with his big body.

She moved her lips to his ear, pressing a kiss there before whispering the words her heart urged her to say.

"I love you."

His body stilled, the arms around her tightening. When he looked at her, there was a new intensity in his gaze. Then he said the words she longed to hear.

"I love you too."

Something in her heart cracked, but in the best possible way. It was the cracking of the casing that she'd put around it to protect herself. The cracking of the shield that had kept men at bay for so long.

Her hands went to his cheeks, his breath whispering over her lips as she dipped her head. "Kiss me."

His eyes turned black. So black they were as dark and stormy as the sky. Then his lips were on hers. Moving. Caressing.

She barely felt the cold now. All she felt was him.

CHAPTER 20

*L*ittle fingers touched Courtney's leg from behind. She turned, two empty coffee mugs in hand, to see Mila standing behind her, other hand tucked behind her back.

"Excuse me, Courtney."

Popping the cups on the empty table beside her, she crouched down, eyes level with the girl's. "Yes, honey, what do you need?"

She shuffled from one foot to the other. Adorable. "I've got no more sprinkles left, but I still have half my chocolate milkshake."

Courtney clenched her jaw to keep from smiling. "I see. That sounds like quite the problem."

"It is! The sprinkles are my favorite part. I was wondering"—a small breath—"could I please have some more?"

"Hm, have you asked your dad?"

Courtney shot a quick look over her head to see Blake looking their way, a ghost of a smile on his lips as he gave a slight nod.

"I have. Daddy took some of my sprinkles, so he said it was okay for me to have some more. If it's okay with you?"

Could this kid get any cuter? Courtney could just about feel her ovaries exploding. "Of course it's okay, sweetheart."

Mila's grin was almost as wide as her face. "Thank you." She skipped back to her table.

Courtney followed closely behind. "I can't believe he stole your sprinkles."

Blake leaned back in his seat with no remorse.

Mila sighed like she was four going on forty. "To be fair, I offered. But I was kind of hoping he'd say no."

She climbed into the booth and reached for her drink, passing it to Courtney.

Courtney leaned down, pretending to whisper to the girl. "I do that too. Offer out of politeness but hope they say no."

"Women," Blake muttered under his breath, a smile on his face. Then he spoke louder. "I'll know better next time."

"Or you could ask Courtney for your own sprinkles," Mila said, leaning against the table.

Courtney chuckled. "Good idea. I'll be sure to bring you your own sprinkles next time, Blake."

He gave a short nod. "Appreciate it. Could you put that in a to-go cup? Callum's going to be here any minute."

"Sure."

Courtney headed back to the front, stacking the two coffee cups she'd abandoned and taking them with her. Blake never stayed at the cafe for long when he was with Mila. Not with the trouble that lurked. In fact, she had a feeling he was only there now because Mila might have begged him.

Callum chose that moment to step inside the shop. He nodded her way before heading to Blake and Mila.

Courtney added the extra sprinkles, giving it to one of her servers to take to Mila. The place was packed today. And every time a new customer stepped inside, she was left hoping, wishing, to see one person.

It was crazy. She'd seen him a few hours ago, woken up right beside him. But she couldn't help it.

Last night, kissing in the rain, telling him she loved him… yep. It was definitely the most romantic moment of her life, just like she and Jessica had predicted it would be. And the shower afterward hadn't been too bad either.

Her body heated at the thought.

She sidled up beside Joey, nudging him in the shoulder as he plated cakes. "Busy again."

"Yeah. That media coverage is still bringing customers to the shop in waves." He gave a tight smile, not looking up.

She frowned, touching his shoulder. "Everything all right?"

"Of course." His response came quickly. Too quickly?

Oh, no. It wasn't more money issues, she hoped. Or was it his mother? Her health?

She lowered her voice so that her words only reached his ears. "Is your mom okay? Are you still affording her bills?"

There was a slight pause. Then he continued plating the desserts. "Everything's fine, Courtney."

She dipped her head, trying to study his face. The store was busy, this really wasn't the time, but for him, she'd make time. "Remember, I'm here and happy to help if you need—"

"I know." He straightened, lifting the plates and a glass of juice from the counter. "Thank you."

Then he was gone, moving around the counter and out to the customers before she could get another word in.

Something wasn't right. He'd always been pretty happy and laid-back. This wasn't the Joey she was used to. But if he didn't let her in, how was she supposed to help? She didn't have a heap of money, not with how much she put back into the business, but what she did have she'd willingly offer.

Courtney looked up to see Blake and Mila leaving. As they did, someone else walked in.

She almost groaned out loud. Oh jeez. Amy.

She hadn't been in since Courtney had caught the woman in Jason's office. She'd assumed she wouldn't be seeing her face again. Which would have been A-okay with Courtney. She'd said she didn't mind Jason keeping her on at Blue Halo until she found another job, but that didn't mean she wanted to see the woman here.

She looked around, noticing that everyone else was on the floor delivering food or tidying tables.

Dang it. That just left her.

Amy stopped at the counter right in front of her.

"Hello, Amy."

"Hi." Amy wet her lips, pausing before speaking again. It was the first time Courtney had seen her look anything other than self-assured or smug. "I was wondering if I could talk to you."

Like in private? Yeah, that was a no. "We're really busy. Maybe another time." Or never. Whichever was further away. "Can I get you something?"

"I can be quick. I just need to apologize. I'm sorry. I shouldn't have tipped my coffee and…"

"Tried to create a situation where Jason kissed you?"

She grimaced. At least she had the gall to look uncomfortable. "Yes. I'm sorry."

Courtney raised a brow. "Really? You're sorry?"

"Yes," she said firmly. Courtney was almost convinced she was being honest. "I acted on one-sided feelings and it wasn't fair to you. He's not interested in me. It won't happen again."

Her words seemed genuine, but they also sounded stilted. Almost rehearsed.

"I can tell you don't believe me," Amy continued. "And that's okay. I probably wouldn't believe me either, what with how I've been acting. I just needed you to hear me say it."

She dipped her head. "I appreciate the apology."

Did she forgive her? No. Would they ever be friends? Big

capitalized No. But did she believe the woman was sorry? Possibly.

"Thank you."

Courtney sighed. "Can I get you something?"

"Just a bottle of orange juice to go would be great."

It was the first time the woman hadn't ordered something for Jason and made a pointed comment about it. Courtney turned, grabbing the juice from the fridge before handing it over.

Amy passed over her card. "I'm happy for you and Jason."

Courtney wasn't sure she believed that, either. Still, she gave the card back, nodding to the woman before she walked away.

She was just turning away when a soft cry, followed by a loud clatter, sounded through the shop.

Spinning around, Courtney's mouth dropped open at the sight of Amy and Joey on the floor, shattered glass and spilled liquid all around them. Running around the counter, she shuffled through customers. Callum was already there, on his haunches at Amy's side.

Courtney lowered. "Are you both okay?"

Amy grabbed her ankle, pain etched across her face. "I think I twisted it."

Callum gingerly took her calf in his hand. "I can already see swelling."

Crap. "I'll go grab an ice pack."

Pushing to her feet, Courtney ran to the back room. Opening the freezer, she started to step inside—and stopped. A chill that had nothing to do with the temperature swept through her limbs. Joey had moved most things out of the walk-in freezer. Ice packs weren't one of them.

Sucking in a deep breath, Courtney took a step. Then another. Quickly, she reached for an ice pack.

Before she could even turn, the room suddenly plunged into darkness and rough hands shoved her against the shelves. She opened her mouth to scream but it got stuck in her throat. Jagged breaths seesawed in and out of her chest, each shorter than the last.

She was locked in the freezer. Again. Only this time, instead of being shut in with a dead body, she was here with a man. A man who had the sharp edge of a knife pressed to her throat, hard, threatening to cut into her skin.

"Where is it?" The man's voice was low and deep with a gravelly undertone. It was one she'd heard before.

The dark encompassed her as a lightheaded fog began to seep in, leaving her knees weak. Her hands were clammy and trembling where they clutched a frigid shelf.

The guy's chest vibrated against her back. He was talking again. But the words weren't making it to her, not with the blood rushing between her ears, so loud it was all she heard.

Pain stung her neck.

Good God, he was cutting her. And she was going to pass out. She'd be completely at this thug's mercy.

She tried to make her voice work. Her hands. Her legs. Anything. But the chill skittering over her skin sank deep into her muscles, her bones, rendering her completely motionless.

The last thing she saw was light beginning to filter into the freezer. But as quickly as it had come, it was gone, her world turning black.

JASON BURST through the doors of The Grind. The shop had been cleared of any customers. Two young girls sat at a booth near the window. Servers. He barely saw them. Courtney was all he saw, sitting on a barstool at the counter, eyes glazed, and bandages on her neck and forehead.

Callum was there, standing beside her.

Jason was there in seconds, tugging her close. Holding her.

She remained seated, but her arms wrapped around his waist, head pressed to his chest.

"I'm so glad you're here." Her words were muffled against his shirt.

He pressed a kiss to the top of her head. "What happened?"

He'd gotten the CliffsNotes on the call from Callum, but he needed to hear the words from her. Then he needed to find that fucker Lima and murder him.

Jason was just pulling back when the door opened behind him. He turned his head to see Agent Peters walking in, trailed by his guys. The man was staying in town at a local motel, so it wasn't a surprise he'd made it here quickly.

"Hello, everyone." Peters made eye contact with each of them, before landing on Courtney. "Miss Davies, I'm sorry to hear you were attacked again."

She gave a small nod. Jason kept one arm around her waist, watching the agent closely.

"Can you tell us what happened?" Peters asked.

Courtney swallowed. "There's not really much to share. A customer ran into one of my employees, rolling her ankle. I ran to the back kitchen to get some ice from the walk-in freezer. The door closed, then he was behind me, pushing me against the shelving and pressing a knife to my neck. He asked me where it was."

Jason took her hand and stroked the inside of her wrist, keeping the intensity of his rage caged within his chest.

"I started to panic from claustrophobia, so I didn't hear anything else. I just remember the door opening before I passed out."

"Is that how you got the cut on your forehead?" Peters asked.

Jason had been told that neither of her cuts were deep enough to warrant a hospital visit, but she shouldn't have been hurt at all, damn it.

She touched the small bandage on her temple, just below her hairline. "I think I hit my head on a shelf when he ran out."

Peters made notes on his pad. "And who opened the freezer door?"

"Annabel." Courtney indicated to the booth by the window. "She's the brunette. She came back to see if I needed help getting the ice. My employees all know about my claustrophobia. When she opened the freezer door, he released me and knocked her out of the way while he ran out the back door. She was stunned, so it took her a few seconds to call out for Callum." Courtney paused. "She's only eighteen, and a bit shaken, but I asked her to stick around to give you a description of the guy."

Peters nodded. "I assume the guy came through a back door, as well?"

Courtney grimaced. "Yeah. It's supposed to be locked."

Peters nodded to some of his guys to head out back.

Jason frowned. It wasn't just supposed to be locked, it was also supposed to be alarmed. He had arranged for the alarm to be installed after the initial freezer incident a few months ago. The one involving Grace's attacker, Kieran.

Courtney rubbed a hand over her face. "One of my employees, Joey, opened it to take out the trash. He forgot to relock and arm it."

Forgot? Courtney almost had her throat sliced open because someone *forgot* to lock and arm the door? No one should even be using that door. Trash was supposed to stay in the back until it could be taken out the front. That was what they'd all agreed to.

As if sensing his unease, Courtney touched his chest. "It's not his fault. He's had a lot on his mind."

Yeah, well, that distraction almost got her killed. Not good enough.

When she leaned into him, he released her hand, curving an arm around her waist.

"And you said you couldn't hear him? So you're not sure what he wanted?"

Courtney shook her head. "I was seconds from passing out. I couldn't make out anything he said."

The lines beside Peters's eyes deepened as he frowned. He didn't even try to hide his frustration. The small pad in his hands flipped shut. "Well, Miss Davies, it sounds like you had a lucky escape."

Fresh anger burst to life in Jason's chest.

Again, it was like the woman sensed it, pressing a hand over his heart, her gaze on the agent. "Thank you for coming."

The detective gave one short nod before moving across the room to the girls.

Asshole.

It was about time Jason did his own check on this guy. Find out why exactly he was so quick to believe Courtney wasn't being honest.

He made a mental note to call Wyatt. The guy was a damn good hacker and a friend of their team. If there was any shady information on Peters, he'd find it.

Jason would also be looking into Joey. Maybe even have the guy followed. Today's mistake should never have happened.

Turning to Courtney, he took her into his arms, not quite feeling like she was close enough. "I'm so damn glad you're okay."

"Me too." She sighed. "I think it's time I made an appointment with Grace to deal with this phobia."

He pressed a kiss to her head.

CHAPTER 21

"Annabel identified the guy. It was Lima. So what are you doing to find the asshole and take him down?" Jason almost growled the words over the phone.

Peters sighed, and dammit, that just spiked Jason's rage. Like he was trying to placate him. "We're doing all we can to shut the entire family down, Jason. You need to trust us."

"Trust you? After my woman almost gets her throat sliced in a freezer?"

"Hey, you said you wanted to take care of her protection. Today was on *you*."

His blood heated, breath whooshing from his chest. The guy's words damn near brought him to his knees, because he was right.

"So, you don't have a location for him?" Jason asked quietly through gritted teeth.

"I'll let you know when we have information to share."

The line went dead.

For a moment, Jason remained still, holding the phone and fighting for calm. Patience.

Did that mean he might already have Lima's location?

He quickly dialed Aidan.

"Jason."

"We've given Peters a chance to find him. He hasn't. It's our turn."

"Done."

Some of the suffocating rage eased. That's why he loved his team. There were no questions. No hesitation.

"I'll let the team know that we're stepping everything up," Aidan said. "Putting more guys on the search. Watching the streets and the stores. The group clearly has a place here in Cradle Mountain. We'll find out where."

"I want someone put on Joey, too. I want him watched and tracked."

"No problem."

Another sliver of anger eased. "Thank you, brother."

Jason hung up, stepping out of his home office and into the living room. Courtney was the first person he saw, standing by the kitchen island, Eddie in her arms. They'd picked him up on their way here, as well as a bag of her stuff.

Grace stood beside her, and Logan beside Grace. Logan looked Jason's way, giving him a small nod, telling him he'd heard the entire conversation. That he understood what was going on.

Jason moved to Courtney's side, wrapping an arm around her waist and pressing a kiss to the side of her neck. Touching her, having her close, had never felt so good. So necessary.

"You want us to stay?" Logan asked.

Jason shook his head. "This place has good security." He'd set it up the second he moved into the house. Plus, he himself *was* security. He'd wake at the first sound of someone attempting to tamper with a door or window.

Grace pulled Courtney close, giving her a hug before leaving with Logan. When it was just them remaining, Jason locked the door before moving around the house and checking all exit points.

When he returned to the kitchen, it was to see Courtney

exactly where he'd left her, still holding Eddie, a pensive look on her face.

He stalked toward her slowly. She didn't even seem to notice when he stood in front of her, she was so deep into her own mind.

He slid his hands around her waist. "I'm so sorry someone attacked you today."

She blinked, finally looking up. Carefully placing Eddie on the floor, she pressed her hands against his chest. "Why are you sorry? You're not the criminal who held a knife against my throat in the freezer."

His muscles tightened at the mention of it. "No. But it was my team protecting you."

Jesus, but that tore him up inside.

She lifted a shoulder. "They assumed the back door would be locked and alarmed. It wasn't their fault."

He was still beyond pissed about that. How could Joey have been so stupid?

"I know what you're thinking. Please, he feels bad enough. He didn't know the danger I was in, since we haven't told anyone." She drew circles on his chest with her fingers. It was the only thing to loosen his muscles.

"From now on, you can consider me and the guys your personal shadows. There will be no space between us and you."

"Hm." A small smile tugged at her lips. "I've always wanted a shadow in the form of a tall, dark, and handsome man."

He nuzzled her hair. "Well, now you have one." He straightened, shifting a lock of golden hair off her face. "Are you sure you're okay?"

"Yeah." She paused, eyes going to his chest. "I spoke to Grace about doing some sessions with her to get over this whole... claustrophobia thing. I can't help but think that maybe if I hadn't freaked out, I might have been able to protect myself. At least thrown the ice pack at him or something. Kicked him."

Jason's blood ran cold at the thought of his woman fighting a man from the Mafia. A man used to killing without thought or conscience. A man who was armed. Deadly.

"I've never done any self-defense lessons, though."

"Maybe we should do some sessions. Not because I want to see you fighting any criminals." Fuck no. "But because I want you to have a way of defending yourself should the need arise."

"I think that sounds good. Although, I don't think I'll have much hope of fighting seasoned criminals."

He placed his hands on her cheeks, demanding her attention. "Self-defense isn't just about hand-to-hand combat. It's about learning how to disarm an opponent. Even if someone has a knife, the right moves can turn the situation to your advantage."

Humor sparkled in her eyes. "Will you train me to beat *you* in a fight?"

He leaned closer, his mouth hovering over her own. "Baby, you destroy me in every other way, why not add hand-to-hand combat?"

~

COURTNEY WALKED through the door that Aidan was holding, stepping out of McKenna Counseling and onto the street. First session with Grace was done. A session that had been both challenging and empowering.

Aidan's gaze darted around the area. He'd waited right outside Grace's office with the door cracked open. "How did it go?"

She looked up at him, one eyebrow lifting. "You heard."

With the door left ajar, it would be impossible for a *normal* person not to hear, so someone with Aidan's advanced hearing... yeah, he'd heard everything.

It was the reason Jason hadn't come with her. She hadn't known what questions Grace would ask or how she'd respond. But she'd wanted to put her everything into it because she wanted to overcome this phobia, and a large part of her had known that if Jason was on the other side of that door, she wouldn't have been able to be as... vulnerable. Open. Real.

"I tried really hard not to follow the conversation. Just listen out and make sure you were safe."

She nudged his shoulder with her own. "Thank you. I appreciate that."

She didn't know if she believed the guy, but she appreciated his attempt to put her at ease. Although it had been hard to relive the most traumatizing experience of her life, it had also been like reaching into her chest and physically lifting one of the unbearably heavy weights off that she'd been carrying around.

She looked up at Aidan. "Did you guys speak to therapists? After you got out of the Project Arma compound?"

He shook his head. "Nah. We were pretty open with each other while we were in there, talked a lot over the years. That didn't change when we got out." He lifted a shoulder. "I mean, we all handled it differently. If anyone had reason to be distrusting or angry after, it was Jason. Working for a company, only to find out that you're not working for the good guys. Then to be taken... have his *sister* taken."

Yeah, it sounded terrible. "He doesn't seem too angry or distrusting, though, considering."

Aidan nodded. "The guy's always been good at regulating his emotions. Making sense of things that shouldn't make sense and forgiving those who probably don't deserve it."

"Do you think he forgave the guys who took him?"

Aidan chuckled. "Hell no. We all agreed they needed to die, and when they did, it was a celebration. But it was a job for him. Get rid of the threats, move on to the next ones."

Interesting. "What about you?"

For a second, his eyes narrowed. The veins of his neck popped out a bit as he swallowed. "I definitely hold more... resentment than Jason."

She watched him, wanting to ask, but not wanting to over-step. In the end, she didn't have to. He spoke before she uttered a word.

"I was dating someone when I left. A woman who I thought I was going to marry."

Oh, no. Courtney could already tell this wasn't going to have a happy ending.

"She was married to someone else when we got back."

Pain laced his words. It tore at her heart. Poor guy. She touched his elbow. "I'm sorry."

They stopped in front of Blue Halo and Aidan tugged the door open, waiting for her to go in first. "That's life."

That was *his* life. Being torn from the woman he loved—because he *had* loved her, she could tell—only to have her find happiness with someone else. It was heartbreaking.

She opened her mouth to offer some kind of empathy, but she quickly shut it again. What should someone say to that? You'll find someone else? That just seemed... inadequate. Disingenuous.

She moved up the stairs, stepping inside Blue Halo. Amy looked up from behind the computer screen, smiling at them. Her foot was propped up on a chair, a bandage around the ankle. "Hey, guys. Jason's waiting for you in the gym, Courtney. How are you doing after yesterday?"

"I'm okay, thank you." Everyone knew her sad Mafia story now. Amy. Joey. The rest of her staff. There'd been no way around it. She shifted her gaze to the raised ankle. "How about you?"

"Just a fat ankle. It'll heal."

Nodding, she turned to Aidan. "Thanks for this morning."

"You got it." He gave her a warm smile before moving down the hall. Courtney headed to the gym. She stepped in just as a shirtless Jason threw a hard punch at a heavy bag. The bag rocked. The muscles in Jason's arms, his back, rippled.

Her mouth went dry. God, the man was ripped. Like, muscles-on-top-of-muscles ripped.

He turned, his lips tilting up. "Hey, gorgeous. How was your session?"

"Good." Did her voice just crackle a little?

His eyes twinkled with silent laughter as he tugged the gloves off his hands, tossing them to the side. "Just good?"

"Are you, ah, going to teach me how to punch, without a shirt on?" Because if so, she'd need some help tearing her gaze from his chest.

He stepped forward, his musky, woodsy scent filling the space. Good God, he even smelled good working out. "I was planning on it. Why? Is that a problem?"

Only if he wanted her to learn something. "It's just a bit… distracting."

He chuckled, hands going to her hips before leaning down and kissing her. "If I can concentrate while you're around, I think you'll be okay."

She scoffed. That was like comparing a daisy to a rose. She wasn't saying she thought she was ugly, but he was every woman's dream.

Releasing her waist, he turned, grabbing another pair of gloves. He put them on her and began strapping them to her wrists. "I thought we'd do a quick warmup first, then get into it. Ready?"

No. "Sure."

This time when he smiled, his dangerous dimples came out to play. Christ. She was screwed.

Jason spent the next ten minutes taking her through a series of jumps, squats and arm rotations, before facing her toward the bag. He surrounded her, his warm chest touching her back.

"It weighs about a hundred and fifty pounds, so I doubt you'll move it much."

A hundred and fifty pounds? Holy heck, he'd just sent it flying.

She cleared her throat, pretending the thing didn't faze her. "You have so little faith in me?"

His breath whispered in her ear. "Prove me wrong, sweetheart."

A shiver rocked her spine. She felt him straighten, then he used his foot to shuffle her legs farther apart. "Feet should be shoulder distance and at a forty-five-degree angle from where you're aiming the punch."

His fingers closed around her wrists, lifting her hands in front of her face. "When you punch, I want you to use your core, shoulders and hips to control your movement. Put speed and force behind the hit."

She nodded, focusing entirely too much on his fingers on her skin. On his naked heat pressing against her back.

"When I say go," he continued, "I want you to take a step toward the bag, transferring your weight forward, then swing hard."

That was it? Step forward, swing hard. Sounded easy enough.

Jason stepped back. "Go."

Courtney stepped forward, shifting her weight and swinging at the bag. Just as he'd predicted, the thing didn't move at all. Like, not even a whisper of movement. It was like hitting a padded brick wall.

"That was good, it just needs more force."

Ha. The man was a good liar. "I'm pretty sure I felt that impact more than the bag."

His hands snaked just below her breasts, fingers spanning across her ribs and down to her belly.

Her mouth went dry. His fingers were like tiny shots of electricity.

"You just need to engage your core. I want you to really tense and engage this time."

She nodded, grateful the man was behind her and couldn't see her tomato face.

When he stepped back again, she took a breath and tightened her core. Then, stepping forward, she threw everything she had at the bag.

It moved. The teeniest, tiniest bit, but... it moved.

She spun around. "Did you see that?"

"I did." He cracked a smile. The smile lasted for less than a second. "Now do it again."

Her own smile dropped. "You're a bit of a dictator in the gym."

She heard the soft chuckle behind her seconds before she was throwing her next punch.

CHAPTER 22

"**J**ason, I can't move. I think you're going to have to carry me up the stairs."

He could even throw her over his shoulder firefighter-style for all she cared, as long as it required no effort on her part.

Her muscles groaned as she climbed out of the car. It had been a long week of daily self-defense lessons. A week of muscle pain, dead limbs and zero energy. How long did fitness take to build up? Whatever the answer was, it was too dang long.

She moved slowly to the backseat, lifting the casserole. Good Lord, even that was an effort. Her quads protested. Her biceps screamed. Maybe the self-defense life wasn't for her.

She'd barely straightened when she was whipped off her feet. Courtney yelped as her side pressed into Jason's chest. The casserole dish only just remained horizontal in her hands.

She looked down, noticing the heavy bag of dog food was hanging from one of his wrists. And his muscles weren't even straining.

"Jason, I was joking." At least, she was pretty sure she was.

"I don't mind." He pressed a peck to her forehead as he walked inside the apartment building. She was relieved when he bypassed the elevator and took the stairs. All four flights of them with her in his arms.

"Hm, so if I told you I needed to be carried around all day—"

"Then I guess you'd be stuck in my arms like superglue."

Superglue? More like Lois and Superman. And she might just be able to get used to that. "You wouldn't care about people looking at us like we're lunatics?"

"Not one bit."

Ha. In that case, on the way back down to the car, she might just pop her hands behind her head, cross her feet and relax.

The elevator stopped on the fourth floor, and Jason carried her all the way to Helen's apartment before depositing her on her feet.

Courtney had been bringing her neighbor food regularly since she'd been released from the hospital. She'd also been picking up her specially ordered dog food and treats. She'd continue doing so for a while. At least until the older woman's ribs healed, but more likely until Courtney's guilt subsided... so forever and always.

Jason had changed all the locks in Helen's apartment and installed an alarm system. If her apartment was breached, Jason's team would be directly notified.

He knocked. Barking immediately sounded from inside the apartment. Poor Bernie. He'd recovered a lot quicker than his owner, but had stayed at the vet until she'd returned home.

Helen opened the door, Bernie in her arms. "Hello, dear." Then her eyes softened, a smile touching her lips as she looked up at Jason. The older woman loved the guy since he'd helped make her apartment more secure. "Jason. Come in."

Courtney barely held in her chuckle. "We made you chicken casserole." And it really was a "we" situation. Truth be told, Jason had probably done more than her.

She headed into the kitchen and set it on the stove.

Helen's apartment was almost a mirror of her own. Only where Courtney had filled her place with color and patterns and modern decor, Helen was more a fan of beiges and whites. Not to mention the dog figurines. So many dog figurines.

"I've told you, Courtney, you don't need to cook for me." Helen walked into the kitchen, filling the kettle and switching it on. "Bernie and I are quite capable."

Courtney crossed her arms. "I know, but I want to make your life just a little easier." She wasn't a good cook. Like, at all. But for Helen, and with the help of Jason, she was putting in the effort.

The older woman sighed, placing Bernie on the ground before opening a cupboard and pulling out three mugs. She did this every time they visited. Made them all tea with a dollop of honey. She was pretty sure Jason hated the stuff—it was pretty sweet, even for her—but he always drank it, God bless his polite soul.

Bernie came over and started sniffing her feet. She lifted him, giving him a cuddle. "And I'd still like to pay for Bernie's vet bill, if that's okay?"

She shook her head. "No need, dear. I have money and we both have insurance. And it's not like I have anything to spend my money on other than Bernie."

"But—"

"No. Courtney, you didn't ask that man to come into my apartment and attack me." Courtney grimaced. "You didn't ask him to hurt poor Bernie or ruin your apartment or chase you into your bathroom. If anyone should pay, it's those no-good criminals."

They were in agreement about that. Unfortunately, the chance of that happening was looking more and more like zero.

Helen placed tea bags into the cups before filling them up with hot water.

"Would you feel safer having one of my guys watch your apartment?" Jason asked.

He'd offered before, but Special Agent Peters had insisted on having one of *his* guys watch the building, and Helen had flat-out refused two guards.

"Goodness, no, that would just be too much. That guy only wanted somewhere to wait for Courtney. Now that she's gone, I don't see him coming back for me. Plus, with the FBI out front, and that new swanky lock and security system, I'm safer than I was before." Helen took the tea bags out of the cups. Courtney put Bernie back on the floor as the older woman handed a mug to her and the other to Jason. "And that agent told me the same thing—that I'm safe."

Courtney frowned as they moved into the living room, taking a seat on the couch.

"When he questioned you at the hospital?" Jason asked.

The older woman took a sip of her tea. "Yes, then. And also when he came over earlier today."

Courtney watched as the tea stilled halfway to Jason's lips. "Peters came to see you today?"

"He did indeed, and he had some questions about Courtney."

Courtney was careful to keep her features neutral. "What kind of questions?"

Helen stirred her tea, brows tugging together as her eyes went to the ceiling. "Let's see. He asked if you'd ever spoken about a woman called Jessica. I told him the truth, that I'd never heard her name come out of your mouth. He also asked if you'd ever had any other visitors like the man who attacked me."

Okay, so the guy *really* didn't trust her. Why? What had she ever done to earn any kind of distrust?

She glanced at Jason. His jaw was so tight it looked carved from granite. He already thought Peters was hiding information and spending too much time questioning her instead of looking for Lima. She was starting to agree.

They remained for another fifteen minutes, Jason barely

saying a thing. Courtney nodded and smiled at Helen as she spoke about Bernie and her potted plants.

When they stepped into the hall, Courtney snuck a peek up at him for the first time in a while. Yep. Still looked about as hard as Michelangelo's "David".

"Are you okay?"

When he took her hand, his touch was gentle, in complete contrast to what the rest of him looked like. "I'm okay."

They stepped over to her apartment door, and Courtney pulled out her key. They'd both agreed it was important for her to continue living with him, for a while at least, so she needed to grab more of her things. The few shirts, pairs of jeans and a couple of dresses just weren't going to cut it long-term.

Jason took the key from her fingers, unlocking the doors. She tried to step inside but he placed a hand on her shoulder, halting her. Then waited.

He was still as he listened. A nervous trickle crawled over her skin. She almost expected someone to jump out of her place and for Jason to transform into deadly protector mode.

Another beat of silence passed, then finally he lowered his hand. She breathed a sigh of relief, trailing him inside.

No big terminator fights. Not today.

She went straight to her bedroom, grabbing a suitcase from under her bed and unzipping it. She started with her top drawer.

"What do you want me to do?"

She grinned at his question. "You can stand there and look pretty. I won't be long." She grabbed a handful of tops, moving back to the bed and dumping them inside.

Jason laughed. It was the first smile he'd cracked since entering the apartment building. She liked it. "You aren't going to fold anything?"

"Do I look like a folder?" She shook her head. No. No she didn't. "Life's too short to fold clothes into a suitcase. Especially when said clothes are going to be in there for, what, ten minutes?" If even.

Nope. Not gonna happen.

She went back to the drawer, grabbing handfuls of socks and underwear.

Jason leaned his shoulder against the doorframe. "That would be true, *if* you planned to unpack immediately. Do you plan to unpack immediately?"

Crap, the man was onto her. She should probably be offended. If he wasn't so dang accurate, she would be.

"Maybe." *Probably not... definitely not.*

Another chuckle.

She smiled, moving on to her jeans' drawer. After adding some to the suitcase, she was just turning toward her closet when she stopped, gaze zeroing in on the framed photo of her and Jessica that sat on a bedside table.

She swallowed, looking across to the other nightstand and back.

"Have you been in here since we left?" she asked, not turning.

"No." She heard his footsteps as he drew closer. "Why?"

"I keep the photo of Jessica and me on the right side, not the left." Always had. She might not be super tidy, but all the important stuff had its place. And Jessica's picture lived on the right side of the bed. The side Courtney slept on.

"Everyone pitched in to help us clean up the night of the break-in. Maybe they put it in the wrong spot."

She shook her head. "No. I picked it up and put it where it needed to go."

She drew closer, lifting the frame and turning it around. Small goose bumps rose across her skin. "And someone opened it."

His voice came from right behind her. "How do you know?"

"I only ever close two of the clips." She specifically remembered checking them on instinct, the night they'd tidied the apartment. Her fingers grazed over the four that were now shut.

Why would someone open it? To look for something inside? To hide something? A bug maybe?

Jason reached over, taking it from her fingers and unclasping the clips. He studied every inch of the thing. No bug.

So they'd been searching for something.

When she looked up, it was to see Jason looking around shrewdly. "Is there anything else different or out of place?" he asked.

She opened the first drawer of her bedside table. She'd straightened most of her bedroom, while Jason's team had helped with the common areas.

"This drawer is neater than usual." Like, way neater. Someone had even gone to the effort to place the books in a neat pile. They were usually a mess. In fact, she remembered just shoving them in there, in such a rush to clear the floor after her space had been violated.

She moved into the bathroom, opening the drawers. "*Every-thing's* too tidy."

As if things had been taken out and placed back in the perfect spots.

Courtney moved into the living room, noticing everything there was also placed to perfection. Frames at exactly the right angle. Canisters in the kitchen perfect distances from each other.

"Someone's been in here." Her skin prickled.

Was it the Mafia? It didn't look like them. Heck, they'd messed up and destroyed almost every item they could get their hands on. But who else could it be? She didn't have any enemies...

"Let's finish packing your bag." There was a deadly quiet to the way he spoke the words.

She moved back into the bedroom, packing quickly, no longer feeling comfortable in her home. Everything felt... tarnished. Touched.

When they stepped into the hall, Jason placed a hand at the small of her back, guiding her downstairs. It wasn't until they were in his car that she broke the silence.

"Do you think it was the Mafia?"

"No. They wouldn't have left the place so clean," he said, confirming her thoughts.

When he didn't continue, Courtney pushed. "What should we do?"

He started the car. "I'll contact my team. We'll check for bugs. We'll also check for prints and send them to Wyatt. He can hack government systems, and if the prints are in there, he'll find them. Maybe if they put everything back and assumed you wouldn't notice, they weren't wearing gloves."

Government systems. That could mean criminals, or…

"You think it was Peters?"

Anger. It flashed through his eyes, dark and stormy. He pulled onto the street and immediately reached out, threading his fingers through hers. "I think the guy doesn't trust you and is putting too much time into investigating the wrong person, and not enough into protecting you."

CHAPTER 23

*S*oft music played within the Blue Halo Security conference room. The space was large, and the long table was pushed against a wall and covered with food. Chairs scattered around the space.

Jason leaned against another wall, watching Courtney from across the room as she sat in the corner with Grace.

They'd closed Blue Halo early today and the team, as well as Courtney, Grace, Willow, Mila, and Amy, were having a pizza night. Most of the team, that was, except for Flynn and Tyler, who were chasing up a lead on the Mafia's location, and Aidan, who was sending prints from Courtney's apartment to Wyatt.

Like Jason had conjured him up, Aidan entered the room, stopping beside him. "Got the prints to Wyatt."

"Thank you, brother. I appreciate it." He was pretty certain they belonged to Peters. "Hopefully by the end of tonight, Tyler and Flynn will have an address for us."

Aidan turned to look at him. "You think he's sitting on it?"

"If he is, he's a dead man," Jason said under his breath.

Callum stepped up beside them. "Who we killing? Actually, don't tell me, just point me to where we're digging the grave."

Jason wished he could laugh, but really, there wasn't anything funny about any of this. He already had trust issues after Project Arma. If the fucking FBI agent, a guy supposedly working *with* them, was instead trying to incriminate Courtney…

"Agent Peters," Aidan said quietly.

Callum grunted. "Yeah, the guy needs to do his job."

Damn straight.

Aidan scoffed. "Who knows, maybe the new boss is paying Peters to incriminate her, or to help him remain hidden. People never fail to surprise me anymore."

At the blatant anger in Aidan's voice, Jason turned his head. He knew that last comment wasn't just in reference to the agent. It was more. It was anger at a woman whose memory Aidan tried to keep buried deep. A woman who'd moved on.

"Have you made contact with Cassie?" Jason asked carefully.

Another quick flash of anger, there and gone.

From what Aidan had told them, they were deeply in love. Then Aidan was kidnapped along with the rest of them. When they escaped the Project Arma compound, he still had to keep his distance until their enemies were dealt with. Enemies who hadn't hesitated to use their loved ones against them.

Hearing that she'd married someone else had damn near torn Aidan in two.

"No. And I don't plan to."

Callum frowned. "Aidan—"

"Finding out she got married so soon after I disappeared was hard enough," Aidan interrupted, scanning the room. "I'd just be punishing myself if I had to see her, happy with another guy. She clearly knows I'm alive. Hell, we made national news. She could have sought *me* out. Called."

Jason hated the pain lacing his friend's words. But he understood it. If he saw Courtney with another man, he'd feel exactly the same.

He pressed a hand to Aidan's shoulder. "Let us know if you need anything from us."

"Hm." His gaze paused on someone across the room. "Besides, if Blake and Willow can't work out their shit, I don't know how the rest of us have any hope."

Jason followed his line of sight. Sure enough, Blake and Willow were talking beside the food table. They were actually smiling, which was rare.

"They'll find their way back to each other." Any fool could see they belonged together.

"I agree." Callum nodded.

Aidan grunted. The man obviously didn't believe in *everyone* getting their happily ever after. Not anymore.

Mila ran up to her dad and started tugging at his pantleg.

Watching Blake and his daughter made Jason want kids. Lots of them. Little Courtneys who tugged at *his* pantleg and looked at him with adorable multicolored eyes.

Callum nodded toward the back of the room, where Amy was talking to Logan and Liam. "At least she's calmed the hell down."

The man wasn't lying. Since the incident in his office, Amy had been nothing but professional. She still hadn't found other work, but at least she'd signed the formal warning and was doing her job.

"Mind if I sit with you?"

Courtney and Grace both looked up to see Willow approaching. Courtney pointed to the spare seat. "Of course, join us, please. Help us stuff our faces with food."

She and Grace had planted themselves in the corner of the room. Courtney had a bowl of corn chips and some guacamole, whereas Grace had a gigantic plate of pizza slices. And when she said gigantic, she meant *gigantic*. Slices piled upon slices.

As if she'd heard Courtney's thoughts, Grace held out her plate to Willow. "Please, take one. Or five. Logan brought this over for me. He must think I have the stomach of a six-and-a-half-foot man."

Either that or a blue whale.

"Ooh, yes, please." Willow reached out and took a slice of pepperoni. "I keep forgetting to eat. I swear this never happened before I became a mom."

Courtney scoffed. "The one time I forgot to eat, ever, was in eighth grade when I caught the flu so bad I was in bed for a week. But don't worry, I more than made up for it the following week."

She was pretty sure she'd almost eaten her parents out of house and home.

Willow chucked. "I used to be like that." Her gaze beelined to Mila. "It hasn't been easy, but God, I love her. She's my entire world."

Courtney looked over to see Mila in her father's arms by the food table. She was feeding him potato chips. Every time she popped one into his mouth, he scrunched his face and made loud, dramatic chomping sounds. Mila's delighted laugh had her head tipping back and her entire body vibrating. Okay, if that wasn't the most precious thing she'd ever seen, nothing was.

When Courtney looked back, it was to see Willow still watching them, but there was almost a sadness to her smile. Because Mila and Blake had lost time together? Or because Willow wasn't with him anymore?

"Do you see things working out with Blake?" Courtney bit her lip after she asked. Maybe she shouldn't have. They weren't that close, and it wasn't her place, but the wonder was killing her. *Had* been killing her since she'd met the couple.

Some of the smile left Willow's lips, her gaze darting back to the pizza in her hand. "I don't think so. Things were great before Mila was born… not so great after. None of it was Mila's fault though. It was all on us."

Grace tilted her head. "If you want to talk about it, we're happy to listen."

Courtney didn't think Willow had many, if any, friends in town. She'd moved here when the guys had, just a few months ago, and seemed to spend all her time working or studying and caring for her daughter.

Willow took a moment to respond. Courtney could just about see her mind moving, figuring out how to word what she wanted to say.

"Becoming a mom was the most magical and beautiful experience. You never know a love like the love for a child." A small pause. "But it was also hard. We *both* found it challenging." She shook her head. "Me in particular."

She looked up, but not at Courtney or Grace. She watched Blake across the room.

"Mila needs stability. Heaven knows, losing her father at two and getting him back at four was complicated enough. I don't think us getting back together, only to possibly break up again, would be good for her."

There was sadness in Willow's words. She wanted him. Probably still loved him.

Courtney was certain there was more to the story. A lot more.

"You're doing such a wonderful job of raising Mila," Grace said quietly.

This time when Willow smiled, it was wide and genuine. "Thank you. I can't believe she's almost five. It's true what they say. Time's a thief. You blink and they're walking, talking, and all grown up."

Courtney snuck a peek at Jason. She wanted kids. Would kids change things for them? Well, of course things would change, but would it be in a way they could handle?

When his gaze met hers, his eyes darkened. Something intimate passed between them. She quickly looked away, reaching into the bowl to grab another chip. Her hand came up empty. Dang it. Had she really eaten all of them?

Yes. Yes, she had.

Courtney stood. "I'm going to grab some water." And maybe some more chips and guacamole. "Anyone want anything?"

Both women shook their heads. Courtney headed to the small kitchen down the hall. She'd just stopped in front of the sink when thick arms banded around her waist.

Jason nuzzled his nose into her hair. "I was just thinking I needed some alone time with you."

Courtney chuckled, leaning back against his strong chest. "Funny, I'm always thinking that."

In the blink of an eye, Jason flipped her around and lifted her to sit on the counter. Then he was kissing her. His lips the perfect combination of firm and gentle, hands gliding over her hips.

She moaned as his tongue slipped between her lips, causing her head to swim. She laced her ankles behind his back, squeezing herself closer to the man.

Jason growled as he tore his lips from hers. They remained close as he spoke, breaths mingling. "If my team wasn't here…"

Her heart jumped. What? He'd have his way with her right here and now?

"Well, let's get the people out!"

His laugh rumbled from his chest to hers. She tightened her legs again. Did he think she was joking? She ground her core against him.

This time, his growl was louder. Wrenched from his chest and pulsing through the air. "You're killing me, woman."

When her lips lowered to his neck, she pressed a small kiss there, lingering. "But what a sweet death it would be."

She'd barely raised her head before he was kissing her again, his tongue driving into her mouth, tangling with her own. When he palmed her breast, a shot of desire zipped down to her core. He pinched her nipple lightly and she whimpered against his lips.

She wasn't concerned about someone seeing. Knowing that, if he heard anyone near them, he'd pull away.

She was just about to tear the man's shirt off when his phone rang in his pocket. This time, they both groaned.

"Ignore it." But even as the words left her lips, she knew that wasn't possible. Not with the danger surrounding them.

He pressed a final kiss to her lips before tugging the phone out. "Flynn, you got news for me?" A small pause. Then a nod. "Good. Let's brief and leave tonight."

He hung up, helping her down and lacing his fingers through hers before leading her back into the other room.

He went straight to Aidan. "We've got an address."

"For the Bonvicin family?" someone asked from behind.

Courtney didn't miss the way Jason's entire body tightened. Then, slowly, he turned.

Peters stood there, two of his guys behind him.

How had Jason not heard them entering the building? But then, Courtney was pretty sure she knew the answer to that. He'd been too distracted by *her* and probably only listening for someone to enter the kitchen.

"What are you doing here?" Jason's voice was hard.

"Just dropping by to see if there's been any activity I should know about. I haven't heard from you guys in a few days."

"We don't have any new intel to share," he said carefully.

Peters took a small step forward. "Did you get their address?"

"No."

That was all he offered. One word.

A short, tense silence followed. Courtney wanted to squirm.

The agent's eyes narrowed. Did he not believe Jason?

CHAPTER 24

The engine was loud, melding with the pitter-patter of rain hitting the car like white noise. The sun had just gone down and the road was almost empty as they made their way toward the Pioneer Hotel. It was the location where the guys had pinpointed the Mafia family members.

Jason touched his fake mustache, shooting a quick glance across at Aidan, who sat behind the wheel. The two of them were wearing black business suits and wigs. The outfits were uncomfortable, not just because he wasn't used to wearing a suit, but also because the mustache and wig were both scratchy as hell.

Lima's men were staying in rooms eight and ten on the fourth floor. Interconnecting suites. According to the hotel blueprints, the rooms were right beside the staff stairs and adjacent to an emergency exit.

They would no doubt have chosen those rooms specifically to be near more than one exit option.

Callum and Tyler were also driving to the hotel, but in a different car. Whereas Jason and Aidan wore suits as a way to disguise themselves from any watching Mafia members, Callum and Tyler wore hotel staff uniforms and would take the employee entrance. They even went as far as to add padding to their uniforms.

The team had booked room six on the fourth floor, right beside the Mafia's.

All four of them were armed but their goal wasn't to injure or kill. The goal was to find out what the Mafia wanted from Courtney and get them out of Cradle Mountain for good.

Of course, if that didn't work, then they weren't afraid to resort to more extreme measures. They were very aware, though, that if they killed a handful of the family, more Mafia would no doubt come to town. And that wasn't something any of them wanted to risk. Not when they had loved ones.

"You think Peters knows we got their location?" Aidan asked quietly.

The fact that his team had found it so quickly just confirmed to Jason that the information was accessible. Peters already had it. He had to.

Why hadn't he acted on it? Shared it? Done something to drive these criminals out of town? They were all questions Jason needed answered.

"Who the hell knows." He watched the trees speed past the window.

Peters hadn't been happy when he'd left Blue Halo that afternoon. Jason didn't give a shit. Courtney was his priority.

Aidan pulled the car into the hotel parking lot. They studied the area. Watching. Half expecting a member from the Bonvicin family to pop out.

Callum's voice sounded through their earpieces. "We just arrived. Pulled into the staff parking lot at the back."

Jason nodded. "Us too." The microphone was attached to the inside of his shirt. No one would be able to see it. "We're going in." He climbed out, the icy coolness of the rain slamming him in the face.

"Damn, I hate these things," Aidan muttered, straightening his suit.

"You're not the only one." It would be the first thing to go when he got home.

They entered the hotel, covertly surveying the area. There were no guests around. Wasn't surprising though. It was early evening. People were probably out at dinner or doing whatever they came to town to do.

They stopped in front of reception. Jason smiled at the lady standing behind the desk. "Hi, we're here to check in. We have a reservation under Roberts."

The woman gave them a warm smile. "Good evening, gentlemen. Of course, let me find your room."

She clicked a few keys and her smile slipped. Just a fraction, but Jason noticed.

He leaned against the counter. "Hotel's pretty quiet tonight."

When she looked up, there were strain lines beside her eyes. "It is. We're not very busy at the moment."

"So we can expect our room to be fairly quiet."

Her neck bobbed just slightly as she swallowed. "Unfortunately, we can never guarantee these things. But if you have any trouble, we're happy to move you."

Trouble? Oh, he was almost certain there would be. And by the clerk's remark, the woman knew exactly who was staying there.

They went through the check-in motions, Jason handing over his fake ID. An ID the guys had procured for themselves when they'd opened Blue Halo Security, should the need for them ever arise.

When check-in was done, they moved to the elevator, continuing to scan their surroundings.

"Just going up to the fourth floor," Aidan said under his breath to Tyler and Callum once the doors closed.

A second later, they opened to an empty hallway. They walked down to room six.

Jason frowned, trying to listen through the doors but hearing nothing. Was the floor empty? Had they intentionally kept people off this floor?

"If they aren't placing guests on this floor, I'm surprised they put us here," Aidan said, obviously coming to the same conclusion.

"They didn't want to. I pushed the matter." He'd used some bullshit line about having stayed in that room before and it being the only one he was willing to accept.

When they reached room six, they used their card to open the door but didn't walk straight inside. Both Aidan and Jason stopped and listened. Silence.

The room was empty.

They walked into the suite, entering a lounge area and kitchenette. An open door sat to the left, where Jason could just make out two queen beds.

He dropped his empty suitcase onto the couch and moved toward the wall connected to room eight. At the same time, Aidan moved out to the balcony. When they caught each other's gaze, they both shook their heads.

Dammit to hell.

"There's no one in room eight," Jason said quietly to the guys downstairs.

"We just swiped the master key." There was the sound of light footsteps in the background. "We'll go to the doors to rooms eight and ten."

"And we'll climb onto the balconies," Aidan finished.

No one being there wasn't ideal, but they'd planned for it. Enter. Search. Ensure it was in fact where the Mafia family was staying, and wait.

Jason and Aidan went out to the balcony. Once Callum and Tyler confirmed they were outside the doors and couldn't hear anyone inside the suites, Jason climbed onto the railing and jumped onto suite eight's balcony. The balconies weren't close, but they weren't too far. His enhancements made the distance attainable.

He heard Aidan leap onto the balcony behind him just as he continued onto suite ten's balcony.

His hand went to the doorhandle, easily snapping the lock. He didn't care about a broken lock. If this was where the Mafia was staying, he and his team would be waiting until they returned anyway.

Jason stepped inside. The space was exactly the same as the suite he'd just left. It was also completely dark. And it would remain dark. He had perfect night vision. That was an advantage he wouldn't give up.

Tyler stepped in from the hall, closing the door behind him and scanning the space.

At first glance, the room looked empty. But that didn't mean no one was staying here. He went over to the drawers beside the couch, searching, while Tyler checked the cupboards. He could hear the faint shuffling sounds of his teammates next door.

Nothing in the drawers. He systematically went through the living area, Tyler doing the same to the bedroom.

"Are you sure this is where they're staying?" Jason asked softly, not finding anything. Not a single thing. Even the bathroom looked unused.

Tyler straightened, moving out of the bedroom and going to the door connecting the two suites. "We tracked one of them back here. Staked out the place all day, saw more than one in these very rooms from the windows." He pushed the handle down.

An ear-splitting explosion tore through the room.

Jason was torn off his feet and thrown back against a wall. Pain ricocheted through his limbs, but he pushed it down, rising to his feet.

Fire blazed around him, smoke billowing through the room.

He searched through the smoke. Where was Tyler?

When he scanned the floor, his gaze stopped on Tyler's still form. He lay on his stomach, blood pooling around his body.

Jason didn't stop to think about what all the blood meant. He was at his friend's side in under a second, lifting him into his arms and tearing out of the room. A smoke alarm screamed through the hotel hallway, water spraying from the ceiling.

Aidan and Callum met him in the hall. Both uninjured. They didn't stop to talk, instead moving down the stairs and out of the hotel.

The fuckers knew they were coming. They'd set this up as a warning.

Jason would make sure they paid. The Mafia—and whichever double-crossing asshole had warned them.

CHAPTER 25

ourtney nervously paced her kitchen, trying not to dig her fingers into the flesh of her arms. Trying and failing. God, she was a nervous wreck.

When the milk on the stove began to bubble over, she cursed softly under her breath before turning the heat down.

Her gaze shot across to the living room. Blake sat on the couch watching a Louis Theroux documentary. She wasn't paying attention. Heck, she couldn't even tell someone what Louis was investigating. All she could think about was Jason. Was he okay? Was he coming home soon? Was he coming home *unharmed?*

Blake, on the other hand, didn't look like he had a care in the world. She'd even caught the guy laughing a few times during the program. Whatever he was on, she needed some of that.

She opened the jar of cocoa, spooning out a few heaping tablespoons and stirring them into the milk. Next, she went to the fridge and grabbed the maple syrup, pouring in a mountain of the stuff.

Hope Blake likes his hot chocolate sweet...

"Maple syrup?"

Courtney yelped, spinning around and finding Blake right there. Like an inch away. "What the heck, Blake? Do you make a habit of sneaking up on unsuspecting women holding glass bottles?"

He lifted a brow, a smile just visible on his lips. "I think you were just distracted."

Maybe... definitely. But still...

She poked his chest. "Make. Some. Noise. Sheesh, you're lucky I have the grip of a ninja or you'd currently be wearing this syrup."

He chuckled. "There are worse things I could be wearing."

Shaking her head, she turned back to the stove. "And yes, I prefer adding maple syrup to cocoa over sugar because it gives me the illusion that I'm being healthier."

"Heathier?"

"The stuff comes from a tree, so it's basically a vegetable." She dared the man to correct her.

Another chuckle. "I don't know if that's how it works, but if it's any good, I might try it for Mila." He sat on a stool at the island.

She grabbed some mugs, dividing the cocoa between the two. "Oh, she'll love it. Maybe add some sprinkles too."

Could a kid overload on sprinkles?

"I think she's getting her daily dosage of those from you." He took the mug from her fingers, trying a sip. Then he nodded. "Not bad."

Pfft. "Not bad my ass. It's awesome and you know it."

One massive shoulder lifted. "It's pretty good."

The guy was clearly downplaying his enjoyment. The stuff was amazing.

She leaned against the island. "Is Mila with Willow tonight?"

"Yeah, she's been staying at my place Saturday to Tuesday, then with Willow for the rest of the week. Both Willow and I are pretty flexible though if anything needs to change."

Courtney nodded, both hands wrapped around the warm mug. "Must be a bit tough. Having her only half of the week."

Less than half the week.

"It's not ideal, but I grew up with divorced parents so it's not a new concept to me."

"Mila was two when you were... taken?" Was that the best way to word it?

Blake didn't seem to care if it wasn't. "Yeah, two. But I was away a lot before that. On missions."

There was regret in his voice. The man had been a SEAL. She was sure a lot of his time hadn't been his own. The sacrifices he made for his country—the sacrifices many made for their country—should never be taken lightly.

Reaching across the island, she squeezed his hand. "Thank you for your service, Blake." He gave a short nod. "I'm sure Willow understood."

When she pulled her hand back, he scrubbed his face. "I should have taken more time off once Mila was born. Made myself more available for her. I didn't realize she had..." He shook his head. "I should have taken more time off," he repeated.

There it was again. A hint that there was so much more to their story. "Was Mila planned?"

"No. She's what we call a happy accident."

Courtney threw her head back and laughed. "I was the same, but in my house, I was referred to as 'the whoopsie child.'"

She didn't mind. She liked to think of herself as the gift her parents never knew they needed.

"Oh, yeah. That's Mila too. It's crazy. That someone you never planned for can take up such a huge part of your heart."

Courtney's own heart softened at those words. "Crazy, but not surprising. That kid is gorgeous." She took a sip of her cocoa, the sweetness filtering through her blood and dimming some of the worry. "I'm sorry you lost those years with her when you were with Project Arma."

A steely intensity filled his gray eyes. "Me too. I missed a lot. Willow gave Mila everything she needed though."

Yeah, but he'd been robbed of precious years he'd never get back. Mila had been robbed of a father and Willow a co-parent. Not to mention what he'd lost with Willow, as well. A relationship he may never get back.

"You love her," Courtney said softly, almost to herself. She wasn't talking about Mila, and Blake knew it.

"I've loved her for most of my life."

Willow's words from earlier that night played back to her: *It was also hard. We both found it challenging.*

It sounded... complicated. But sometimes, it was the most complicated relationships that were worth fighting for the hardest. "I think you'll find your way back to each other."

"Maybe." She heard what he didn't say—*hopefully*. Then he gave a small shake of his head. "Look at you and Jason, though. From barely talking to living in each other's pockets."

They basically were, weren't they? "Yeah, I'm pretty head-over-heels obsessed with the guy." She leaned farther forward, whispering, "But don't tell him."

Blake laughed. Yeah, she didn't need him to tell the guy, because Jason a hundred percent knew.

The smile slipped from Courtney's mouth. "You're really not worried about your team tonight?"

"Why would I waste my energy worrying? They're the toughest sons of bitches I know."

Yeah, but they're not bulletproof. The words were right there on the tip of her tongue. But she didn't dare say them out loud, because then the universe might hear and play right into her fears.

Blake frowned, no doubt seeing the anxiety on her face. It was probably hard to miss. His tone softened. "If something did happen, the rest of the team is a phone call away, and so is medical support. We heal fast, don't forget."

She nodded, gnawing at her bottom lip. That did give her some comfort.

He took another sip of his drink. "I changed my mind. This is really good."

Courtney straightened. About dang time the man caught on. "I know. It's the bee's knees. But you know what we're missing? Cookies to dunk."

She went to the pantry, rummaging through the food. Where were they? Jason had to have at least one package. Everyone kept cookies in the pantry, didn't they?

There were plenty of protein bars…

The ringing of Blake's phone cut through the room. Courtney straightened, nonexistent cookies forgotten as she returned to the island. She grabbed the edge, fingers wrapping tightly around the granite.

"Aidan, what's happening?"

Blake's features darkened. The energy in the room shifted.

Dread swam in her chest, stealing her breath. Oh, God. Something was wrong.

"He's okay?" More tense silence, then he nodded. "Got it."

Blake had barely hung up when she was asking, "What happened?"

Strain lines creased the edges of his eyes. "There was an explosion."

Her stomach dropped, nausea crawling up her throat. "An explosion?"

"Jason's okay. But Tyler was in the thick of it when it went off. They've taken him to the hospital."

Oh, Jesus. If something happened to him… She pushed off the island. "Let's go."

Blake shook his head. "We're waiting here."

"Are you serious? Blake, Tyler is lying in a hospital bed! I know you want to check on him yourself. Not to mention find out from your team exactly what happened. And I need to be with Jason."

She said need because that was exactly what it was. A need to support the man she loved. Make sure he was okay.

When he didn't budge, Courtney moved closer. "And if the other guys are with him, I'm more protected there than I am here."

Heck, for all they knew, it could have been a distraction and the Mafia were on their way here right now.

Blake's jaw tensed. He lifted his phone, sending a quick message, no doubt to Jason.

If the man said no…

A second later, Blake's phone beeped with a response. He scanned the screen before pushing the phone into his back pocket. "Let's go."

～

JASON PROWLED the small hospital room, his mind a dark haze of anger. He needed to cool down before Courtney got here. He probably should have told Blake to keep her at home, but the truth was, he needed her. He needed her softness. Her goodness. Her everything.

Tyler lay in the bed while Callum and Aidan were in the hall dealing with the police, telling them this was an FBI matter.

He swung his gaze over to his friend. He'd woken up for a short period of time, but was unconscious again because of the drugs the doctors had given him to keep him under and help him heal faster.

The burns already seemed to be healing, which was a goddamn miracle, but the truth was, none of them had suffered from burn wounds before. They had no idea whether his body would fully heal. Whether he'd scar.

Jason's phone buzzed, and he looked down to see a message

from his sister. She and Mason were on their way to the airport. The doctors here were good, but they didn't have the years of experience studying altered DNA that Sage did.

He was just putting it back in his pocket when it started to ring. "Wyatt," he answered.

"Mason told me. How's Tyler?"

"Stable. The doctors are amazed that he's still here, given the intensity of the blast." Any normal man would have died. It sent more shards of rage pummeling through Jason's blood.

"I'm glad to hear that, my friend."

"Did you run the prints?" Jason wasn't sure he was in the right headspace to hear this, but he needed something to focus on. Take his mind off his friend.

"They don't match any in the system. They don't belong to Peters."

Jason stilled. He hadn't been expecting that. He'd been so sure Peters or one of his guys had been in her apartment.

There was always the possibility Peters had *also* been in there and had just worn gloves.

One thing he was sure of, Peters had to have known the Mafia's location. And he hadn't shared it.

"Okay. Thanks." Jason breathed through his anger. Every part of him wanted to hit something. Lash out. He pushed it down. Buried it for the moment.

"You need anything else?"

"Not today. Thanks for all your help." God knew, he was the only person outside the Blue Halo team giving it.

"You got it."

Hanging up, Jason walked over to Tyler. He'd never seen his friend like this. Usually so large and commanding, now so still and pale. It tore at his damn chest.

"I'm gonna find out how this happened, brother."

Not just the men who'd set the explosion, but also the person who'd tipped them off.

He was just turning when the door opened. Callum and Aidan stepped inside, followed by men in suits. Including Peters.

Jason was across the room in a second, grabbing the agent by the collar of his shirt and shoving him against the wall, lifting him off his feet. Guns were immediately drawn around him, pointed in his direction. He ignored them.

"How did they know we were coming?"

"Jason."

He ignored Aidan. He also ignored Peters's men, demanding he release the guy.

When Peters didn't respond, Jason's voice rose. "Let me rephrase that for you. Did you, or one of your guys, warn them we were coming?"

Because what other explanation was there?

Peters held up a hand to his men. From his peripheral vision, Jason saw the weapons lower. "No."

He spoke the truth.

Jason refused to believe it. The Mafia had been expecting them tonight. *Someone* was responsible for that. "Then how did they know?"

"I don't know."

The calmness in his tone combined with the complete lack of reaction had Jason's temper rising. He lowered his voice, letting his words skitter through the silent air. "You knew their location. You had to have. Why didn't you share it? And why have you been asking Courtney's neighbor questions about her?"

A tense beat of silence ticked by. "I talked to her neighbor because it's my job to cover all bases."

"And the location?"

More silence. Then the words he'd known were coming.

"I *did* know where they were."

His fist tightened on the guy's shirt, blood rushing between his ears.

"I didn't tell you because I knew you'd do something stupid—

like raid their fucking rooms." For the first time, a flicker of anger flashed over the agent's face. "My job is to identify their boss and take the organization down through him. How do I do that without eyes on them?"

"It's also your job to protect anyone the Mafia is threatening."

Peters was silent for a beat, his gaze narrowing.

The door opened, and Courtney entered the room. Her feet came to an abrupt stop when she saw Jason.

He dropped Peters. Stepped back. Then her feet were moving again, her chest slamming into his, arms wrapping tightly around his waist.

Jason hugged her back, breathing her in. Instantly, some of the suffocating anger and frustration dulled.

This was why he wanted her here. Why he needed her. And this was why he wouldn't stop. Not until he ensured she was safe.

CHAPTER 26

"*I* actually stepped into the freezer the other day." It was scary as hell but she'd done it, and she'd been so dang proud of herself.

Grace's lips tugged into a smile. They sat opposite each other in the patient room at McKenna Counseling.

"That's amazing, Courtney. What did you feel when you stepped in there?"

This was their fifth session together, and Courtney was already feeling good about her progress. She'd thought that it might be hard to work with Grace, with them being friends and all, but it wasn't. The woman was good at her job.

"At first, I felt like I was about to lose my breath. My heart started to beat faster, but I put my hand to my chest like we practiced, and I took deep breaths. I reminded myself that I was safe. That I could leave the freezer anytime I wanted and I wasn't stuck. I was in control."

That was something that Grace had helped her understand. That her fear wasn't just about being in a small space, it was about being *stuck* in a small space. Kieran, the guy who had shoved her in that freezer, had zip-tied the door closed. She hadn't known if she was going to freeze to death beside a corpse before she was found.

"And that helped the panic subside?"

"Yes. I was able to go in, get what I needed, and leave. I was only in there for a few seconds, but…"

Grace leaned forward. "Don't downplay your progress, Courtney. You did something that a week ago you couldn't. And you did that because you've made your recovery a priority. You're putting in the work."

God, she loved this woman. "You're right. I'm badass."

"Yeah, you are." Grace closed the laptop. "Well done. Should we do the same time on Thursday?"

Courtney stood, already feeling better than when she'd entered. It seemed a regular occurrence for these sessions. She swore Grace had magic powers or something. "Definitely. And coffee at The Grind tomorrow. No claustrophobia talk."

Grace chuckled, moving around the desk and hugging her before whispering into her ear, "You're doing so well."

Courtney hugged her friend back. "Thank you."

Walking out of the room, she met Flynn beside the door and they headed out together.

"Good session?"

It was almost comedic that the guys always asked her that. They could hear the session just fine. She knew it. They knew it. But everyone pretended that wasn't the case.

"Grace is a magic worker. We may as well give her a wand and call her Hermione."

"Harry Potter?"

Courtney gaped at him, almost stumbling over her own feet. "That was really a statement, right, not a question? Because *everyone* knows who Hermione is."

"I'll take that as a yes."

Good Lord. This boy needed some education. Or just a few movie nights. What else had his childhood been deprived of? "I think you need to get your butt home and watch some Harry Potter tonight."

"Can't tonight. I'm visiting Mom. Although, there's always the chance she'll watch it with me."

Her smile slipped. His mother had dementia and was the reason his team had moved to Cradle Mountain. Apparently, she barely left her house, and Courtney had never met her.

"How is she?"

"Yesterday, I got there before her caregiver and found raw chicken in the microwave. I don't know how long it had been there, but it was room temperature." He shook his head. "It's getting worse. I hate that one day she won't remember me."

She gave his arm a gentle squeeze. "I'm sorry."

He dipped his head.

She tried to keep the rest of the conversation light. When they reached Blue Halo, she went straight to the kitchen. She'd barely eaten that day and had her session with Jason coming up. There was no way she could do it without sustenance. Heck, even on a fully nourished day, the man exhausted her.

He'd scheduled it for after hours, just the way Courtney liked it. No one would hear her heavy elephant breaths near the end of her session. No one but Jason.

Man, it was a wonder the guy was still attracted to her.

The second she tugged open the fridge door, she saw it. Chocolate cake and milk.

Hell yeah. That was the energy food her body needed.

A small part of her brain said that maybe she should go for the carrot sticks in the container beside the cake, but she shut that voice out. That part of her brain was small for a reason.

Courtney was turning away from the fridge, cake and milk in hand, when a gigantic figure appeared right in front of her. She yelped, both items flying from her hands. She stumbled back a step, her foot slipping on the milk that had crashed to the floor.

With lightning reflexes, Jason grabbed the cake before it hit him then lunged for her, spinning them around so that instead of landing on hard, wet floor, she landed on him.

They didn't stay that way for long. Almost as soon as they were down, Jason flipped them over, the cake miraculously disappearing from his hand. Fortunately, the section of floor he'd flipped her onto wasn't wet.

When he looked down at her, he wasn't happy. "Really? After all our sessions, your response to a man surprising you is to throw cake in his face?"

Courtney's hand went to her chest. "Just give me a minute while I learn how to breathe again."

One brow lifted. "If I were the bad guy, you wouldn't get a second, much less a minute."

She tilted her head. "You're not the bad guy." Hang on a sec, he didn't... "Did you sneak up on me on purpose?"

Because if he had...

"No."

Hm. She didn't know if she believed him or not. But she also didn't hate the way his body was pressed against hers.

A noise down the hall snapped her back to reality. Anyone could pop in. "Okay, I'm ready to get up now."

"So, get up." He remained perfectly still above her. Didn't move a single muscle.

She pushed her hips, tiny beads of awareness shooting through her system at the contact. "Jason..."

His mouth went to her ear, nipping. More toe-curling awareness. Desire. Heat. "Make me." His words were almost a challenge, his breath like hot lava traveling from her cheek to her core.

The man wanted her to remember how to flip an attacker off her while she was under him? Lord, give her strength, because there was a good chance she'd remember squat.

"Jason, I'm not playing around." She tried to push him again. He was like a big old rock.

One of his hands trailed down to her breast, thumb grazing over her nipple.

She gasped.

"I'd do it soon, darlin'. Anyone could walk in right now."

He nipped her ear again. Another shot of fire.

Gritting her teeth and ignoring the storm of desire zipping from her breast to her core, she tried to recall the sequence of movements he'd shown her. They'd just practiced it the other day. But her brain hadn't been mush then. Or maybe it had, and that's why she didn't remember.

What had he said? Wrap an arm around the waist...?

More flicking of his thumb. Her spine trembled.

"Tick tock," he whispered.

The hand finally left her breast. She almost breathed a sigh of relief. But then he moved it to the base of her shirt, creeping up. Ah, crap.

Think, Courtney.

Closing her eyes, she forced herself to remember his instructions. Lean forward. Wrap one arm around the attacker's waist and the other around their shoulder. Drive the knee and hip up, then swing over.

Okay. Got it.

His hand was almost at her bra. Crap.

She locked it down, opened her eyes and concentrated. Then she did it. Executed those same moves, exactly as he'd taught her.

Leaning forward, she wrapped one arm around his waist and the other around his shoulder, and she drove her knee and hip up, swinging them over.

A smile a mile wide stretched across her lips as she looked down at him.

She wasn't stupid. She knew he'd only rolled because he'd chosen to. Because she'd done what he taught her. But still, had he been a normal man, there was a very real chance she would have moved him. Or at least jolted him to the side. She wouldn't be going down without a fight.

"Gotcha."

His smile wasn't quite as wide, but the way he looked at her was... intense. "You do."

~

COURTNEY THREW ANOTHER PUNCH. Again, it was blocked. Extremely easily.

"I don't think I'm making any progress." In fact, it was entirely possible she was regressing from exhaustion.

After Jason's quick shower to clean off the milk, they'd gotten straight to the session. How long had they been at it now? Hours? It had to be because it sure as heck felt like it.

Jason's hands dropped. "Tired?"

"No. Exhausted."

One side of his lips tilted up. He stepped closer, taking her by the shoulders and turning her. Then he began to knead her tired muscles.

Her eyes fluttered closed. A groan that she should probably be embarrassed about dribbled from her lips.

Oh, sweet Jesus, the bliss.

His breath brushed her neck, and a small shiver rocked her spine. "It's when you're most tired that you need to hit the hardest."

It took her replaying his words in her head a couple of times before they made sense. The bliss of his hands on her sore muscles was sucking up her attention like a sponge. "Jason, my shoulders are on fire. I can barely lift my arms."

He pressed a kiss to her neck. "If you're tired, imagine how your opponent feels. It becomes more of a mental battle than a physical one."

She snorted. "If my opponent has a hundred pounds of

muscle and stands a head taller, then it's probably still a physical battle."

His hands trailed down and began to massage her upper arms. Pure. Heaven. "Then fighting through the exhaustion becomes even more important for you. It becomes survival."

The idea of ever actually being put in that position was kind of terrifying. "Let's hope it never comes to that."

Another kiss, this time pressed to her neck. She threw a hand back, hitting him playfully. "Jason..."

He sighed. "Remember the days when you barely looked at me? Now you're hitting me. And you can't take your eyes off me."

She spun in his arms. "That's because I thought you were a big deal back then. And can't take my eyes off you?" She giggled, attempting to duck out of his arms. He was too fast, flinging them around. She remained on her feet but he caged her to the wall.

"You don't think I'm a big deal anymore?" He took a half step closer.

"Okay, so maybe I think you're kind of a big deal."

But that was it. She wasn't admitting to anything else.

His mouth hovered over hers, his breath searing her lips. "You're kind of a big deal to me too."

"I don't think there's any 'kind of' about it."

The smile vanished, his eyes darkening ten shades, filling with heat. Passion. Possession. "There really isn't."

She couldn't stop herself—she lifted to her toes, kissing him. He dove straight in, tongue swiping inside her mouth, causing liquid heat to pool in her abdomen. One of his hands went to the back of her neck, his hold firm but gentle. His intoxicating scent surrounded her.

Her breasts ached with the need to be touched. Attended to.

Like she'd spoken her needs out loud, his other hand traveled down, slipping beneath her shirt and inside her bra, a thumb grazing against her nipple.

Courtney whimpered against his lips, her back arching, urging him closer. Her senses were in overdrive. Every part of her consumed—mind, body and soul. Desperate, she tangled her fingers in his hair, tugging and pulling harder with every flick of his thumb against her peak.

He growled deep in his throat. "We should stop." The words sounded torn from his chest between kisses.

"No. We definitely shouldn't." There was a good chance she'd combust right there and then if he pulled away.

Reaching down his body, she snuck a hand inside his shorts and briefs, wrapping her fingers around his thickness.

God, he was already so hard.

His hand stilled on her breast, his entire body tensing. Was the man even breathing?

A grin tugged at her lips as she started to move her hand, sliding it up and down his length. Stroking. Massaging.

His breath shuddered on her cheek. "Courtney…"

There was plenty of warning in his voice.

She ignored it, tightening her hold on him. Quickening her pace.

A growl was the only hint of his intentions before she was tugged off her feet, shirt yanked up, bra pulled down, and his lips latched around her nipple.

Courtney's head flew back, the most delicious bliss sweeping through her limbs. Her body urged her to move against him. *Grind* against him as he nipped and sucked at the pebbled bud.

Her entire body trembled when he jerked down the other side of her bra. Then he switched, torturing that breast in the same way he had the first.

"If we're stopping," he said in short bursts of breath, "then you need to tell me now."

She would rather saw off her right arm than have the man stop what he was doing to her. She wriggled her body, wishing she could reach the part of him she craved to touch.

"Not stopping." Not slowing. Not anything involving losing what she felt right now.

The words were a gasp as his tongue continued to play with her. His chuckle was like a vibrator against her sensitive skin.

He lifted his head, but only long enough to remove the top and bra. Then he was back with her.

At the feel of his fingers dipping inside her shorts, she went still. Then they slid beneath the thin material covering her. The second his rough, warm finger ran across her clit, her heart jackhammered against her ribs. Then he was moving. Swiping up and down her core, his mouth continuing to work her nipple.

A throbbing need built, consuming her.

Her cries were loud, guttural. "Jason, please, I need you."

"Soon, baby."

She wanted to protest, until a thick finger slid deep inside her.

Pleasure swamped her and Courtney nearly screamed. She dug her nails into Jason's back, seeking an anchor, and hoped she wasn't drawing blood.

His finger moved in and out in a slow, torturous rhythm. Wet heat engulfed her core. Her eyes threatened to roll back in her head.

Jason surrounded her, heating every inch of her body.

When he inserted a second finger, desire rippled through her, almost tipping her over the edge. She couldn't think. Could barely function.

"Jason." This time, his name was a desperate growl.

Suddenly, he withdrew his fingers and lifted his head. She wanted to cry out when her feet landed on the floor.

In seconds, he rid both of them of their clothes, then she was in his arms again, the hardness of the wall against her back, his chest to her front.

She felt him at her entrance, big and hard and hot, but he didn't move.

He kissed her cheek lightly. Then her ear. "I love you."

Her heart sang. "I love you, too." So dang much.

The words had barely left her lips when he plunged inside her, impaling her in one thrust.

She moaned deeply, at the edge of the precipice there and then. He pulled back, then thrust back in. He did it again. And again.

Desire, hot and thick, pooled in her lower stomach.

His mouth returned to hers. Their tongues dueled as they tasted each other. As his thrusts grew faster. Harder. Deeper.

He nipped her bottom lip and slid one hand to her breast. Lightly pinched the nipple. Sensation stabbed through her.

Her breathing altered, stopped for just a second before she exploded. The orgasm tore through her entire body, causing her to tremble and jolt in his arms.

Jason pumped another two times, then he tensed, his deep growl all she heard, all she ever wanted to hear, as he pulsed inside her.

CHAPTER 27

*J*ason stroked Courtney's hair, watching the soft rise and fall of her chest. They lay on the couch in Blue Halo's conference room. It was getting late, definitely past any kind of respectable dinnertime, but hell, the need to hold the woman overrode any hunger he should be feeling for food.

Courtney sighed. "This is nice."

Nice wasn't quite the word he'd use to describe holding the woman he loved. "It's perfect."

Yeah, that fit.

She snuggled against his chest under the blanket. He'd found it in a cupboard and said a silent thanks to whichever teammate had thought to store it there.

"Yes." She stroked her fingers across the indents between the muscles of his chest. "I'm glad Tyler's going to be okay."

"Me too." He'd felt her guilt since the explosion. She blamed herself because Tyler had been in that hotel to help protect her. "It wasn't your fault."

"Mm." A short pause. She didn't believe him. "I'm glad he won't have much scarring as well."

"It's pretty incredible really. That a blast that should have killed him, didn't even send him to intensive care."

They were still learning about everything their bodies were capable of after Project Arma. Every new element they encountered just amazed them more. "Some days, I almost feel like we're indestructible."

Her fingers paused. "Don't say that. I want you to act like you're a fragile wineglass teetering on the edge of a counter. Got it?"

He chuckled. "I'll be careful, honey."

She gave a small nod against his chest. "Good. And what about Peters? Feeling any better about him?"

Better? No. Frustrated that he couldn't find anything to incriminate the guy? Yes. "The guy seemed to be telling the truth about your apartment and not tipping off the Mafia. But if neither were him, then I don't know who it could have been. And just because he was telling the truth about that, doesn't change the fact he's done a shit job looking out for you."

The FBI had been trained to lie, and to lie well, so he wasn't discounting anything. The Mafia had a way of getting to people, with threats or bribes. Who the hell knew what was going on?

"So... keep one eye on him?"

"Keep two eyes on everyone."

"Gosh, I'll run out of eyes."

He tickled her side and she squeaked, rolling onto his chest and looking down at him.

He brushed some hair from her face. So fucking beautiful. "How are your sessions with Grace going?"

Her eyes softened. "I love that woman. She's an amazing therapist. So calm, always saying exactly what I need to hear. The first few chats were hard, I didn't want to relive being locked in that freezer with Nicole. But once I did, it was like taking a weight off my chest. The words were out there. I could start recovering from this ridiculous fear of mine."

"It's not ridiculous."

She nodded. "Yeah, that's what Grace says. I was telling her that I stepped into the freezer at work without turning into a sobbing mess the other day. I didn't stay in for long, but I'm going to work on increasing my durations."

He pressed a kiss to the top of her head. "You're not a mess. And that's fantastic."

Courtney chuckled. "Thank you." A small frown bunched between her brows. "I know I've said this before, but I wish I'd taken self-defense classes earlier. Like before Kieran had thrown me into the freezer."

And just like the last time Courtney had said it, Jason felt the debilitating fear creep over his muscles. Fear of her fighting a criminal of any kind, Mafia, or sex trafficker... it was fucking terrifying, self-defense lessons or not.

CHAPTER 28

*C*ourtney tapped her fingers on the old oak bar. It was the most popular bar in Jacksonville. The place where she'd spent many Saturday nights. Too many. Having drinks with friends. Dancing. Laughing.

Tonight felt different. It should feel different good, shouldn't it? Of course it should. It was her twenty-ninth birthday and a dozen of her friends surrounded her. Everyone had big smiles on their faces and drinks in hand, and some were even working the dance floor like they were Beyonce's backup dancers.

So why on earth was she standing here on her own, untouched mimosa in hand, feeling... unfulfilled? Yes, unfulfilled. That was it.

She watched her friend Elke shake her ass against a guy she'd met less than an hour ago. The joy on her face was an expression Courtney should be wearing.

Maybe she was having a quarter-life crisis, because, really, who the heck would feel their life was lacking when they had what she did? A great job working at her father's architect firm—a firm that she would one day take over. A spacious city apartment. Money in the bank. Christ, she was the poster child for "has her life together".

She lifted the mimosa to her lips, taking her first sip. The fruity drink caused her tongue to tingle. She was just about to take a second sip when a large, heavy arm swung around her shoulders. When she looked up, she almost groaned out loud.

Trent.

She tried to force a smile to her lips but was sure it looked nothing like it should. "Hey, Trent."

He smiled back, his glazed eyes sliding over her face. Her chest.

Argh, kill me.

"Dance with me, beautiful."

She almost rolled her eyes. The guy hit on her regularly. Like just-about-every-day regularly. He worked as an accountant in her dad's firm and Courtney almost spent as much time avoiding him as she did working.

"No, thank you. I don't feel like dancing."

Or having you grind up against me.

He leaned down, the stench of beer and cigarettes almost causing her to gag. "Come on, one dance."

Going for the sweetest, most phony smile she could muster, she repeated, "No, thank you."

She waited for him to walk away. Of course, he didn't. Instead, he leaned his head closer. God, why did this guy have such a problem understanding that no meant no? Did he have peanuts for brains?

"What if I say please?"

Oh, well, then that would change everything. The sleazeball would miraculously turn into the prince she'd been waiting for. A prince she was dying to wrap her hands around and dance the night away with.

Courtney swished the contents of her drink, watching the orange liquid, seconds away from throwing it right into his smug, arrogant face, when a hand curved over his shoulder.

"Unless you want to be wearing that mimosa, I'd walk away."

Courtney's hand stilled, disbelief mixed with excitement crawling up her spine. It couldn't be...

She took a step to the side. Trent's arm dropped, and he mumbled *something before walking away. Courtney barely noticed, happy for the first time tonight.*

"Jessica!"

Her drink barely touched the bar before she was flinging herself at her cousin, arms wrapping around her best friend's shoulders, holding her tightly. Jessica's arms went around her in return.

She hadn't seen the woman in... God, months. Since the funeral. And Lord, but it felt good to hug her.

Pulling back, Courtney held Jessica's shoulders in a tight grip, like if she held too loosely, the woman would disappear. "What are you doing here?"

Her cousin lifted one bare shoulder, her straight brown bob bouncing with the movement. "I couldn't miss my best friend's last birthday in her twenties."

Courtney shook her head. There had once been a time when they saw each other every day. Often, multiple times a day. They'd known each other so well that words weren't even needed to know what the other woman was thinking.

How often did she wish for those days back?

"I've missed you," Courtney whispered.

Jessica's smile faltered. "I've missed you too, cuz."

For a moment, they just stood there, drinking each other in. Appreciating that they really were in each other's presence. Then, smile still intact, Courtney turned to the bar. "Let me get you a drink. Are you still loving the strawberry daiquiris?"

Jessica chuckled. "I'm supposed to be buying you a drink. It's your birthday."

"Nonsense. You traveled all this way." Courtney called the bartender over, ordering her friend the drink she knew was her favorite, before swinging back to her cousin. "Now, tell me everything that's been going on in your life. Don't leave a single detail out."

For a second, the edges of Jessica's mouth pinched, and her brows drew together. The anxiety was only there for a fleeting second—a second of pain, uncertainty, unhappiness—then it disappeared, replaced by an extremely polished smile. "Not much. Still working at Boon Hospital. Still living with Ryan."

Courtney frowned, at both the fleeting moment of vulnerability and the mention of Ryan. The latter probably wasn't fair. She'd only met the guy once, at the funeral, and they'd spent barely any time together. It was very possible she'd read him wrong... but her gut told her she hadn't.

"Everything's going well with you two?"

Jessica nodded. No words. No smile.

It wasn't going well. She may not see her friend every day anymore, but she could still read her like a book.

Courtney opened her mouth to ask more about the relationship, to dig deeper, but Jessica spoke before she could. "What about you? How's work at the big firm?"

Courtney didn't respond immediately. She didn't want to talk about herself, but they had all night together. She had time. "It's fine."

One of Jessica's brows rose. "Just fine?"

"Eh. If I'm being honest, it's a bit mind-numbing."

Mind-numbing.   Could-fall-asleep-at-my-desk-every-single-day numbing. Same thing.

Jessica nodded, a knowing smile on her lips. It was a smile Courtney had seen way too often in her lifetime.

"I know what you're thinking," Courtney said before her friend could. "That you told me not to study architecture. That you told me to do something else."

Jessica leaned forward, touching her arm. "Something more in line with you and who you are. You're fun and quirky and colorful. You're a people person."

Not these days. "You know that Dad wants me to run the business—"

"What I know is that Uncle Gary wants you to be happy. Are you happy?"

For a moment, she paused. Was she? "I don't know."

The honest words slipped from her lips. So damn accurate. She didn't know if she was happy. Which was sad, wasn't it? Surely that was the one thing people should know about themselves.

"If you were happy," Jessica said quietly, "you would know." Her drink was set in front of her, and she took a quick sip. She shook her head, a faraway look coming over her face. Yearning. "Remember the coffee shop we were going to open together?"

Courtney chuckled. "Yeah. We were going to serve the best coffee in town and paint every wall a different color."

Sigh. The dreams of young teenagers.

"We were going to use Nana's mugs." Jessica swirled her drink. "The ones her and Pop collected over the years with all the jokes."

There were so many. Those silly cups had been her grandparents' pride and joy. Even after he'd passed, Nan had continued to collect them.

"Nana would have loved that."

Jessica swallowed. "Maybe one day."

Courtney frowned at the sad longing in Jessica's voice. She leaned forward, touching her cousin's hand. There was the slightest jolt. Her frown deepened, but she didn't bring attention to it.

"Are you still doing okay? It's only been a few months since Nan passed away."

She'd tried to call her as often as possible, but talking on the phone wasn't the same as being there for someone in person. And with both of them working full-time jobs, that just wasn't possible. They'd spent a bit of time together in the days following the funeral, but with Ryan always nearby, conversation had been stilted. Awkward even.

Jessica gave a small nod, taking another sip of her drink. "It's been hard, but she was getting old. Her passing wasn't unexpected."

Unexpected or not, it was still a huge blow.

Courtney studied her friend's face. She didn't like the hints of dark circles beneath the makeup. The missing sparkle that usually brightened her eyes.

Jessica straightened. "Oh, I got you a present." She rustled through her handbag.

"You didn't need to do that—you being here is the present."

She pulled out a little wrapped box. "I didn't buy it. It's something Nan left me. She left me so much, though. I want it to stay in the family, but with you."

Their nan had left just about everything to Jessica, which was exactly the way it should be.

She tore off the black wrapping paper to find a jewelry box. When she opened the lid, her breath caught. A necklace sat inside, familiar, with the most beautiful gem she'd ever seen. It was a deep blue that sparkled in the bar lights.

"Jessica, I can't take this. Nan left it to you."

She tried to hand it back, but Jessica simply took the necklace out of the box and moved behind Courtney, working the latch.

When she came back around, she smiled. "It looks beautiful on you. I knew it would." Her cousin reached to touch it. As she did, the sleeve of her sweater pulled up, and Courtney noticed dark bruises on her pale skin.

She grabbed her friend's hand. "What's this?"

Jessica immediately yanked her arm back, hiding it behind her, out of view. "It's nothing."

"Did Ryan do that?"

Jessica's eyes narrowed. "I said it's nothing. Don't worry about it, Courtney."

"Don't worry? Jessica, is he hurting you?" God, if he was—

"No. It wasn't him. And if you bring it up again, I'm leaving."

"Jessica—"

Jessica lifted her bag.

Courtney's jaw tensed. "Fine. I won't bring it up. Just... just tell me you're safe."

"I'm safe." Her response came so quickly that it left a sour taste in Courtney's mouth. She wanted to push but knew she'd lose her.

"Come on, let's dance." Jessica took Courtney's hand, pulling her to the dance floor.

She didn't want to dance. She wanted to know who the hell had put *those bruises on her cousin's arm. She wanted to know every little thing about Jessica's life, even if it was ugly and hard to take. But that wasn't going to happen. Not tonight, anyway.*

~

COURTNEY'S EYES POPPED OPEN, her heart aching.

The arm around her waist tightened, Jason's breath brushing across her neck. "Everything okay?"

She inhaled deeply. "Yes. I'm okay. I just dreamed about the last time I saw Jessica."

More of a memory than a dream. But it was crystal clear. So too were the bruises on her friend's arm.

A small pause. "Tell me about it."

She didn't like to think about that last weekend together. Because now she could recognize it for what it was. Her last chance to save Jessica. But she hadn't.

"It was my twenty-ninth birthday. She surprised me by flying down." His thumb started a gentle stroke on her hip. "I saw bruises on her arm."

The stroking paused, just for a moment, then continued. "Ryan?"

She wasn't sure if it was a question or not. "I think so, but it was never confirmed. I tried talking to her about it. I brought it up so many times while she was down, but every time she cut me off. Or got angry. Or threatened to leave."

She should have pushed harder.

"I know what you're thinking," he whispered against her neck. "But you're wrong. She knew what you would say. She knew that you would help her. She *knew*. She didn't want help. And you can't help someone who doesn't want to be helped."

He'd said that before. And the words were just as powerful then as they were now. She *had* wanted to help. And if she were honest with herself, she was angry that Jessica hadn't wanted it.

"Why? Why would she stay with someone who was hurting her?"

It just didn't make sense in Courtney's brain.

More stroking against her hip. "It could be a number of reasons. Fear. Shame. Maybe he made her believe she needed him."

God, she hated the guy. Like, really hated him.

"Or maybe she really did love him and thought he'd change."

Tears pressed at the back of Courtney's eyes. "And maybe she'd needed to lean on him after our nana passed, and she felt like he was all she had."

So many possibilities. They'd never know the truth. No one really knew what happened behind closed doors.

She snuggled closer to Jason. "Thank you."

"For what?" he asked.

"For always saying what I need to hear."

Without reply, he pressed a soft kiss against her neck.

CHAPTER 29

houghts of her dream from the previous night continued to skitter through her mind as she removed the remaining pastries from the display case. *Had* been skittering through her mind the entire day. Thoughts of Jessica. Of their last weekend together.

Why had Jessica turned up that night if it hadn't been a cry for help? Had it really been just to celebrate her birthday?

A clatter sounded by her feet. She looked down to see the portafilter from the coffee machine laying there. Joey mumbled something she didn't quite catch before picking it up and going back to cleaning the machine.

"Today's been nice and steady," she said softly, trying to distract him from his grumpy mood.

Joey had been even more reserved lately. Nothing like his usual self. She knew he had stuff going on, big stuff, but God, she wished he'd talk to her about it.

"Hm. The rush of people coming to check out the 'most unique coffee shop in Idaho' might finally be starting to die down."

The store was almost empty now, just a lone customer in a

booth finishing his latte, and it was ten minutes before closing. Blake sat in another booth across the room. He was on the phone, a frown on his face. She thought she'd heard him say Willow's name, so he was probably talking to her.

"I wouldn't be too sad about that." Courtney began to wipe down the inside of the display. "It might be nice to go back to a normal busy."

Fortunately, the store had always brought in enough customers to more than cover the costs of running the place and allow her to live on a good income. A small part of her almost thought it might be Jess looking down on her. Sending some good luck from heaven. Courtney smiled at the thought.

Joey coughed from behind her. "Have you, ah, found your necklace yet?"

She frowned. "Okay, you need to explain your continued interest in the thing." Because it was bordering on obsessive. Since that text on the way to Jason's, the night they'd kissed in the rain, Joey had questioned her about the necklace almost daily.

An uncomfortable, almost fearful look came over his face.

What the hell?

"I'm just… concerned. There's no chance Jason took it?"

Courtney blinked. "You mean so he can wear it out to dinner?" When Joey didn't laugh, she studied him closer. Good God, the man was being serious. "Why would Jason take it?"

"Well, the thing's worth a lot."

Courtney stepped toward him. "What do you mean, it's worth a lot?" *She* didn't know what it was worth. Of course, she knew it would have some value, most gems did. But she couldn't put a dollar amount on it. "Why would you say that?"

Joey stilled, his mouth opening and shutting a few times before he spoke. "It just looks expensive." He went back to scrubbing the coffee machine, this time a bit harder. "You didn't fall over anywhere? Trip?"

"What?"

"The weekend you went camping. Did you fall over somewhere?"

Well, she fell once when she was backing away from that bison. "We searched those places. I—" Courtney stopped. A memory flashed in her mind. "Yes!"

God, how had she forgotten?

Joey turned to look at her. "What?"

"Yes. I *did* fall over." The bell on the door sounded, but Courtney was too caught up in her thoughts to glance over. She stepped up to Joey, grabbing his shoulders. "The spider!"

Joey opened his mouth, but she was already speaking again.

"There was a spider in Logan's truck. I fell over the console and when I went to get back up, something caught. I thought it was my shirt, but what if it wasn't? What if it was the necklace?"

"Necklace?" Peters stepped up to the counter, eyes darting between her and Joey.

"I have to go." Courtney took a step away when Joey's hand wrapped around her arm, stopping her.

"Wait—"

"Whatever it is, it has to wait, Joey. I need to go. Close up the store for me."

Blake made it to the door first, opening it as he slid his phone into his pocket. He glanced back at Peters and Joey, before moving through the door with her.

There was an excited bounce to her step as she power-walked down the street, her steps almost morphing into a run. Blake kept up easily beside her.

She had to be right about this. She couldn't be wrong, not after getting her hopes up. "Logan will be there at Blue Halo, right?" she asked.

"Should be. If not, he's just a phone call away."

Calling first probably would have been smart. She was just so dang excited!

When they reached Blue Halo, she jogged up the stairs. Amy

smiled at them from her seat. "Hey, Blake. Courtney, Jason's in his office."

"Is Logan here?"

Amy's brows rose. "Logan? Uh, yeah, he's around here somewhere."

She moved down the hall. She was passing Jason's office when he stepped out. "Are you okay?"

She grabbed onto his shoulders in much the same way she'd just done to Joey. "I think I know where it is!"

For a second, he looked confused. Then he tilted his head, understanding lighting his brown eyes. "The necklace?"

"Yes! When I saw the spider in Logan's car, I fell forward and got caught on something. Maybe the seat. Anyway, I had to yank myself up. I thought my shirt was caught but now I think it might have been the necklace." She spoke so fast her words were running into each other.

Jason took her hand, leading her to Logan's office. The man was just hanging up the phone. "Ah, two of my favorite people. What can I do for you?"

"We need to check your truck," Jason said.

His brows lifted. "My truck?"

"I think I may have dropped my necklace in there when we went camping." And if the man didn't toss them the keys right the heck now, she might just tackle him for them.

"Ah, okay. Good news and bad news. Bad news, my truck is parked down in front of Grace's office. She still hasn't bought her own vehicle since moving here. Good news, I was just packing up to go."

Courtney's smile was so big it was making her cheeks ache. Was she really going to find it? And, God, she was still kicking herself for not remembering that something had caught in the truck sooner.

Logan stood. They passed Jason's office on the way out, turning everything off before heading into the reception area.

Amy rose to her feet. "Everything okay?" The phone at the desk began to ring, but she pressed a button and it stopped.

"Everything's fine," Logan said. "Blake, are you staying?"

Blake was leaning against the reception desk. "Nah, I'm gonna head over to see Willow and Mila."

Logan nodded, turning back to Amy. "You're the last one. Lock up after yourself."

⁓

JOEY WATCHED as the last customer left The Grind. He'd all but forced the guy out. He needed to call Courtney. He should have told her earlier. So much earlier.

If she'd finally remembered where the necklace was, there was no doubt in his mind that *they* would be close.

With fingers trembling, he pulled his cell from his pocket.

God, he was an idiot. Accepting cash from people he had no business dealing with. Accepting terms that he knew would alter at their discretion.

He'd been directed to find the necklace. All he'd known was that she'd likely lost it at the camping grounds. They'd taken him to the location and they'd searched the area high and low.

His stomach cramped at the memory of them returning to his apartment days later. At the photos they'd shown him... of his mother... sleeping peacefully, oblivious... at the threats against her.

It was the only reason he'd acted on their next request, unlocking the back door to The Grind and disabling the alarm.

He shook his head, bile rising in his throat as he dialed Courtney's mobile number. It rang. And then it rang some more.

Dammit, Courtney, you need to pick up!

When the voicemail picked up, he groaned, leaving a short message asking her to call him back. Then he called Blue Halo

Security. That had to be where she was headed. Where Logan would be with his keys.

It only rang once before it was sent to voicemail.

Joey cursed under his breath before leaving a message similar to the one he'd left on her mobile. "It's Joey, from The Grind. This message is for Courtney. If you find the necklace in Logan's truck, *do not* tell anyone you found it! It's worth millions and the Bonvicins want it." He ground his jaw. "I'll explain how I know all this in person. For now, just... don't tell any—"

The message ended. He was out of time.

The second he ended the call, dread filled him. Leaving a message on the Blue Halo phone probably wasn't the smartest decision. But he couldn't think straight, dammit!

He wished he could turn back time. Undo everything he'd done. Tell Courtney what had happened from the start. *Stupid idiot!*

Taking a breath, he straightened. He could only hope, *pray*, that those guys from Blue Halo could keep her safe.

CHAPTER 30

*T*he street was quiet as Jason made his way to the truck with Courtney and Logan. That wasn't unusual for Cradle Mountain. As it reached late afternoon, most people were home, preparing dinner.

He tightened his hold around Courtney's hand.

They stopped beside Logan's truck. He'd parked in front of Popshaw, which was a few doors down from McKenna Counseling. The restaurant's windows were dark since the restaurant was closed on Mondays.

Courtney glanced at the store with a dreamy look in her eyes before flicking her gaze to Logan. "Bet you guys are eating plenty of dumplings since Grace opened her business."

Jason almost laughed. The woman and her dumplings...

Logan unlocked the doors. "Nah, we're not big dumpling fans."

Courtney's mouth dropped open. This time Jason *did* laugh. "It's unlocked, darlin'."

She shook her head, climbing into the truck through the passenger side.

Logan pulled out his phone, glancing at the screen. "Grace is going to be another ten minutes."

"You know that dream I had last night?" Her muffled voice sounded from under the passenger seat. "It was of the night Jessica gave me this necklace."

Jason frowned. "Jessica gave it to you? I thought it was your grandmother's?" She'd said that the necklace had been passed down in her family.

"It was. She left it to Jess, and Jess gave it to me." Her arm reached beneath the seat. "Do you know something strange? Joey actually said something weird about it today. He said, 'the thing's worth a lot', and when I asked him how he could possibly know that, he said, 'it just looks valuable'. He's been so strange lately."

Jason shot a glance at Logan. The same surprised but suspicious expression crashed across his friend's face. "*Is* it worth a lot?"

"I don't know. Our grandmother never talked about it being expensive. But then, she didn't care about that sort of—" A short gasp escaped her lips. "Oh my God, I can feel it!"

A low hum vibrated in the distance. Car engines. More than one. All drawing closer.

"Do you hear that?" Logan asked quietly, the muscles in his arms bunching.

"Yes." Jason scanned the streets, an uneasy feeling building in his gut.

Courtney was just climbing out when cars careened around corners from their left and right. Two from each direction. All traveling fast and directly toward them.

Jason grabbed Courtney's arm, yanking her behind him. She gave a small squeak.

"What are you—"

"Put the necklace in your pocket, Courtney. Now!" He didn't look behind him to make sure she listened.

Popshaw was closed. No way were they leading them to

McKenna Counseling. Instead, he and Logan positioned themselves in front of Courtney, blocking her from view of their visitors.

Logan quickly dialed a number. Jason could hear Grace's voice on the other end as he told her not to go outside. To lock her doors and hide.

Courtney's quiet gasp sounded behind him. "What are they—"

The cars stopped, surrounding them on the sidewalk. Men climbed out, a handful from each vehicle, all of them with guns raised. Courtney's heart thumped loudly, like a drumbeat cascading through the air. Her arms trembled where she was pressed against his back.

Jason's world narrowed to pinpoint accuracy. He pushed down the rage at finally seeing the men who were responsible for blowing up Tyler, the fury at having guns pointed at them, and he let his years of training take over.

Tommy Lima headed the group. His black eyes were as deadly and dangerous in person as they'd been in the images. The eyes of a killer.

"Hello, gentlemen. Miss Davies."

Jason kept his voice low and even. "What the fuck do you want?"

Lima's eyes remained steely. "Where's the necklace?"

"*Window.*" Logan whispered the word so quietly under his breath that only Jason would hear. He knew his friend's lips wouldn't have moved an inch.

"Say we did have it and we handed it over"—Jason shuffled them back a step—"would you leave us unharmed?" *Leave Courtney unharmed.*

The men edged forward. Jason and Logan edged back again, forcing Courtney to do the same.

Lima's smile grew. "Of course."

Jason's blood ran cold. It was a lie.

The second they acquired the necklace, they'd shoot to kill. Because in the Mafia, leaving witnesses was a mistake.

The safety clicked off a gun. The man had tried to do it silently, but it penetrated Jason's ears like a gunshot.

"Now," he whispered.

A split-second later, they both turned, bodies a blur. Jason wrapped his arms around Courtney, shielding her as he threw them through Popshaw's glass window.

Courtney's scream was overshadowed by the sound of gunshots exploding. Pain seared through his shoulder as a bullet landed a moment before they hit the floor behind the brick wall.

Ignoring his wound, Jason continued to cover Courtney's body with his own. Sticking close to the side wall, he crawled toward the back of the shop, keeping her beneath him the entire time.

At the back of the shop was a long, narrow hall, kitchen, and bathrooms leading off to the sides. He continued to crawl, only stopping once they'd reached the door at the end.

Logan was behind him when he stood. Jason pulled Courtney to her feet, his hand going to the back door, but he stopped before pulling it open.

Movement from outside, right near the back door. And what was worse, the men out front were approaching the window, their steps slow, obviously cautious.

Goddammit.

Plan B.

"I'll hold them off from the front," Logan said, turning and moving back.

It wasn't ideal. But Logan was smart and well-trained. And once they were in close quarters, the other men would have less of an advantage.

He turned to Courtney, hating the utter terror on her face, how pale her skin was.

His hands went to her cheeks. "Baby, I need you to listen to me."

One quick nod from her.

"There are men outside this door. When they enter, I'm going to fight them. Take all their attention. When the door is clear, I need you to run."

Her eyes almost bugged out of her head. "You want me to leave you? With all these men with guns and knives?"

"Yes." Jason reached into his pocket, pulling out a ring with two keys. He pushed it into her cold hand, closing her fingers around it. "The keys to Blue Halo. The alarm code is two-two-five-eight. Repeat it to me."

"Two-two-five-eight."

"Again."

"Two-two-five-eight."

Good. "Once you're inside, lock the doors. We installed the best security money can buy in that place. Once the door is locked, no one can get in unless you let them."

She opened her mouth. She was going to say no. He could see it before the word had even formed. The sounds outside grew closer. Any second now they were going to enter.

He lowered his head. "I need you to do this. I *will* be okay. And I need you to be okay too."

She swallowed, her eyes closing for a moment. When they opened there was determination on her face, sparks of strength. "Okay."

Some of the tension that had been gripping his chest loosened.

Fighting sounded from the front of the shop. He blocked it out, trusting Logan to take care of himself.

Jason pulled Courtney into the bathroom closest to the door, making sure she was out of view. Then he moved into the kitchen, hiding in the shadows. Waiting.

He didn't have to wait long. A second later, gunshots hit the door, then it flew open. Six fully armed men barged in. Jason waited until all six had entered the hall.

Then he stepped out of the shadows, attacking, keeping them away from where Courtney waited.

His shoulder screamed at him, but he ignored the pain. Pushed it down. Focused on survival.

~

COURTNEY'S uneven breaths shuddered in and out of her chest. Her fingers shook, tremors spiraling through her limbs.

Gunshots, followed by the crash of the door splintering, caused her to jump. Then there were footsteps. The men were moving quickly.

She pressed her eyes closed at the first sound of fist colliding with flesh, praying it was Jason doing the hitting.

Her mind threatened to shut down with fear for Jason. He was bigger and stronger, but he was also unarmed, injured and outnumbered.

The sound of fighting moved farther down the hall. Taking a risk, she cracked the door to peek out of the dark bathroom.

"Run!"

Jason's voice thundered through the hallway even as he threw a punch at one of the men.

His voice propelled her feet forward. She sprinted out the back door, all but falling into the street. Then she ran, shoes slapping against the concrete, the stench of garbage filling her nose. The sound of fighting lingering behind her like angry whispers behind her.

She gasped in air, worry for Jason all-consuming. Her heart begged her to slow, her brain wouldn't let her. Going back would just distract him. She couldn't be a distraction. Not when he was fighting for his life. Fighting for *their* lives.

She cut down a dim alley, needing to get back to Blue Halo—

but her feet crashed to a halt when she saw a dead end in the form of a brick wall.

She spun around but immediately stopped again. Footsteps. Loud. Heavy. They pounded against the ground, coming from the direction of Popshaw.

Oh God. Someone was coming! And they were coming fast.

Desperate, she scanned the alley, gaze zeroing in on a door to her right. She tugged on the handle. Her heart stopped when it didn't budge.

She slammed her fists against the wood, pounding it violently, frantic. The footsteps on the street grew louder.

Please, please, please, someone hear me.

When the door opened, she almost fell into a man. He was wearing a white apron. The smells of cheese and dough assailed her. She was at Pizza Malloy.

"Lock the door! Men with guns are coming!" she shouted, pushing off his chest and running down a hall into the main restaurant area. She collided with a young man holding a tray of dishes. Plates crashed to the floor, splintering into a million pieces. She barely paused, air whipping across her face as she ran out the door and onto the street.

She quickly looked both ways, trying to get her bearings. Men were no longer in front of Popshaw. Probably all inside. And she was close to Blue Halo. Two blocks away.

She sprinted again, legs aching, lungs clawing for breath. She pushed herself hard, forcing her body to run faster. All the way to Blue Halo Security.

She could barely breathe when she finally reached the door. Her fingers shook so violently it took four tries before she got a key to fit—miraculously, her first choice for the outside door was the right one. Then she was moving up the stairs. Sprinting.

At the top, she tried the next key. Again, it took her far too long. Half a dozen tries, maybe more. She almost cried when the thing finally opened and she fell into the reception area.

The space was dark as she turned to the alarm, keying in the code Jason had given to her, forced her to repeat—two-two-five-eight. Numbers she could have easily forgotten, but was thanking every God she knew that she hadn't.

She was just turning back to the door to close it when someone stepped in. Her heart catapulted into her throat.

Agent Peters—holding a gun.

"What are you doing here?" She took three large steps back, hands raised, breaths rushing from her chest.

"I was sitting on the street in my car taking a work call when I saw you run in here. Are you okay?" He kept his weapon down as he took a couple steps of his own.

Suddenly, details started slotting into place. Peters had walked into The Grind at the exact moment she'd remembered where the necklace was, overhearing her explanation to Joey. Then, minutes later, the entire Mafia showed up. They somehow knew that she'd found the necklace.

Had Peters known they'd wanted the necklace all along? Did he know it was valuable? Hell, it had to be worth a lot to warrant all this...

"Courtney, I'm here to help."

On his next step forward, Courtney didn't think—she swung. Her fist crashed into his face, sending him stumbling back a step in surprise. She followed with a kick to the balls.

The gun dropped from his fingers and he fell to his knees.

Quickly, Courtney reached down, swiping the gun before running into the hall. She silenced her steps, choosing the fourth office down—Aidan's office, maybe—and crouching beneath the desk.

Closing her eyes, she worked hard to silence her breaths. Her heart.

The gun felt heavy in her hands.

Slow footsteps sounded down the hall. "Courtney, tell me what's going on! I'm on your side here."

She swallowed, one of her hands dipping into her pocket and pulling out the necklace.

This is what they'd wanted all along. And the entire time it had been in Logan's truck.

What did you give me, Jessica? It was beautiful—of course it was —but was it really worth so much violence?

Shaking her head, she placed it on the floor.

More footsteps sounded, this time closer. But then she heard something else. The sound of the lobby door opening again.

Courtney's heart clenched. Was that Jason's team? Were they here?

Peters's footsteps retreated. Muffled talking sounded from the other room. Courtney frowned when she thought she heard a female voice.

Then she heard a gunshot.

CHAPTER 31

*J*ason plunged a knife deep into the guy's chest. Three down. Three to go.

A gun flashed to his right.

Shit, he thought he'd kicked all the guns away.

Jason pivoted, swiping the handgun before the guy could blink, spinning it in his hold and shooting the asshole in the temple.

Blood sprayed the area. Fourth son of a bitch dead. Two left.

Another knife flew at him. He ducked, pointing and shooting number five in the chest before dropping the gun, the mag empty. The guy's mouth opened in a silent scream. His body jerked. Then he joined his friends.

One more.

Jason heard the movement a split-second before the guy jumped out of the kitchen.

He dropped onto his stomach before spinning, kicking the man's legs and sending him to the ground. He lunged forward to grab the guy's head and snapped his neck.

Dead.

He jumped up and moved quickly down the hall, surveying the large dining room. Logan was still fighting three men.

That very second, Flynn and Aidan jumped through the window. The Mafia guys' eyes widened, their fear thick in the dark space. Jason could all but smell it.

He estimated the men would be dead in a minute, tops.

Time to find Courtney.

He returned to the back door, grabbing a discarded weapon and checking the magazine for rounds on the way before running outside.

Immediately, he stopped.

Tommy Lima stood in the street. Gun drawn, pointed directly at Jason's head.

"You killed my family. My brothers!"

The guy's face was contorted in both pain and rage. Not physical pain. No. This was the pain of losing his men.

Jason's grip tightened on his own pistol. He didn't lift it. Not yet. "You knew who you were coming up against when you came here. You knew what we could do."

"I did. But I had to prove I was worthy of being their leader. I had to get that necklace."

"Why?"

He almost laughed. "Why? Because the diamond is worth fucking millions!"

Millions? How had Courtney not known?

"You said you needed to prove your worth... that means right now, there's no boss?"

Peters's entire mission had been to search for someone who didn't exist.

"No. Gianni's wife stepped in until someone could be appointed. That was supposed to be *me*."

Outwardly, Jason didn't react to his words. Inwardly, shock rippled through his system. "Wife?" He was assuming Gianni was the former boss. No one had mentioned anything about a wife, though. Or any female attached to the organization.

"I'm gonna kill you, motherfucker!" The muscles in Lima's forearm flexed a second before the gun went off.

That second was all he needed. Jason dropped to the ground, narrowly missing the bullet. He rolled behind a garbage container as more bullets pelleted the building behind him.

Lima's curse was loud. *"I'm gonna fucking murder you!"*

Not today.

Using strength that no normal man could possess, Jason gave the heavy container a huge shove, sending Lima flying backward.

The second the asshole hit the ground, Jason lifted his gun and shot the guy in the head.

COURTNEY PLACED her hands over her mouth to silence the cry. Had Peters just shot someone? Who?

A few excruciating minutes of silence passed. Every second had Courtney feeling more nervous. Finally, there were footsteps.

"Courtney, I know you're under the desk."

Courtney jolted.

Amy.

And the woman was close. Like, in-the-same-room close.

"I just watched the last couple minutes of video surveillance."

Courtney's breath stuttered in her chest. Then, slowly, she crawled from under the desk.

Her skin chilled at the sight of the woman holding a gun. It wasn't raised. But that didn't bring her any comfort. Not when she was pretty sure she'd just shot Agent Peters. "What are you doing here?"

"I forgot my phone and came back to get it." Amy took a step inside. "Are you okay?"

Courtney's gaze flickered to the gun then back to Amy's face. "How did you get that gun?"

"Peters pulled it from his holster. I didn't have a choice. He pointed it at me and just kept moving forward. He would have shot me if I hadn't wrestled it from him."

Wrestled it?

She swallowed hard. "Disarming an FBI Special Agent couldn't have been easy."

Amy took another step. "He wasn't expecting me to do anything. I took him by surprise."

Courtney studied the woman's face. Her eyes. Looking for something. Anything. Because her story just wasn't adding up. "Well, if you dropped the gun now, I'd feel a bit safer."

Amy glanced down at Courtney's hand. "You first."

She couldn't do that. In fact, her fingers felt stuck, glued to the thing. A beat of thick silence passed. Courtney's heart hammered in her chest.

Then Amy raised her gun, pointing it at Courtney's chest. "Drop the gun, Courtney. And tell me where the necklace is."

Air caught in her lungs, every inch of her skin tingling and icy.

"I mean it. Step around the desk, drop the gun and kick it to me. Or I shoot you in the hand."

She wasn't joking. She would shoot. Who *was* this woman?

"Tell me why first." She needed to buy time. Time for help to come. They had to know what was going on by now. Grace would have called the police or the other Blue Halo men when Logan called her. "Are you part of the Bonvicin Mafia?"

"Part of it? Darling, my husband *ran* the organization. Before he was killed, that is. I'm the boss until someone replaces him."

She almost collapsed. "Boss? So you were... what? Sent here to Cradle Mountain to spy on me?"

"I came here to watch these men. Make sure none of them were close to you."

How had no one realized?

As if she'd heard the question, Amy answered it. "I didn't even attempt much of a disguise. Just some dyed hair. For a man, that wouldn't have been enough. But no one was looking for a woman. I bet Peters didn't even show my picture on that screen of his."

No. He hadn't. "How did you find me?"

"We saw you in that article, wearing our necklace." *The article...* "We knew this place was crawling with those genetically enhanced soldiers, so we needed to make sure they didn't get in our way. I came to work for them, to watch them, while my guys were supposed to get the necklace."

"But you saw how close Jason and I were. Is that why you tried to seduce him away?"

The silence was all the answer she needed. "Drop the gun, Courtney."

"It's just a necklace, Amy."

A silly possession. Was it really worth all this?

Something flashed over the other woman's face. Something dark and angry and violent. "That *necklace* was Ryan's way into the family. He offered it to us. From that moment, it became ours. But then that bitch girlfriend of his hid it. And what did the idiot do? He killed her in a drunken rage before finding out where it was."

Razor blades slashed through her insides at the confirmation that Ryan had killed Jessica.

"That gem belongs to *us*. And I want it back." She took another step closer to Courtney.

"How much is it worth exactly?"

She laughed. "You're so stupid. That diamond is one of the most expensive and rare gems in the world. Ryan had it authenticated. It's worth almost twenty million."

Courtney's jaw dropped, her skin prickling. She'd been wearing a necklace worth a small fortune around her neck for over two years?

"Yeah, I can see you're getting it now. After your *cousin*," she sneered the word, "hid the gem, refusing to tell Ryan where it was, he killed her, then tried to give us a perfectly crafted counterfeit with the original diamond's letter of authenticity. By the time we realized what he'd done, it was too late. She was dead. And he had no idea where the diamond was."

Amy stepped forward again. "Now drop the damn gun and tell me where it is."

Courtney took a deep breath, rounding the desk before bending her knees slowly to place the gun on the floor.

It was midway to the ground when Courtney took a wild shot at Amy, then lunged.

Amy cried out, gun falling from her hand as they slammed to the floor.

Courtney could feel the stickiness of blood as she quickly rose up, pointing her gun. Before she could shoot, Amy swung, knocking the gun away. With a strength Courtney hadn't expected, particularly while injured, Amy spun them around until she was on top, straddling Courtney's waist.

The first punch caught her square in the face.

Pain rippled through her skull, blinding her and rendering her still for a stunned moment. A split-second later, she caught the blurry outline of Amy's fist rising again.

Courtney shifted her head just in time, narrowly missing the hit. Amy let out a strangled cry as her fist collided with the floor. Courtney dimly registered Amy's blood-soaked shirt from the bullet wound to her side.

Fury danced like wildfire over the woman's face, but before she could make her next move, Courtney wrapped one arm around her waist and the other over her shoulder, just like she had with Jason. She put all her strength behind driving her knee and hip up, spinning them.

Amy fell to her back right beside the desk. Courtney threw

her first punch, pain ricocheting down her arm as it collided with the woman's cheek.

Amy's head flew to the side, blood spraying from her mouth. "I'm gonna kill you, bitch!"

Courtney grunted when Amy's fist struck just below the ribs. Coughing, she fell to the side. What the hell had the woman hit? A kidney?

She was still coughing as Amy lurched for the gun. Courtney desperately yanked at the woman's leg, tugging her back. When she continued to claw her way forward, Courtney stretched up, pressing fingers into the bullet wound on her side.

Nausea rolled through her gut at Amy's scream. At the blood that poured from the wound, coating Courtney's fingers.

Amy's cry was followed by a furious growl. Before Courtney could stop her, Amy made a final grab for the gun, turning. She aimed it at Courtney's head.

A shot fired.

Courtney's breath caught. Her heart stopped.

Then Amy's eyes rolled to the back of her head, blood pouring from her temple, and she dropped to the floor.

Courtney's gaze shot up to see Peters standing in the doorway, one hand pressed to his bloodied chest, the other holding another gun. A small one. Maybe one he'd kept in an ankle holster.

He moved into the room slowly, grimacing on every step. Then he dropped to his knees beside her. "Are you... okay, Courtney?"

She nodded, sure that all the blood had left her face. "Are you?"

"I need," he sucked in a quick breath, "paramedics."

She nodded again, forcing her brain to snap out of its shock. She was about to stand when a door somewhere else on the floor banged open.

A second later, Jason burst into the room, gun drawn.

When his dark gaze narrowed on Peters, Courtney flung herself in front of him. "Don't shoot! He's okay! He saved me!"

Slowly, the gun lowered, Aidan and Logan rushing in behind him. Aidan was already pulling out his cell and pressing it to his ear. Logan moved toward Peters while Jason helped Courtney to her feet.

"Are you okay?" He spent a frantic moment searching her face, her body. Then he took in the scene around him, gaze landing on Amy.

"I'm okay," she said softly

When his eyes met hers again, relief flooded them. Relief that matched her own. He was here. Alive. Everything would be okay.

He tugged her against him, holding her close. Courtney dug her head into his chest, surrendering to the safety of his arms.

CHAPTER 32

"*A*re you sure you want to do this?"

Jason watched as Courtney lifted the pen. When she looked up, she smiled, her eyes shining. It wasn't a half smile, it wasn't hesitant or unsure. It was wide and confident and radiant. "I am one hundred percent sure I want to do this."

The tip of her pen touched the paper and she signed the final page of the draft corporate charter for Quinton House. Then, she slid the paperwork across the Blue Halo conference room table to her lawyer, Lucian Pratt.

He scanned the pages before shuffling them into his briefcase. "Fantastic. This should take a few weeks to process, then you're one step closer to becoming the director of The Quinton House."

The Quinton House, named after Courtney's cousin, Jessica Quinton. A nonprofit corporation providing shelter for women escaping unsafe situations across Idaho.

Damn, he was proud of his woman.

When the lawyer stood, he shook both their hands.

"Thank you for all your help," Courtney said, moments before he left the room.

When it was just them, she let out a small squeal, flinging her arms around his neck. "Can you believe what we just did?"

Jason wrapped his arms around Courtney's waist. "What *you* just did. You're incredible."

Not just incredible. She was so much more.

The second everything had died down in Cradle Mountain, Courtney had swung into action. She'd been on a damn mission, first to find a buyer for the necklace—an international diamond collector—then putting most of the money into opening her own charity.

Courtney's eyes softened, a trickle of sadness seeping in. "I wish that Jessica had gotten help from an organization like the one we're setting up, before it was too late."

Jason tightened his arms around her waist. "I wish that, too."

He'd caught Courtney researching the psychology of abusive relationships on more than one occasion. Trying to understand why her friend had stayed. Why she hadn't sought help. The frustration from not understanding had tormented her for a long time. She didn't need to say it out loud for him to know that.

He pressed a kiss to her forehead, lips lingering. He hadn't been able to stop kissing her. Nightmares still plagued him of that day. Of the moment the Mafia had surrounded them on the street. Of sending her out of that building alone. Unprotected. Unarmed.

Fuck. It was torture. He'd had no idea if either of them would survive that day. But they had. And he wouldn't be taking that for granted, not for a second.

"Three centers to be built across the state," Jason reminded her gently. "And one of those right here in Cradle Mountain. You will help so many women."

"I hope so."

He leaned down, hovered his lips at her ear. "I know so."

There was a lot for her to do. They needed to oversee the

building of the centers. Hire staff. There was more than enough money from the sale of the gem to fund all of that.

"Come on, I'll walk you to The Grind." He slipped his fingers between hers, leading them out of the conference room.

The reception desk was empty as they passed. It would probably stay that way for a while. They'd survived fine for the first couple of months without an assistant. He was sure they'd be fine for a couple more.

The fact that Amy had been the wife of the former Mafia boss had shocked all of them, especially Peters. He'd admitted to never even considering a woman could be involved in the running of the family, even for a short period of time.

When they reached the street, Courtney sighed. "I still can't believe my grandmother wore a necklace worth almost twenty million dollars around her neck for... I don't even know how long. Since it was left to her, I guess."

They'd traced the necklace back to English royalty over two hundred years ago. A great-great-grandparent had spent some years living in England, where it was believed she'd dated royalty and was gifted the stone.

"Did you ever consider keeping it?" he asked softly.

The sound Courtney made was something between a laugh and a scoff. "No. Too much blood was spilled over that thing. Selling it and putting the proceeds toward something good, something to help women, was the best decision."

So damn proud.

"How's Peters doing?" she asked.

It was Jason's turn to scoff. "The man almost died and he's just about refusing the sick leave they want him to take." Last Jason had heard, he was already demanding his next case. The stubborn ass.

"I can't believe I thought he was on the wrong side." She shook her head. "Although, he acted shady enough. Still, the guy saved my life."

He had. And Jason would be indebted to him forever.

~

As Courtney neared The Grind, fingers threaded through Jason's, she couldn't help but feel an overwhelming sense of gratitude. The threats were gone. She and Jason were in a good place. And she'd been able to do something good with the necklace.

Although Jessica had never told her why she gave Courtney the necklace, she was sure she knew. She hadn't wanted it to land in the wrong hands. She hadn't wanted Ryan or the Mafia to own it.

Courtney's chest tightened when she looked through the glass window of her shop. Because there was no Joey. After everything that had happened, Joey left town, going back to his mom.

She knew that Jason was angry at him. He'd wanted Joey arrested. But all Courtney could feel was hurt and sadness that her friend would choose to involve himself with the Mafia for money. To put himself, her, Jason... *everyone* at risk like that. All he'd had to do was ask for help, and she would have done everything in her power to give it.

"I'm sorry he hurt you," Jason said quietly.

She tried to smile but couldn't. "Thank you." There was nothing else she could say. She *was* hurting. Someone she cared about had almost gotten her killed. And she suspected that hurt would remain for a long time.

Jason held open the door to The Grind. She'd barely stepped inside when a small person came barreling into her legs. And for a small person, she had pretty good force, almost knocking Courtney over. She probably *would* have knocked Courtney over if it hadn't been for Jason's hand steadying her from behind.

Laughing, Courtney dropped to her haunches. "Hey, Mila."

"Courtney, I've been waiting for you!"

"You have?"

The girl nodded, her pigtails bouncing. "Yeah, I asked Daddy why you haven't been here and he said you got into trouble. Are you okay?"

She shot a quick look up at Blake. He was sitting at the booth with a coffee in front of him, a small smile on his lips. She looked down at Mila again.

"I'm okay, honey. There are some very good people in this town keeping me safe."

Mila placed her hand on Courtney's shoulder in much the same way an adult would to comfort a child. Courtney bit her bottom lip to keep from laughing. "I'm glad. And Mommy will be happy too. She wanted to check on you but wasn't sure you wanted visitors."

That was sweet. "You tell your mom that she's welcome to come around anytime."

Mila's smile widened. Then she nibbled her bottom lip, gaze shooting behind her at the counter before landing back on Courtney.

"Is everything okay with *you*, Mila?"

She signaled for Courtney to come closer. She leaned forward, and the girl lowered her voice. "I don't like anyone else's milkshakes."

Courtney's brows rose, scanning the bar and seeing two of her younger female employees. "How come?"

"They don't put many sprinkles on top. And it's not as thick."

Ah, they probably weren't blending in the extra scoop of ice cream. Courtney only did it for Mila. Easy mistake.

She looked over to Blake. She didn't say anything, but he knew what she was asking. He nodded. She turned back to Mila. "Would you like me to make you a milkshake, Mila?"

The uncertainty fled, the huge smile returning. It was the most pure, heartwarming thing Courtney had seen all day. Heck, all week. And boy, did her heart need it. "Yes, please!"

"You got it."

Mila skipped back to her dad while Courtney went behind the counter and started on the shake. She'd only returned to work last week, and it felt good. Immersing herself in mundane, everyday tasks helped her feel semi-normal.

When she got to the ice cream part, Courtney headed into the back room, opening the walk-in freezer. For a moment she stood there, looking inside. At the spot where Lima had attacked her. Where she'd been shoved when Kieran had thrown her inside.

She felt almost certain that if anything like that were ever to happen again, she'd fight back and have at least a chance of protecting herself.

Suddenly, she felt eyes on her. Turning her head, she found Jason standing in the doorway.

"This feels familiar." His deep, rumbly voice tickled through her belly.

It did. Because he'd caught her in this very position only a few short months ago. But back then, she'd been looking at the freezer in fear, unable to step inside.

"Are you okay?" he asked softly.

She nodded. "I'm okay." More than okay.

Walking in, she grabbed a gallon of ice cream. Not a hint of fear. Not even a tremble in her limbs.

So damn proud.

When she stepped out, it was right into Jason's waiting arms.

His head lowered to her mouth. "I love you so much."

She sank into his body, allowing his warmth and strength to surround her like a winter jacket. "I love you, Jason."

She kissed him. Grateful for how far they'd come as a couple. So much had been thrown at them. And they'd battled it all together, coming out the other end stronger.

CHAPTER 33

*B*lake parked his car on the street outside Willow's house.

"Do you think Mama will let me get a dog for my birthday?"

He chuckled, already picturing Willow's face if or when their daughter asked. "I'm not sure, baby." But he was leaning toward no.

"I'm going to ask." Blake watched in the mirror as Mila nodded from the backseat like she was confirming it to herself. "Jemma has a little gold dog with long furry hair. Her mom walks it to school when she picks her up. She says her dad complains that it gets hair everywhere then sneaks it treats when no one's watching."

He grinned as he climbed out of the car. Yep, sounded like a dad thing to do.

Moving around the car, he helped Mila out, grabbing her small bag before walking up the path to the door.

Willow and Mila lived in a small cottage on the outskirts of Cradle Mountain. It was only a street away from where he lived. Too far. If he had his way, they'd be living in the same goddamn house.

"You could always ask," Blake said to Mila. And then likely be met with a resounding "no."

Willow didn't like messes. It was one of her traits that would annoy a lot of people. Not him. He wouldn't call himself messy by any means, but the woman had cleaned up after him more times than he cared to remember.

They'd only taken one step onto the porch when the door slid open. Blake immediately felt like he'd been punched in the abdomen. But then, he always felt like that when he looked at the woman. Every. Single. Time.

Willow smiled, and his chest constricted. Fucking beautiful.

"She could ask what?" Willow asked.

He frowned. "Wait, is it me who has above-average hearing, or you?"

Mila released his hand and took off toward her mom, throwing her skinny arms around her. Willow lifted their daughter, pushing her face into her hair, breathing in her scent.

"Oh, I missed you, baby girl."

Blake stepped forward, pressing a kiss to her cheek. His lips lingered. He couldn't stop himself. There was a slight reddening of Willow's cheeks before she turned, heading into the house.

"I have so much to tell you, Mama! About Mrs. Pennington and Jemma and her dog. Oh, and I asked Courtney if she was okay, and she said she was so you don't need to worry anymore."

When Willow turned, there was a small crease in her brow before it quickly cleared. He read her like a book. She was wondering how her daughter had picked that up, because there was no way Willow would have told Mila that she was worried about anything.

"I'm glad she's okay, baby." She placed Mila on the floor, remaining on her haunches as she spoke. "How about you take your bag to your room while I talk to Daddy for a minute."

"Okay." Then she leaned up and kissed her mom on the cheek. "I missed you too, Mama."

The smile on Willow's face was all heart. Another pang to his chest.

It wasn't until Mila took her bag from Blake and left the room that Willow's brows pulled together. It wasn't a worried frown though. He recognized that look. Pain.

He was in front of her in a second, hand going to her upper arm. "Hey. Are you okay?"

She sighed. "I'm okay."

Not true. "It's a migraine, isn't it?" Not a full-blown one. Not yet. But it was coming. She'd been suffering from them for as long as he could remember, usually brought on by exhaustion. Sometimes stress. "You're working too hard."

She lifted her right hand, massaging her temple. "I need to work and study, Blake. I've told you this."

Yeah, she had. So she could support Mila. He knew how tough they'd had it while he'd been missing. How hard she'd worked to keep a roof over their heads. And damn but it tore him apart. Thinking about it made him want to growl, rage. Fix it.

"I've told you, *I'll* support you."

Her hand dropped, her lips thinning. She didn't respond.

Shaking his head, he went to the cabinet below the sink, taking out the first-aid kit. He knew it was there, not only because he'd helped Willow and Mila move in, but also because that's where she'd always kept it, even when they were together.

Taking out two aspirin, he grabbed a glass of water and took them to her. "Drink."

She gave him a small smile. "Thank you."

"You need to rest."

She sighed. "I know. I just have a paper to write once Mila goes to bed and I'll be done."

Done? For how long? A couple of days until the next one was due? Maybe not even that.

He looked over her shoulder, seeing the piles of papers from the studying she'd clearly already done. Willow was taking online university courses to get her BA in teaching. She also did online English tutoring for kids all over the world.

Lifting a hand, he gently caressed the lines beside her eye. He could have sworn she let out the softest of sighs. "I wish you would lean on me." He spoke the words quietly, not wanting them to carry down the hall to Mila.

A small pause. Was she considering it?

Then a shake of her head. A tiny step back. "I can't."

"Why?" It was a question he'd asked many times. And he'd probably ask a million more. Because he still wasn't under-standing why they couldn't give it another go.

"You know why, Blake." Her voice was quiet, too. "We weren't great together. Not at the end. I don't want to put Mila through that, especially now that she's older. And I don't want her to get used to us together, only to have us separate again."

He wasn't an idiot. He knew there was truth to their relation-ship being difficult before he'd been taken, between a new baby and his absence during missions. Willow in particular had strug-gled. And he'd missed the signs. Something he'd never completely forgive himself for.

"It'll be different this time. *I'm* different."

Hell, after everything he'd been through with Project Arma, there was barely anything that remained the same. Except his love for Willow and Mila.

She wet her lips. His gaze zeroed in on her mouth. God, how long had it been since he'd kissed her? Touched her in the way he wanted—needed—to touch her?

"I can't take that risk." Even though she said the words, there was an air of yearning about them. A yearning for him? To find out whether they could make it work a second time?

He took a small step closer, hearing her sharp intake of breath. "I'm not a SEAL any longer. My time is more my own. I can be more present. I can be there for you and Mila."

He would be whatever she needed him to be. He'd loved the

woman for so damn long. Seeing her again, but not having her, was the single hardest thing he'd ever gone through. It was hell. And he'd been through a lot of hard shit in his life.

She studied his eyes. She wanted to believe him. He could see it.

Do it, baby. Trust me.

One of her hands raised to his chest, pressing above his heart. The touch burned through the thin material of his shirt, causing fire to tear through his chest. "Blake, I—"

The ringing of his phone cut off whatever she was about to say.

And just like that, the light in her eyes dimmed, the hand whipping away from his chest.

He swallowed a curse. Ignored the ringing. "What is it, darling?"

The ringing eventually stopped. A second passed, and she opened her mouth again, but then his phone started once more. The shrill tone was like a hammer slamming into whatever progress he'd been making.

This time he didn't hold back the curse. Stepping away, he pulled the phone from his pocket, just about shouting to whoever was on the other end. "What?"

"Jesus, Blake, are you okay?"

He took a breath. It was Flynn. The guy didn't deserve his anger. "Sorry. What is it?"

"There's an urgent snatch-and-grab rescue mission Steve needs us to complete. We need you down at Blue Halo ASAP to go through the details."

Blake massaged his temple, feeling a migraine of his own coming on. "Okay. Be there in ten." When he hung up, he almost didn't want to turn around, didn't want to see her face. Because he knew exactly what he was going to see.

When he eventually looked at her, Blake's heart dropped like a bag of sand. She didn't even look angry. She just looked... sad.

"Willow—"

"It's fine, Blake. Duty calls."

He stepped forward, but this time she shook her head, stepping back, keeping the distance between them.

"You save people. It's what you do. Other people need you more than I do." She tipped her head toward the door. "Go save people, Blake."

She didn't say it with malice or sarcasm. She said it with acceptance. Like she'd been expecting him to receive a call from the second he'd stepped inside her house. And somehow, that made it worse.

Mila's soft footsteps sounded as she moved down the hall. She ran up to him and he lifted her into his arms. "I'll see you in a few days, munchkin."

"For chocolate milkshakes at The Grind?" Her brown eyes twinkled with excitement.

"Yeah. For chocolate milkshakes at The Grind."

"Yay!" She leaned into his shoulder, wrapping her short arms around his neck. "I love you, Daddy. Don't let the bad men hurt you."

He tensed at her words. Both Willow and Blake told Mila that his job involved saving good people from bad. So her request shouldn't have surprised him. But it did.

They'd also told her that's where he'd been during the two years he was missing. Saving people.

"I won't." Pressing a kiss to her cheek before placing her on her feet, he stepped closer to Willow, leaning in and kissing her temple. Again, his lips lingered a second longer than they should have, her gardenia scent flooding his system, intoxicating him. "Goodbye, Willow. Stay safe, honey."

He walked out the door, leaving his family.

The family he would get back—and not on a part-time basis. One way or another, he and Willow would be together. It may as well be written in the stars.

Order BLAKE today

ALSO BY NYSSA KATHRYN

PROJECT ARMA SERIES

Uncovering Project Arma

Luca

Eden

Asher

Mason

Wyatt

Bodie

Oliver

Kye

BLUE HALO SERIES

(series ongoing)

Logan

Jason

Blake

JOIN my newsletter and be the first to find out about sales and new releases!

https://www.nyssakathryn.com

ABOUT THE AUTHOR

Nyssa Kathryn is a romantic suspense author. She lives in South Australia with her daughter and hubby and takes every chance she can to be plotting and writing. Always an avid reader of romance novels, she considers alpha males and happily-ever-afters to be her jam.

Don't forget to follow Nyssa and never miss another release.

Facebook | Instagram | Amazon | Goodreads

JUN :. 2023

CPSIA information can be obtained
at www.ICGtesting.com
Printed in the USA
BVHW041652250423
663034BV00018B/263

9 780648 946298